Praise for J. P. Pomare's
Call Me Evie

"Literary suspense as dark and fresh as midnight in winter, with a merciless twist-of-the-knife finale. One of the most striking debuts I've read in years and years."
—A. J. Finn, author of *The Woman in the Window*

"An outstanding debut...Almost nothing will turn out as it initially appears in this devastating novel of psychological suspense."
—*Publishers Weekly* (starred review)

"With a story line that hooks readers immediately and twists and turns galore, this impressive debut is highly recommended for fans of Gillian Flynn and those who enjoy well-written psychological suspense tales."
—*Library Journal* (starred review)

"What a read! It's a tight, compulsive, beautifully written thriller."
—Christian White, author of *The Nowhere Child*

"This debut novel by Pomare sets him up as a writer to watch... Readers looking for a page-turner will be happy, but so, too, will those looking for a work with deeper resonances."
—*Kirkus Reviews*

"An immersive and exciting read."
—Laura Wilson, *The Guardian*

"I felt pure dread reading this book. _____ e dread... There are so many lav_____ they are revealed in the most f_____ ____rk Lake*

"A smart, propulsive thriller."
—Kate Hamer, author of *The Girl in the Red Coat*

"Pomare skillfully controls the drip-feed of information to create a nerve-racking love story that continually blindsides the reader. It's hard to believe this is his first novel."
—Mark Sanderson, *The Times* (UK)

"More than a taut, intelligent psychological thriller. At its core is the story about how family, control, and love shape our choices and who we are. Pomare has written a mesmerizing and heart-stopping novel."   —Sarah Schmidt, author of *See What I Have Done*

IN
THE
CLEARING

Also by J. P. Pomare

Call Me Evie

IN THE CLEARING

J. P. POMARE

MULHOLLAND BOOKS

LITTLE, BROWN AND COMPANY

NEW YORK BOSTON LONDON

Copyright © 2019 by J. P. Pomare
Reading group guide copyright © 2020 by J. P. Pomare and Little, Brown and Company

Mulholland Books / Little, Brown and Company
Hachette Book Group
1290 Avenue of the Americas, New York, NY 10104
mulhollandbooks.com

First North American edition: August 2020
Originally published in Australia by Hachette Australia: December 2019

Mulholland Books is an imprint of Little, Brown and Company, a division of Hachette Book Group, Inc. The Mulholland Books name and logo are trademarks of Hachette Book Group, Inc.

The publisher is not responsible for websites (or their content) that are not owned by the publisher.

The Hachette Speakers Bureau provides a wide range of authors for speaking events. To find out more, go to hachettespeakersbureau.com or call (866) 376-6591.

ISBN 978-0-316-46293-8 (trade pb)
LCCN 2020933494

10 9 8 7 6 5 4 3 2 1

LSC-C

Printed in the United States of America

For my father, Bill

I love children.

Anne Hamilton-Byrne

IN
THE
CLEARING

— Amy's journal —

Here are two things I learnt today:

1. My brothers and sisters were all saved from the world outside.
2. I have a meanness in me, something black and rotten that swells like a lymph node. That's how I imagine it, as a growth you could cut out.

I don't know why, but I wanted the girl to feel pain — I wanted to see her vulnerable but only so I could comfort and soothe her. People can be kind and mean at the same time.

Adam shared the plan with us this morning. It sounded so simple; all we had to do was stop the van by the edge of the road, pull her into the back, then fly away with her to the Clearing.

Riding in the jolting van, I was so giddy that I couldn't keep my hands still. Adam, sitting up front with Susan, was opening and closing his blade. It's about an inch long and when he punches it between your ribs it sucks all the air out of you and replaces it with a burning.

Twenty metres from the bus shelter we waited under the shade of the big eucalyptus until we heard the school bus groaning along the road. The bus was nothing like I'd imagined. It was longer, with windows all along the sides. Adam folded his blade away and picked up the stopwatch. He knew exactly where the girl sat, up towards the front. Even if the rest of the bus was empty, she would always be there on the left side, looking out at the trees whirling by.

Adam knew that most days she had a ponytail swinging down over her pink backpack. Adam had what he calls a 'watcher'. Someone out there studying the movements of the people around the child.

That's how he knew that today, and every Wednesday over summer, the girl's grandfather had a tournament at the bowls club that didn't finish until three-thirty, so he wouldn't be home for another twenty minutes.

Their neighbour, Roger, was out in the paddock most days feeding the calves on his farm. Roger normally waved, and the girl waved back. Adam knew that today Roger was meeting with his accountant in the city.

Adam knew everything. He always knows everything. He made us recite the distance she had to walk once she got off the bus: one hundred and sixty-one metres. There were three straights and two corners. The first straight, where trees hang over the road, was seventy metres, ending in a gentle hill. We couldn't grab her there because you could see it from the main road. The next straight was forty-eight metres. That was where it needed to happen.

I was nervous at first to see the world outside; it was all so strange and new. On the drive out there, we passed through towns and I got to see all the cars and the houses. Then we were driving beside endless plains of pale grass. It reminded me of the story about Freya in the woods.

Adrienne told me about the woman who calls herself Freya. She is free, she cares for nothing but her family. Freya has a secret. Adrienne said her secret is so sharp it could cut her. Adrienne wants me to understand something about Freya, but I don't know what it is yet.

Adrienne knows everything, too. Adrienne makes things happen just by thinking them. I love my mother.

We were ready in the back of the van. I knew the plan by heart, and I could repeat it back to Adam in his words. Our sister was coming home to us. Susan started the engine again as the bus lurched around the bend towards the shelter. I was squeezed in between two of the minders, Tamsin and Indigo. Tamsin is small and wiry; she has strong arms and a mole with a single hair poking out beside her nose. I could smell her sweat. Indigo is shaped like the fridge in the Great Hall but with rounded shoulders. She was so calm, like she had done this many times before. Tamsin and Indigo were nurses at the hospital where Adam used to work. That was before Adrienne changed their lives.

Adam turned around to face us. I knew he was the same age as Adrienne but he looked older. He had two wrinkles running up from between his eyes when he said, 'The first impression is the most important. We don't want the child to fear us. Her caveman instincts will be flight or fight. We cannot calm her down out here and we do not want her to develop any associations with us, negative or otherwise. Not yet.' He turned back to face the front, still speaking. 'Capture a child's trust and you will have its mind.' I have heard that before at the Clearing. If she didn't remember us or the collection, the child would simply wake up in her new home as if placed there by the hand of God. Which, now that I think about it, is true.

Her grandfather hurt her. She was my sister, and someone was hurting her, so I had a duty to help. It was my duty to Adrienne and to God.

The bus shuddered to a stop on the side of the road, the door hissed open. The weather was hot and the wind pressed the side of the van. We're in drought, Adam had told us, and today was hotter than I can remember it being. Sweat trickled down my forehead and into my eyes. I swept it away with the back of my hand. I needed to be able to see the child.

She was big for a seven-year-old; even bigger than Annabelle, who is eight. She shrugged her schoolbag onto her back and started walking up the road towards her house.

In the front seat, Adam had his eyes fixed on the girl. I wasn't breathing at all in that moment. I had to tell myself to inhale, to focus. Adam looked at the stopwatch, then at the girl. When I gripped the brown bottle in between my thighs, I could barely turn the cap. My hands were too sweaty.

When she was around the first corner, the van moved forwards.

'Wait,' Adam said. He raised his hand, his eyes still shifting between the watch and the girl.

My heart was thunder, but my breath was an ocean tide.

'Now,' he said, and the van moved again.

The road was all shimmering with heat but there were no other cars. I opened the bottle as we started up the hill. Liquid spilt over my knuckle and the pungent sweet smell filled the van. It stung my eyes.

Adam said my name. 'Amy.'

The van hummed along. I held the bottle up to see how much of the liquid was left. It was half full.

'There's still enough,' Adam said. 'If she remembers the collection, it will take longer.'

The van engine was humming like it wanted to give up. I tipped the remaining liquid over the cloth, bunching it up in my hand like Adam had showed me.

Hold it against her mouth until her eyes have been closed for two seconds, no more, no less.

My own eyes began to water from the vapour, but I blinked the tears away and focused on the world outside.

The van turned. We were close. It was magical; I knew the engine and the wheels were loud, but it seemed silent inside, as if even the van was holding its breath.

I could see her. A smudge of blonde and pink, a yellow skirt, walking in the dappled shade of the trees on the side of the road.

The van was moving slowly, but it still squealed when we stopped. She turned. I saw her eyes. Did she know what was about to happen? Was she afraid? Did she realise her life was about to become so much happier, safer, better? Was her heart thumping in her chest like mine?

Her blue eyes widened, her mouth became an O. The door scraped open. Hot air rushed in. It was over quick. Quicker than I thought possible. Tamsin and Indigo tore her from the road's edge into the van, wrestling her like a lamb. Her head rested on my lap with Tamsin's dirty fingers covering her mouth, just how we had planned. It was perfect, everything in place.

She looked up into my eyes. I hesitated.

'Go!' Adam screamed at me.

I pressed the cloth down hard over her nose. She began jerking. It was taking longer than it should; there wasn't enough liquid on the fabric, I wasn't pressing hard enough.

Everyone was watching me, except Susan, who was driving again. The world outside blurred by. I looked down into those gas-flame blue eyes, disappearing and reappearing as the girl's eyelids fluttered. I was jealous of her long lashes. She looked so much like Adrienne then. So beautiful.

Her blinks slowed. Eyes closed for a second. Open again. Closed for two seconds. Barely opening. Then she was gone.

The liquid had spilt beneath me and the van was full of the fumes. Adam wound the window down to let in a gust of fresh air. The girl's body was limp now. Lashes long and thick, cheeks pink. I peeled the cloth away, and leant back to ease the tension from my fingers, my arms, my neck and back. It was done. Our sister was coming home.

PROTECT THE QUEEN.

PART ONE

GOOD GIRL, KEEP GOING

FREYA

Four days to go

A CHILD WAS taken, it was on the news, and I just had to get out of the house. You see, there are some things Freya Heywood – that is to say, *I* – can't see without changing. I'm like you, but then again I'm different.

I wear the skin of others the way you wear clothes. Not in a *Silence of the Lambs* kind of way – although, now that I think about it, I *do* have something of a dungeon, and a dog that I care about more than I do other people. No, this layer of skin I wear is pure metaphor.

I learnt how to behave by watching others, slowly building up an ideal of a person, but if you were to slide a scalpel from my head down to my toes, an entirely different woman might climb out. There's an art in the small details, the idiosyncrasies that make someone convincing. It's not easy to be this person twenty-four seven, while everyone else is just *so* natural.

I could be the neighbour you've only met a few times, or the woman you've seen reading the nutritional label on a box of muesli at the supermarket, or someone at your local cafe, rocking a pram with her foot while she googles the answers to the crossword. If you watch me for a day, you might be fooled, but if you watch me closely for long enough you would see the moments when the other woman comes out. They are only brief, these moments, but they are impossible to miss. When I saw that news story about the missing girl today, the skin began to slip.

We all act; I'm just *better* at it than you. You do it when the service station attendant asks how your day is, and you smile and say, *Good, thanks*, because that's what's expected. You're doing it with every small lie, every interaction in which you must consult that ideal inner version of yourself before you respond. Unconsciously you are always asking, *What would a normal person say or do?* You're exactly like me; the difference is I'm prepared to admit what I am. I'm doing it right now, as I walk my dog down to the river. In a way I'm like an actor, except that most actors yearn to be seen while my aim is to disappear.

Freya Heywood drinks kombucha and believes that it will counter the effect of last night's two glasses of pinot noir. Imagine being so gullible; as if a fermented tea could really make up for washing alcohol, a known carcinogen, through the sensitive human digestive tract. I want to be one of the normal people with their strange and fickle ambitions, the types that become accountants or chefs or, in my case, yoga instructors. Normal people eat organic, if they can afford it, and stop having sex somewhere in their forties when they have had children or have given up trying for children. People don't need to know about the violence beneath the surface, the coils of razor wire turning inside like the inner workings of a watch. That's all I ever wanted: for people to know and love Freya Heywood. Is that so much to ask?

•

Today is different. I can feel it in my bones, feel it in the scar below my belly button. The air is weighted. Maybe there's pollen on the hot breeze, maybe it was the news report about the girl, but as my Rottweiler, Rocky, disappears around the bend ahead, I feel an avocado stone grow beneath my sternum, my limbs tingle like the moments after you take a drug. Something is going to happen.

The sky is a hard ceramic blue. The heat seems to flow down from the hills, collecting in the valley among the native bush lining the river. It's been hot for weeks but this afternoon the temperature crashed through forty-five degrees. Those few leaves still on the trees are frayed and curled. *Leaves are the respiratory organs of trees.* What attracted me to this place was the private river access, the isolation – sometimes I could go weeks without encountering strangers.

The air is so thick with humidity that it barely fills my lungs and only the flies seem to have the energy to move in the heat, hovering in a cloud over something dead near the track's edge. The flies, and the indefatigable Rocky, whose tongue drips as he huffs away from me. The bush opens a path down to a mud flat beside the river where the water is still and silty. This is where I expect to find him rolling about, snapping at the nub of his tail. I carry the chain in my hand and the tennis ball with the receding hairline in my pocket.

Instead, Rocky is growling low and fierce. Has he seen a snake? Or a wallaby in the scrub, maybe?

Squeezing the clip of the leash in my fist, I pick up the pace. Beside the river I see Rocky, his body angled low, fur bristling, his lips drawn back to reveal the white stones of his teeth. Only then do I notice the smell, something that casts my mind back to my late teens. The tangy herb, as rich and potent as body odour. I think of the back seat of Wayne's Datsun. Carpet on the dash, cigarette butts stuffed into the ashtray. I can almost taste the cheap beer sipped from dusty cans, feel the heavy Doc Martens on my feet. I can almost see the Melbourne cityscape from Ruckers Hill. I once loved Wayne so much – or I wanted to – which is exactly the same thing.

'What is it, Rocky?' I say, striding towards him.

A shape steps out from the shadows in the enclave of trees. A man.

'Oh,' I say, resisting the impulse to apologise. I clear my throat. 'Hi.'

Sitting behind him in the shade is a young woman, nude but for her white cotton underwear. They seem young, despite the man's patchy facial hair.

'Can you get him away from us?' the man says.

'Rocky,' I say, stern. On my command he would latch on to the man's forearm, and I can't say I'm not tempted. The man wears mascara and his earlobes are stretched to the size of a five-cent piece. His nose is drawn up in a sneer but there is something vaguely familiar about him.

Rocky backs away.

'What are you doing here?' I ask.

'Having a swim,' the man says. 'Free country.'

'Right.' I let my eyes linger on them for a moment longer.

A hot breeze pulls through the trees and the smell of dope fades. Did they know to put the joint out and bury it in a matchbox? Did they know that when the bush is this dry just a single spark could devour hectares in minutes? I imagine the undergrowth exploding, the trees aflame, fire spreading like spilt ink and the sky disappearing in smoke.

'Follow, Rocky,' I say with force, showing these people that my dog is trained and obedient. *This is private property,* I could add for effect. The river's edge technically does not belong to me – anyone could come via kayak – and the land across the river and north of here form part of North Tullawarra National Park, but this pair has walked across my land to get here. I whistle and jerk my head. Rocky barks once then runs to my side.

The couple will move on. Rocky has given them enough of a scare. They're harmless, I'm sure, yet I can feel the man's eyes following me as I walk away.

I fiddle with the tennis ball in my pocket, scratching it with my fingernail. As I climb the next hill, I bounce it once on the hard earth, thinking about Billy.

I can't help but imagine Billy choking, or drowning, or swept up from a roadside. Perhaps that's an affliction of motherhood, the way we evolved; mothers must always consider the worst scenarios in order to prepare for them, to keep us alert. It was the same with Aspen, until one slip and he was gone.

My connection with Billy is not something you can fake, the bond forged in childbirth; the earthy mud smell, the feeling of being split in two, the overwhelming sense of relief when the nurse wrapped him in cotton with my blood drying in his hair. I think about my own mother, how her indifference tempered me. The brief glimpses of love she did show drove me into a frenzy for more; the slightest hint of affection could make me buzz.

I bounce the ball again and Rocky leaps up, barking. 'Just a little further,' I tell him.

The trail follows the curve of the river, the incline levelling out. Looking down, I can see the couple still watching me. Their voices are low, reaching me as a hum. So long as they're gone by evening it will be okay. So long as they leave and don't come back.

I continue on, walking much further than I'd planned to, all the way to the next gap in the shrub. I hurl the ball into the water for Rocky, who swims out, ploughing through the mirrored surface.

Eventually, I clip him back on to his leash and head for home. The leash is for show; he obeys every command. I could take him anywhere and he would only listen to me, but people feel more comfortable when he is leashed.

Four eyes track me down around the bend beside the river, then through the bush. Their voices are quiet and rushed over the trickle of the river. Rocky walks stiffly beside me. That grey washing sensation in my gut comes back.

'Good boy,' I say. 'Good boy, Rocky.'

Inside, the clock reads 1 pm. I look out over the sun-bleached yard to Rocky who flicks his legs back with military decorum, his post-shit dance. I've locked him out so he is lingering down in the shade at the fence line. Even in the cool breath of the air-conditioning, I still feel the burn of the walk. Despite the efforts of surgeons and the 'wellness' industry, we all age, we all wither. After exercise, I'm reminded of my age by the tightness in my muscles. Yoga helps, I suppose, but seeing all the petite yoga-toned mums in their late twenties doesn't.

There's a white-tailed spider in the corner of my bedroom. I use a glass from the kitchen to trap the spider before sliding a piece of paper underneath. I carry it out into the garden to set down near the paperbark tree.

Back inside in the lounge, I do my push-ups, three sets of twenty, then step into the cold shower, my skin prickling and my legs becoming blue. You don't get used to cold showers; even when the mercury hits the forties, it still feels like hands slapping all over my body.

I turn the TV on and head to the room to get dressed. A quirk of the open-planned home means my kitchen, dining room and lounge are all one giant L-shaped room – I can watch the afternoon news while I down my tonics and eat a chia bowl at the kitchen bench. On TV, they're talking about the Great Barrier Reef again, sixty percent bleached and not coming back any time soon. Run-off from a new coalmine in Queensland will hasten the decline. I open the fridge and pull out my bottle of kombucha, twisting off the cap.

Another news story is running: '. . . *the girl went missing yesterday afternoon between three and four . . .*'

I face the TV as the news cuts to an aerial view of a paddock with a line of people walking slowly, heads bowed, scanning the long grass. I rush to the remote and snatch it up.

'. . . *police are asking for members of the public to come forward with any informa—*'

I mute the story and turn to watch the backyard, feeling the anxiety continue to churn within. *The girl went missing.* I know what the parents are going through.

Rocky stands at attention, watching something on the other side of the fence. Maybe it's the couple walking back up to the road? I want to wait, to be certain that they have left, but I have a class soon and a boss – or she prefers 'spiritual coach' – named Milly who is all Lululemon, meditation and sunshine until you are late, then she is Old Testament wrath. When I had a flat tyre she reminded me that it might have been 'negative energy' that caused it, and that it was something I should work on. I sense the studio is just a tax write-off for her wealthy husband.

I sip my kombucha and turn back to the TV. There is an image of the child on the screen now, a school photo, hair back in a ponytail, wide grin, blue eyes shining. The type of child designed for the twenty-four-hour news cycle. I drum my fingers on my lips. *It won't happen again*, I tell myself.

I open the door, call to Rocky, then aim the hose at the grass to clear it of hot water before filling his steel bowl. I lock the house and, for the first time in years, I set the alarm and roll down all the external aluminium shutters over the windows and doors – to keep the house cool, but also for security, because Freya Heywood doesn't trust strangers and those people at the river were verifiably strange.

My front door opens into the dining room, and when I go to leave I find a bouquet on my doorstep. My heart stops. I glance up towards the road and about the house. A spray of yellow wattle, bunched in native fern. I don't pick up the flowers; I simply kick them away from the door. There is no note, nothing to indicate who has sent them or why. Heat floods my cheeks. Anger or fear? Is this a sick joke? Taking a few deep breaths, I manage to calm myself, the facade restored. I walk out to the car, alert but not tense. I watch for movement in my periphery.

When I shifted out here all those years ago, the road to the house was muddy and my hatchback got bogged. Derek, the stooped retiree from next door, backed his truck up and winched me out.

'Gunna need something with a bit more guts out here, I reckon,' he had said. I looked at his Land Rover, the badge on the side reading *Discovery*. 'Good rig, especially when the river floods or the track is washed away. You ever need to get out of here in a hurry, you're gunna need something like this,' he said, patting the bonnet.

Thank you, Derek. I went out and bought my own Discovery. The *very* had chipped off the side leaving only *Disco*. Now I tote my cork yoga mat out to the Disco and take off, gravel spitting out from beneath my wheels and a dragon of dust rising in my wake. I love all the euphemisms I have picked up from that old man, pocketing the vernacular like pretty flowers or perfectly shaped river stones. *Bogged* – now there is a word that Freya Heywood loves. *Roo, Disco, crikey*; I could never speak them out loud myself, but I love the sound of them when they come from Derek's tobacco-stained mouth.

My road is too narrow for cars to pass, so I pull onto the shoulder with a wave as a car comes the other way. Derek must have visitors. I'm running late so I speed along.

At the dip where the drain runs out beneath the road, I slow and glance at the flattened road's edge where visitors to the national park leave their cars. There is an old white kombi van parked with tinted windows. I repeat the first three letters of the number plate to myself. *OUP.* It sounds like a mantra. *O-U-P. O-U-P.*

In the rear-view mirror the van disappears in the dust.

AMY

'TAKE IT EASY, both hands on the wheel, eyes ahead. Don't speed. Indicate. Everything is on your shoulders now, Susan.'

I can feel the warmth of my new sister in my lap as she sleeps the deepest sleep. I cradle her head, thumbing her tangled hair back behind her ears.

'Forty-eight hours, then we're in the clear.'

Forty-eight hours.

I feel so warm and happy. We have her. The van eases back onto the main road, merging into traffic. We all stay low in the back, holding the girl still, while Indigo takes the needle and syringe. She holds it up as the van jigs from side to side, eyeing the liquid in the light before plugging the needle into the girl's arm.

'The hard part is over, Susan. Eyes on the road. Deliver us home.'

We stay flat against the floor of the van for an hour or more. All the while I stroke the girl's face, holding her against me, making sure her head is cushioned and her body is comfortable.

As we drive along the gravel track towards the Clearing I sit up. The entry is well disguised. A barred steel gate crawling with blackberry bushes. On the other side of the gate, the grass is flat-tened where the wheels roll over it. Branches squeal against the sides of the van. The trees are tinder-dry with curled leaves. I miss Autumn, when the bush is cooled and green, when mushrooms ladder up the sides of fallen trees.

We keep driving.

Tamsin climbs out and opens the last gate, and we drive through, crossing the expanse of grass where the bush has been cleared away. As we near the Great Hall, where the kitchen and our classroom are, I see my brothers and sisters and the other minders burst from the building and rush towards us. Everyone knows the precious cargo we are carrying and their palms bang on the windows as we pass. My chest fills with pride. The enthusiasm of the others is infectious. Susan honks the horn, waving to the children outside, and then we are heading around the Great Tree, then beyond the Burrow, where we sleep and bathe, making our way to the Shed at the south-east corner of the property.

We pass the child through the door of the van and into the waiting hands as though delivering a baby. Her small body seems to float into the Shed. We lay her down on the stained cotton cloth covering the bench. Adam has rigged a square in the sheet-metal roof on a pulley so when my brother Anton – the only child older than me – turns the wheel near the door a perfect diamond of light falls through the ceiling and across the girl. We circle her, to be close, to look at her.

'That's enough,' Adrienne says. 'We need to get to work.'

I know that soon the child will wake and when she does she will be hungry and thirsty. I know we have chores to do, but it is so hard to walk away.

•

I know that when we liberate a child from the world outside, the minders become tense and agitated. Susan was chewing her nails today and now, as I'm peeling potatoes, looking out the kitchen window, I watch Tamsin in the yard with the young girls. She is near the vegetable garden, squatting down and pointing at something in the earth. The children stand and watch. The peeler catches on my knuckle and a pearl of blood seeps from the flap of skin, distracting me momentarily. When I look back up I see Tamsin rise and strike one of the younger girls. It's so sudden, like a cat's paw. The girl clutches her cheek as Tamsin stands over her. Tamsin slaps the child once more, then shoves her to the ground. The other children remain completely still. I know the heat of those slaps.

I turn my gaze towards the Shed. Adam is there with our newest sister, Asha. Anton is in there, too, and Adrienne.

How different will Asha's life be here with us in the Clearing? I think about the road she was walking along to her old house. If it was so bad there, why would she keep walking back?

But I chase the thought out of my head. That is a deviant thought, something evil. It is my duty to confess thoughts like this, to be purged, or they might burn me up inside. We only have room for the Truth. Deviant thoughts will bring about the apocalypse for our little world.

I wonder if Asha will remember the collection when she wakes. I hope she doesn't remember me putting her to sleep. I think about the journal Adrienne gave me to write in. I will return to it tonight.

FREYA

Four days to go

IN SUMMER I spend my life dashing between air-conditioned spaces. The house, the Disco, the yoga studio, the grocer. There was a time when I loved the heat, leaping into the waterhole while the sun drew colour to my skin. As I got older, when I first had a mole removed and noticed the spots and creases, the creped texture of my forearms, I realised I couldn't control the simple fact of my biology; I was getting older and would continue to get older until I died. I began to wear longer sleeves, slathered on sunblock.

I put on some music and take a long drink from my water bottle. Wedges of lemon float within; it *alkalises* the body. I might be the oldest instructor at the centre but I am also, as I remind others, the most experienced.

Our place is a decent drive away from Tullawarra town, far enough removed from civilisation to be alone but close enough to have access to all the trappings of a modern urban society. Still, my side of Tullawarra – north of the bridge and further from Melbourne city – is mostly populated by small-town people, with small-town attitudes. When a set of traffic lights was being put in down near the bridge, people petitioned and protested (yes, protested: placards, t-shirts with anti-traffic light slogans, meetings at the town hall).

The southern side of town is newer, closer to the city. It's full of people like Karen, who is at yoga today, swollen with a baby. Most of the yoga mothers live on the south side. They have husbands who commute an hour to the Melbourne CBD so the family can afford to live on one white-collar income.

'In,' I say, drawing a breath. The arms of the class rise in unison. 'Hold . . . and now out.' I do this a dozen times until the oak-panelled room, the building, seems to breathe with us. All the bodies rise in a sort of tidal movement then fall as we move through a series of sun salutations and on to the next poses.

Yoga mothers, I've found, are the least self-aware, least forgiving gaggle of women you will meet in your entire life. They ask what *organic* sanitary pads you use (and remind you that menstruation cups are *actually* better for the environment). Without guilt they explain why they chose not to vaccinate their children. They choose everything *natural* but fail to see the irony with their sports bras and legs shrink-wrapped in lycra. They disarm you with their questions, their nauseatingly kind eyes. They are like me in that way, I suppose.

The class huffs and heaves along with me. I move about the room, pausing to correct the position of anyone who needs it. I rest my hand on an older man's spine, using the weight of my palm to make a minor adjustment to his pose. 'Don't push too far if it feels unstable,' I whisper. This is a man who listens, not like some men, who see yoga as a competition.

Taking yoga classes is not about the money; I don't need money and I would volunteer my time if it didn't contradict what people think they know about me: that I'm kind and hardworking, but not wealthy. No, yoga instructing is a nice, normal job and I'm good at it. And the only studio in town, a neat white-washed brick building, happens to back onto a car park across the road from Billy's school, which helps.

I move through flows and, finally, into a meditation. Five minutes. The meditation is a time for me. A time for the real me to reset. Meditation is shown to *actually* work; neuroplasticity studies suggest the brain *can* change itself.

I attempt to clear my mind, scan my body, but I keep thinking about the girl who was swept up. My subconscious won't let go of the nagging suspicion that something is going to happen to Billy and me.

•

I get to school just as the other mothers are arriving and sit in the car for a moment, waiting to hear the school bell. I check my various social media accounts. My brother has posted holiday snaps. He's somewhere hot and sunny in Indonesia. The bell sounds and I climb out of the car. I cross the street towards Sandra and Cassie. They look *exactly* how a Sandra and a Cassie should. They usually stay the extra five minutes chatting to the teacher, as if it's going to affect how much attention their children get in class.

'Hi, ladies,' I say. All the botox in Cassie's face makes her smile look as if she's smiling through an embolism. I push down my loathing and smile back. They've lived out here for years but still have the city-stance, heads tilted over their mobile phones with reusable coffee cups in their other hands.

The Forrest Entrance Primary School is the only decent school in a thirty-kilometre radius, so it's one of the rare places where people like me from north of the bridge and people like Sandra and Cassie from closer to Melbourne intersect.

The kids fly from the classrooms like leaves swept by a gale, funnelling through the gates. The school bus is waiting across the road.

Billy is walking with another boy, his blond hair ruffled. I touch his shoulder when he gets close. 'Come on,' I say to him. 'See you, ladies.'

Billy sits in the back and as we drive home, he keeps his head turned away from me, blue eyes fixed on the paddocks outside.

'How was school?' I ask.

He shrugs one shoulder.

'Good?'

'It was okay.'

It's a twenty-minute drive, winding up through the hills then back down towards the river. I turn the radio on to break the silence.

After a while, I try again. 'How's Mr Holden?'

Mr Holden is the new teacher: young, curly hair, a little over-weight. I've met him once; I could tell he was nervous by the sweat rings on his cheap shirt and the sharp rising notes in his voice.

'Billy?'

'What?'

'I asked you a question. How is Mr Holden?'

'He's okay.'

'Can't shut you up today, can I?'

No response. He's probably a bit young for sarcasm.

I feel something on my lip. I touch a hand to my mouth then hold it in front of my eyes. A slug of crimson blood is crawling down my palm.

'Fuck,' I mutter.

'Mum!' Billy says.

I look up, drag the steering wheel to the left, my foot finding the brake. Something flashes by. Grey-brown, leaping from the road. The Disco slews one way, then the other. The tyres grip again and I don't resist the pull of the wheel. I accelerate through the slide, the defensive driving lessons coming back. The truck straightens and I pull off the road, coming to a stop in the tall grass. Billy breathes in short high-pitched gulps.

I let my head fall to the steering wheel. The Disco is still, the engine ticking. When I sit up, I see a dash of blood on the leather wheel.

'I didn't hit it,' I say. 'It's okay. Just a roo.'

I turn towards him, reaching out to run my palm down his face, forgetting for a moment about the blood. His skin is as cold as silk. When I take my hand away, I have left a red trail on his cheek.

'It's okay,' I repeat.

I start the Disco again, pinching my nose, tasting the blood and steering with one hand back out onto the road. My knuckles are bleached from strain and my fingers tremble with adrenaline. I wind down towards the river, over the crossing. The white van is still there. *O-U-P.*

Trees extend over the narrow road from either side as if reaching out to embrace. It has been eighty years since fire last ripped through here. It's only a matter of time before it happens again.

Soon we pass the mouth of Derek's driveway and his barley-can letterbox. At the end of the road I turn through our gate and ease the Disco down the drive. Gravel shifts beneath the wheels as I pull in beside the house. Billy opens his door and is already halfway out when I say, 'Wait.'

Rocky would normally be rushing up to the car, leaping about in a frenzy, but he is nowhere in sight. I lean forwards, scanning the backyard. The sense that something is terribly wrong is stirring again in my gut. I brace myself for anything.

'Stay in here,' I tell Billy.

He turns his big blue eyes towards me. 'Why?'

'Because I bloody well said.'

Billy slouches back in his seat and crosses his arms. I take the keys from the ignition, open the door and climb out, locking the car behind me. I stride towards the yard, my eyes searching ahead for movement.

'Rocky,' I call. 'Rocky?'

Then I notice the back gate is open.

AMY

SHE WAS SCREAMING all through the night, stopping for hours then starting again. With all my brothers and sisters in the same room lying in their bunks, no one spoke. We just laid there listening to her while we waited for sleep. That's where I sit now, daylight warming my skin through the window of the Burrow, on the edge of my bed brushing Annette's hair – one stroke with my fingers, one stroke with the brush. I hear Asha's screams start again out in the Shed. The sound rises off and on.

I wonder if the realignment would happen quicker if I had put her to sleep faster. Maybe if I hadn't hesitated it would be over by now. *If she remembers the collection, it will take longer.*

I wince again as another cry comes from the Shed. Asha will come out of this healthier and happier. It will all be worth it. It's about the ends, not the means.

•

I'm in the classroom at the back of the Great Hall that afternoon when, gazing out the window across the Clearing, I see Asha emerge from the Shed. We have been studying geography, learning about the world, the wars and violence. Ozone depletion and melting ice sheets. Our education is not to be taken lightly, Adrienne says. Jonathan, our teacher, is preparing us for the new age. Under Adrienne's instruction, he is preparing us to lead. When our brother arrives, we will be twelve, and we will be complete. We will be ready for the new age when it comes.

Asha steps out tentatively into the glare of the sun. She looks pale; her eyes are fixed on the ground. Her entire body rocks. She balls her new dress in her fists at her sides and, when she stumbles, Adam bends over to lift her back up. We all watch as she crosses the Clearing towards us.

When the door opens, Jonathan, who is standing at the front of the room, stops talking.

Adrienne enters. 'Amy,' she says, 'come with me, please.'

I follow her out of the classroom, closing the door behind me. She pauses and turns to face me.

'The full moon is coming. This year it aligns with a leap day. What a special time.'

'Yes, Mother.'

'You still haven't bled. You're too skinny. You need more protein; you need more fat.'

I swallow. She steps closer. Her face is beautiful, her blue eyes shining down on me. 'That means extra food at dinnertime. Soon enough, you might be ready for your own child. One you can keep and raise here with us in the Clearing.'

'My own?'

'Would you like that?'

'Yes, Mother.' I feel myself smiling, listing towards her. 'I would love that.' I imagine holding a baby, feeding it, carrying it against my shoulder.

'But before that happens, I want you to make Asha appreciate what she has. You must help to raise her, even if that means correcting her behaviour at times. Can you do that?'

'Yes, Mother.'

'Come on then, this way.' She leads me out into the Great Hall. Asha has been moved inside and is sitting on a knitted beanbag. I can hear Jonathan begin to speak again in the classroom.

'Show her your deepest love. Obliterate any fear or doubt she has with love.'

Asha's fingers clutch her jaw, nails chewed to the quick. Her eyes don't seem to fully open. I can imagine what it must be like, this great cavernous room, all the plain wood, and all the new smiling faces.

'Protect the Queen,' Adrienne says.

'Protect the Queen,' I repeat, smiling up into her eyes.

I lower myself to sit beside Asha on the beanbag. When my arm touches hers she retracts with a small gasp, as if I've burnt her.

'It's okay,' I say softly. 'No one is going to hurt you anymore.'

I wrap my arm around her and she pulls away again, a slow twisting struggle, but she has no strength. When she speaks I can barely hear her.

'I want to go home.'

'Shh,' I say. 'You are home.'

The other children must be scorching with jealousy. *I* am the one who gets to hold Asha first. I squeeze her against me, leaning forwards to kiss her head. I bury my nose in her hair and can smell something clean and sweet. It's blonde enough already, I note; she won't have to go through those stinging purifying sessions where minders soak our scalps in chemicals to whiten our hair.

'The hard part is over,' I promise.

I know what she has been through. The drops they place on your tongue. The room shifting as the colours become louder. The Truth with which Adrienne fills your ears. In this way, you experience an entirely new dimension. The room bends and sparkles, things leap out in a thousand shapes and colours. To learn the Truth, we need to access that other world – the place only Adrienne can take us.

When I woke after the first time I was realigned, I was five or maybe six. The smell was thick and choking; vomit, blood, other body fluids. As I began to come to, I felt the cold blast of a hose. After hours of hallucinations, hours spent in that other place, I was hosed down like an animal.

I take Asha's hands and tenderly kiss the bruises and scratches from when she tried to hammer her way through the corrugated iron of the Shed.

•

At dinner that night, I can feel Anton's eyes on me from across the table. He's huge and stooped, his hands strong and callused. He's no longer a boy at all. I glance up to see that he is frowning down at my plate. I follow his eyes and find that, for the first time, he doesn't have the most food; I do. Potatoes, carrots, peas, broccoli. More than all the younger children combined. My stomach knots.

'Eat,' Adrienne says. As one, we take up our cutlery. The hunger is painful. I eat quickly, protective of my larger portion. I have seen my brothers and sisters chasing spiders and eating them; I have seen children clutching handfuls of grass and chewing on it like cattle or scraping up crumbs into their palms. Food is worth fighting for. I glance up from my plate again. Anton is still watching me.

FREYA

Four days to go

I RUSH TO the back gate, eyes scanning the bush. It had been closed when I left that afternoon, hadn't it? *Think, Freya. Think, you bitch.* Yes. I had definitely closed it. That meant someone had opened it, someone had let Rocky out. I think about the flowers at my door.

'Rocky!'

'Mum,' Billy says. I turn around to see him standing behind me on the lawn.

'Get back in the bloody car, Billy,' I order. 'Lock the door behind you.' *Nice. Locking a child in the car again.* This is different.

I rush out the back gate towards the river. If the man is still there, I don't know what I will do or say. It's moments like this that I can feel the skin beginning to slip. Who else could have opened the gate?

Then I hear Rocky rustling in the undergrowth. He emerges with his head down, a sorry look in his eyes.

'Get home *now*.' I point and the dog scampers past me. I fish for my phone in my pocket. Dial and hold it to my ear. It rings and rings.

'Derek speaking.'

'Derek, it's Freya from next door.'

'Freya, what's going on?'

'I was just wondering if you'd noticed anyone loitering around today?'

'Like who?'

'Like anyone you've not seen before. I had someone cross my property to get to the river.'

'Ah, right. No, I didn't notice anyone.'

'Okay.' I scratch my neck. 'Strange question, but you didn't happen to open my back gate today, did you?'

'Me? No, I haven't been near your gate. What's going on? You think someone's opened it?'

'Oh, I'm sure it's nothing. I probably opened it myself.' I laugh lightly. 'I might be losing my memory.' *I do, after all, have a family history.*

'Well, we all lose it one way or another eventually.' He laughs too.

I say goodbye and hang up. I close the gate then cast my gaze over the lawn and up towards the house, looking for anything out of place.

There are always sounds: birds, the distant hum of Derek pushing the lawnmower or line trimmer, the trickle of water, critters rustling in the bush. I know no silence. I climb up onto the back deck and look about the yard, the scrolled bark the pale eucalypts have shed. There is an invisible cord between me and Billy that stretches the further apart we become. I feel it tug now. *Shit, Billy.* I hurry around the side of the house to the Disco.

Billy is sitting inside with his arms folded tight across his chest and his face turned away from the window. I use the keys to unlock the door.

'Come inside now,' I say.

'I don't want to.'

'*Get inside*,' I say, glaring.

I see the shine of his cheeks. Maybe I am being too harsh on him; he is probably still shaken up from the near miss with the roo. But in an emergency it is best to be clear and direct. Others need to understand who is in control. Granted, this isn't exactly an emergency, but it's *something*. I just don't know what.

He slides out from the back seat and walks towards the house. I follow. The bouquet of wattle still sits near the doormat. I kick it out towards the garden.

Inside, I open the roller shutters on the windows; the light expands in growing rectangles across the wooden floorboards.

Rocky is standing at the back door.

Billy rushes over to let him inside.

'Careful,' I say, as Rocky skips past him. Last year Rocky had knocked Billy over when the two of them were playing and Billy had broken his arm.

In the kitchen, I begin chopping the vegetables for dinner while Billy sits on the couch and turns on the TV. If you don't believe in the zombie apocalypse, I'm sorry to tell you that it's already arrived; put a child in front of a screen and see for yourself. Billy sits with eyes and mouth wide open. One of his front teeth is missing; it fell out yesterday.

'Billy,' I call, 'go put your tooth under your pillow. Don't forget again tonight, or the tooth fairy won't come.'

'Soon,' he says, eyes still fixed on the screen.

I walk over and take the remote from him, turn the TV off. 'No more TV,' I say. 'Do something else.'

He drags himself to his bedroom and returns towing the mini easel I had bought him. In the room next to his, my study, I've hung lengths of brown butcher's paper covered with Billy's watercolour houses and cats on the walls for his own exhibition. He believes he will be a painter. In my mind, Billy floats somewhere between talented and prodigious, but don't all mums think that?

What had my mum thought? When I decided to study art, she was disappointed. 'I think you should study something more normal,' she said stiffly. Children learn from their parents' mistakes. I will let him find his own path. I was always so afraid of letting Mum down. Jonas, my brother, is much better with her than me. Forty-one years old and still adores his mum. No wonder he's single. He's bought fifty acres way out in the country and doesn't work at all these days; I guess he's a farmer now. He's got his hippie ideals and enough of Mum's money to get by on.

Billy is struggling to open a tube of paint. I take the pliers from the toolkit beneath the sink and help him.

When I think of Billy's father, I imagine a child obsessed with soccer or basketball, rather than a child who would one day endure the rigours of neurosis that come with being creative. He might grow out of it. He tangles himself around my legs whenever strangers try to talk to him, and he still likes it when I pick him up and carry him in public; he's seven years old and seems intent on causing me a serious spinal injury.

He manages to get hurt a lot for a quiet boy. When Rocky bumped him down the deck stairs, it took eight weeks in a cast for his arm to heal, and in that time Billy – who is right-handed – learnt to use his left hand for most things. I wonder what Aspen would have been like as a seven-year-old?

I have been thinking about Aspen more and more today. I guess it has something to do with the missing girl. The familiar feeling when I reflect on that time: a sinkhole opening in my gut. When I lost Aspen and was alone again, I would occasionally drive to playgrounds and kindergartens to simply sit in my car and watch all the happy children. I haven't done that since Billy was born.

I finish chopping vegetables then reach for my phone and check my emails. I see I have an email from Corazzo, an old friend. It's a news article about Henrik but I'm not in the mood to read it. I know what it's about already; he's being released from prison in just a few days. I don't know how Mum met Henrik but he was the closest thing I had to a father.

Billy is painting Rocky, who is lying in a square of sun on the floor. The nib of Billy's tongue sits in the corner of his mouth as he concentrates. I should start painting again. One of these days I will. I've got all that unsold art out in the fire bunker. Oil on canvas, scenes of the bush with a black square obscuring the centre of the image. I hate them, but they're an insurance policy. I could sell them if I run out of money.

I take my chopped vegetables and a tray of eggs and make frittata. I put it in the oven before heading outside to the yard in my boots. Sweat rises instantly and runs down my cheeks. Fingers of late-afternoon sun pass between the trees. I rake the leaves, the eucalypt bark and other debris, weary of the long grass. I'm always on the lookout for brown snakes at this time of year.

The heat is a presence. It presses down on my skin. The drone of the air-conditioning unit thrums over the yard.

Despite countless visits to Olivia, my psychologist – when I first lost Aspen I was ordered by the court to see her – the sense that disaster is imminent blooms inside. Olivia would tell me that my fear is irrational, borne out of trauma from the past. She would tell me I shouldn't be afraid because there is nothing to fear. But what if she is wrong? I know the heat is flustering me. I need to cool down.

I finish raking, then hose down the lawn all the way to the door of the fire bunker. From where I stand, I can see through the bush to a patch of river.

'Billy,' I call, without turning around. 'Billy!' Louder still.

The door opens. 'Yeah?'

I turn. He's standing half in, half out, like a child dipping his foot into a hot bath.

'You want to go for a swim?'

'No.' He twists as he says it.

'Why not?'

'I'm painting.'

'Right. Well it's hot and I feel like a swim.'

'Can I stay and paint?'

I don't know why I feel so reluctant to leave him alone. Yesterday it wasn't a problem. Freya Heywood isn't a helicopter parent . . . or maybe she is. Maybe when I think of Aspen and the past, when I think of the girl who was taken, I become a helicopter parent. It will only be ten minutes, I tell myself. *Is this what a* good *mother would do?* the other voice in my head says.

'Alright,' I say, stripping down to my underwear there on the lawn. 'I won't be long. Could you lock the door while I'm gone?'

He nods enthusiastically, happy that he got his way. The door closes. A moment of concentration on his face as he twists the lock.

'And the front door too,' I call through the glass. I just need to cool down, gather my thoughts.

He looks serious as he nods again and rushes towards the front door.

When I see he is back at his easel, I make my way down to the river.

There's no sign of the couple I'd seen earlier. Relieved, I step out of my underwear and unhook my bra, let it drop to the ground. I walk into the cool water. My neck feels stiff and tense, a tingling sensation spreads. I am not self-conscious about my scars and my naked body, the skin rippled with lightning storms of stretch marks at my belly and my breasts from Aspen first, then Billy later.

The wind comes on strong, bringing the heat down from the hills. The drought has driven the river level lower, rocks long submerged now breach the surface and still pools are isolated from the flow of water. I suck in a breath and turn over, holding my head beneath the surface for as long as I can.

I think about Aspen's father – my ex, Wayne. I think about what he took from me. I think about Henrik Masters. He'll be out of prison soon enough. I stay under the water, feel the pain starting deep in my brain; my arms and legs ache. My heart is thudding. Just a few more seconds. Someone is watching me. Is someone watching the house too? I rise, drag a breath deep into my lungs, feel the ache begin to subside.

When I climb out of the water, I reach for my underwear and pull it on without drying myself.

I run back to the house, my heart knocking, but it settles when I see Billy at his easel. I watch for a moment without disturbing him, pulling my clothes back on.

As I climb the back steps, Billy turns. He comes to the door to let me in. Then his mouth shifts, his eyes widen. He raises one finger and points behind me.

My pulse racing, I turn to see a man striding across the lawn. I quickly swing about, my arms coming up in defence. I am casting about for a weapon when I recognise the dark face beneath the Akubra.

'Hey, Karate Kid!' he calls.

I let out my breath. 'Derek,' I say. Billy unlocks the door behind me. The adrenaline is fading. 'You gave me a fright.' *You silly old perv.*

'You're alright. Just checking in. You sounded a bit shaken up on the phone.'

'It's nothing,' I say. 'Just these people that were at the river and then finding my gate open. It creeps me out to think that someone was on my land.'

'That's fair enough.' He scratches his right cheek. He has a jawless face, everything softening in old age, and he's wearing gardening gloves. 'I mean when you say *on* your land—'

'They were trespassing.'

'They shouldn't be leaving gates open.'

'They shouldn't be on my property regardless of what they do with the gate.'

'Yes. Right.'

My voice sounds harsh to my own ears. I smile, wanting him to leave but not wanting to show it. I keep up the good hospitable neighbour act. 'Have you eaten? I've got a frittata in the oven.'

'Not yet,' he says. 'Frittata sounds great.'

Shit, I think, as I widen my smile. 'Come on in then.'

Inside, Derek scrubs Billy's head with his palm and crosses to the table, taking a seat. 'Hot out, isn't it?'

AMY

MY SKETCHING CLASS takes place outside of regular learning hours. Jermaine Boethe is a famous artist, Adrienne told me. He has exhibitions. While the others are in the Burrow, I am in the classroom with my charcoal pencils and a sheet of paper. Jermaine closes the door behind us. This has been a regular class for me once a week and we have been working on sketches of humans and animals. He is always ready with a compliment, both for me and for Adrienne. He says things like: *Your mother is doing wonderful, amazing, incredible things in the world. She is controlling everything.*

I can hear the cicadas outside and the moths at the windows as Jermaine says, 'I have a very special project for you today.'

He places a chair behind the door, the seat back beneath the doorhandle. I watch him walk towards me, his pot belly pressing against his shirt.

'I cannot bring a model down to the Clearing, but it is an important part of the artist's development to understand the human body and to draw it.'

He loosens the buttons of his shirt, one at a time. Black hair runs down his chest, thicker at his belly button, circling it like a blocked drain. He breathes in so his chest rises, then he lets his shirt slip from his body. He unbuttons his pants. They drop to his feet. Finally, he peels off his socks. I'm struck by the shape of him – I had only seen the naked bodies of boys, all bones and skin drawn tight. Jermaine Boethe is different. The roll of skin hanging down over his penis, the curls of black hair everywhere.

'Okay, Amy?'

I nod.

'Begin.'

I dip my head. I don't know where to look, but it is hard to turn away. He sits over the edge of the desk. Then I see his hand slide across the top of his thigh to hold his penis.

'Keep sketching.'

His breathing is ragged and hoarse. I imagine his throat all phlegmy and half closed.

I can't believe that this great artist is doing this, I wonder if he has done this for other students? This must be part of the process.

I take the pencil, glancing up at him, then back down. When I sketch, I am also imagining the scene before me. It's not enough to refer back to it; there is a gap between when my eyes look away from the subject and my pencil moves across the page. I keep imagining him, building the image in my brain so I barely have to look up at all.

I fill the page with his shape first, just like he had showed me. Arms, legs, torso, head. They all begin as elongated circles, prisms. I begin to form the contours of his arms and legs, his fat knees and hanging ankles while he pulls away at himself.

'Good girl,' he says, like this is a normal class. 'Good girl, keep going.'

I take a finer pencil and fill in the details: his eyes, the stubble, the black curls that are scrubby at the shoulders but thicken at the chest, and up his thighs. Then I draw his penis, the grip he has on it.

He slows his movement, and pulls his clothes back on quickly, so quickly I can't even finish the sketch. He takes the piece of paper on which I am drawing and shoves it into his pocket.

Normally my sketches remain in the classroom, in the drawer with the rest of my schoolwork. I feel a pang of frustration in my chest, it seems so silly.

'I'll hold on to this,' he says. 'Let's keep this lesson between us. You're not much of a talker anyway, are you?'

He leaves the room, leaving me sitting there. I look down at my blank sketchpad. I had pressed so hard that the outline of my drawing has gone through to the next page.

The lesson is over, I can go to bed. But I don't.

Instead I take up the pencil and begin the sketch again, following the outline at first and then filling in the details from memory. This time, the drawing is even better, the thighs more proportionate, the eyes gazing towards me instead of looking down. I sign my name at the bottom like a real artist, like Jermaine Boethe would, and place the sheet of paper with the rest of my artwork in my school drawer. I stack my desk away and pack up my pencils, my mind still whirling with what had just happened.

I had seen my brothers and sisters without clothes on. And, of course, Adrienne. But I had never seen a man like Jermaine Boethe. It is interesting, and now I have all these deviant thoughts. I have a secret – and we're not supposed to keep secrets.

PART TWO
THIS IS HOW IT ENDS

So the Lord God caused a deep sleep to fall upon the man, and he slept; then He took one of his ribs and closed up the flesh at that place.

Genesis 2:21

**POLICE LAUNCH HUNT FOR MISSING SEVEN-
YEAR-OLD GIRL SARA MCFETRIDGE, LAST SEEN
ON JACKSON ROAD AT 3:19 PM YESTERDAY**

Victoria Police has launched an urgent search for a child who vanished yesterday afternoon near her home south of Nimbi Flat.

Sara McFetridge was dropped off at the corner of Jackson and Moonah roads, and was later reported missing by her grandfather at 4:22 pm.

Sara has blonde hair and blue eyes. Officers say she was wearing a pink t-shirt, a yellow dress and a pink backpack, which is also missing.

Search and rescue teams, along with local volunteers, have been deployed in the surrounding paddocks, and police are calling on members of the public to come forward with any information.

Senior Sergeant Jared Grant said: 'Sara's disappearance is completely out of character and we are all concerned for her welfare.

'It's snake season out here, and it's not safe for a little girl to be wandering around alone in this heat.

'We haven't ruled out abduction, but our first priority is to canvass the surrounding areas to see if anyone noticed anything out of the ordinary.'

FREYA

Three days to go

HAVING A TRAINED guard dog is a little like having a sixty-kilogram toddler that can crush a human forearm on command. Rocky was trained almost a decade ago now; he's getting older, but he still listens and still knows to respond when a command is given.

Now he is howling, a long winding groan between barks. I reach for my phone, shine the light into the room and climb from my bed. I try to chase the fear from my mind with logic. It's just a possum or something outside bothering him.

It was Corazzo who arranged for Rocky to be trained. He knew a guy. I was shown how to control him, taught what visitors should do when they enter the house. Rocky was trained to be a house alarm and a defender without losing his affectionate side. A house alarm with something of a hair trigger, I should add. When he came back from training he had a new vocabulary. Not only did he know *food*, *walk* and *sit*, but *search*, *release*, *lay*, *attack*, *stop*, *stay*. Most commands come with a hand gesture. The only humans on the planet this big idiot dog knows to trust are me and Billy. I suppose he is used to Derek by now, too.

When I reach the lounge, I hit the lights and squint against the sudden brightness. I thought the light would help with my fear, but it somehow makes me more afraid. Rocky's low growl continues, growing more certain now that I'm in the room. I wouldn't normally bother checking the yard, assuming it was a possum, but after today I decide to have a look.

'Quiet, before you wake the child up.' *The child*. The child has a name. Billy's room is at one end of the house, through the dining room and lounge. I quickly open his door a fraction and check in on him. Still asleep. I go back to the lounge and the back door opening out into the yard.

I know if I open the back door, if I raise my palm and utter the word *search*, Rocky will be out there as quick as a shot. Rocky is brave, but blind bravery comes from ignorance of the real threat. My heart is still slamming in my chest and I can barely see outside. The windows only reflect me back to myself. Dark shadows around my eyes, my cheeks drawn and anaemic – *you're a ghost*.

I reach for the switch to the outdoor light and turn it on. The yard is illuminated. I exhale. What was I expecting? I thumb the knot in my chest, imagining wide eyes staring back at me from somewhere down at the tree line that fringes the river. A lone moth is already caught in the gravitational pull of the light.

This house is so much glass, so many windows. *A perk of the sixties architecture*, according to the real estate agent. It's as good an alarm clock as I have ever had. Without curtains for every window, light fills the house, making it impossible to sleep past sunrise. The roller shutters installed on the exterior windows and doors block it out, but the walls of aluminium slats make me feel like I'm in prison, so I often choose to leave them up, particularly in my bedroom. On the plus side, my body always aligns with the sunrise and I maintain a natural circadian rhythm. On the other hand, all those windows make hangovers considerably worse. But when was the last time I drank enough to get a hangover?

I don't know why Rocky is howling. I imagine Henrik out there watching me, but it can't be him. He won his appeal but won't be released from prison until later this week. He'll be wanting to see me and Mum, I'm sure.

It's times like now, when I realise how isolated I am, that I wonder why I chose this mid-century behemoth over something smaller, easier to hide. In the dark of the night, when the house is lit up from within, anyone could be out there watching. But I have Rocky, and I have a couple of months of self-defence classes under my belt.

In the still room, staring out into the night, I remind myself of all those movements, the small muscles that activate when you are throwing a man off you, how your elbow automatically flies up to your ear, covering your neck, when you sense someone is going to choke you from behind. The exact reaction I had yesterday afternoon when Derek turned up.

'You're a very courageous thing, aren't you?' I say to Rocky, reaching down to rub his neck. I flick the switch and watch the roller shutters descend, sealing us off from the world outside.

I think of all the reasons I *should* feel safe. Rocky; the roller shutters; the remoteness; the only man I truly fear is still in prison, for now; I haven't heard from Wayne in years; my self-defence training; Derek is close enough to help. No one wants to hurt me anymore; my family will always protect me. (This last one I'm not so sure about. Jonas is overseas, and Mum has her own battle with dementia.)

But it's not about me. I am not afraid for my own safety as much as I fear for Billy. I fear that I won't always be there when he needs me. It's a cliché, I know, but it's true. What if something happens at school, or in the middle of the night? Which reminds me – the tooth.

I take a two-dollar coin and go to his room. Gently sliding my hand under his pillow, I find the tooth, a porcelain stone, and replace it with the coin.

In the kitchen, I hold the tooth up to the light; there is a tiny chip in the corner. I go to my room and place it in the top drawer of my dresser.

I call Rocky through to my room and pat the end of the bed. He leaps up. His big meaty shape circles then falls down against my legs.

'Let's not make this a thing, eh, boy? One night on my bed then back to yours.'

I've always measured distances between me and Billy in terms of how quickly I could get to him if he was in trouble. If he ever choked, for example, or collapsed suddenly. I'm only seconds away from his room. The morning will be here soon enough. *Close your eyes, Freya, breathe, relax, let sleep take you.*

•

Billy is awake before me. The birds are singing out there in their trees. I don't have time for a swim or a walk. I barely have time to slurp down my breakfast smoothie before we're racing out in the Disco. At the lights down near the bridge into Tullawarra township, I look in the mirror. My skin sags beneath my eyes. I finger it, dragging it out to flatten it, and see the blue fish-scale veins just beneath the surface. I hate losing control, I hate when something puts me out. I couldn't sleep last night, and so I overslept this morning. Now I'm trying to regain control, to look and feel like Freya Heywood. *Pull yourself together, stop being weak.*

'What are you doing, Mama?'

'I'm trying to make it look like I had more than three hours sleep.'

The light changes and I accelerate away.

After I drop Billy at school, I head to the grocer. The white-haired shopkeeper is leaning on the checkout counter, shaking his head at the newspaper.

'G'day, Freya,' he says, glancing up as I enter.

I pick up a basket. 'Hey, Paul, what's news?'

He taps the newspaper with his finger. 'See this?' he asks. 'The missing kid?'

'Yeah,' I say. 'Sad, isn't it?'

'I'll say. Some cruel' – a yawn overtaking him – 'cruel people in this world.' Then, as if realising who he is talking to, his eyes spring wide open, the colour drains from his face. 'Sorry. You don't want to hear about this . . .'

'No, no, it's fine. They think she might have wandered off, right?' I stroll towards the bakery section and pick up some croissants for Mum, then turn to look at him. Paul is a true local. Six decades in this town. His parents saw the fires.

His eyes are fixed on the counter now. 'Uh, I think they're saying it's a kidnapping.'

I'm reaching for a bottle of mineral water when the bell above the door sounds. Someone else is in the shop.

'Hey, mate, I just wanted a bottle of juice.'

A knot of panic passes through me as I recognise the voice. I try to breathe but the air is stuck in my throat. It's Wayne. It has to be him. It's been eight years, but I would know his voice anywhere. *Keep the mask on, Freya.*

'In the refrigerated section down the back.'

'Thanks.'

I am in the refrigerated section. I quickly move away and duck down the next aisle.

What is he doing here? I think of Aspen, what Wayne did, how he left me broken. What will he do if he sees me? What might he say? I listen, trying to map his movement about the store. I could abandon the basket and flee for the door, I think.

The scanner beeps and I exhale. He's back at the front now.

'Two ninety, thanks.'

The cash register opens, slots closed.

I feel a trickle of sweat run down my cheek. I have a secret, and if Wayne finds out he could ruin my life again.

'See ya later.'

'Yep.'

The bell at the door sounds again. I wait a few minutes before taking my basket to the counter. Paul rings up my purchases.

'Plans this afternoon?' he asks while I punch in the pin of my credit card.

'Oh, nothing special.'

'Right.'

I can tell he is staring at me, but I keep my gaze fixed on the screen of the card machine.

'Are you alright?' he probes.

'Me?'

He swallows. 'I didn't mean to bring up the missing kid, you know.'

Hold it together, the voice says. *Don't crack now you bitch.*

'Yeah,' I say, aiming a smile at him. 'It's fine, don't stress. I didn't think anything of it.'

He stuffs the receipt in the bag. 'Well, sorry all the same.'

'I'm just feeling a little off. Must be the heat.' I take the reusable shopping bag and walk quickly to the car park. My heart is still hammering. Wayne is back. I feel eyes somewhere watching me, but I keep my head up and pace directly to my car.

•

Olivia is waiting for me when I arrive at her office ten minutes later. She smiles and guides me into her room.

I saw her for years after Aspen, then I stopped. But since Mum has become ill, I've started to see her again. For the last year or so she has made constellations of all the things that have happened in my life. Once upon a time, all we spoke about was Wayne and what happened with Aspen. When he and I were set to face off in court, our names had been suppressed, but the case was in the newspapers. They were talking about Aspen and what I did to him. Wayne had told his lawyer about the small acts of neglect, things I put Aspen through that were admittedly a little unconventional, but they were taken so far out of context that by the end of proceedings they made me a monster. The soft slaps I used to punish him with, the way I had shaken him to quieten his sobs.

Olivia helped me work through that difficult time, I even let her get close enough to see glimpses of the real me. I'm trying to be honest with her so she can help me come to terms with what I am. Now we tend to speak about my relationship with my mother and untangle the yarn ball of neurosis I carry in my head.

Today Olivia sits me down and smiles that close-lipped smile that fans the skin about her eyes.

'So, what has been happening lately, Freya?' she begins.

Soft Balinese chimes wind through the speakers. Olivia, who sits across from me in her wingback chair, reaches forwards to the coffee table for the pot of chamomile tea, pouring us each a cup.

'I've decided I'm going to try to paint again.'

'That's a great idea.'

'Yeah. I've been exercising a lot. Walking every day. Some swimming.' I pick up my cup and take a sip, scalding my tongue.

'Well, it sounds like you have some good healthy habits at the moment. I hope you're not exercising too much?'

'No. Not too much. I still give myself enough space and time to cook and think.'

She gives me a warm smile. 'Good, good.'

'But I saw something on the news . . .' She is nodding as I speak. 'A girl . . . a girl has been taken. Well, she's missing.'

Olivia raises her eyebrows over her glasses, so her forehead corrugates. There's a pause in the music as the track ends and for the first time I notice the purr of the air-conditioning. 'I can see how that could be . . .' she squints as if she might read the word she is searching for in the distance '. . . significant. How did you feel on hearing about that?'

I think for a moment. 'I was afraid, I suppose.'

'Afraid for your son?'

'Yeah,' I say, my eyes gliding away towards the window. 'And afraid of Wayne.'

'Mmm,' Olivia says. 'Well, I guess we've got a bit to work through, huh?'

'I know bad things happen to people. But I've had my share of bad things already. I don't want to be on the lookout all my life, always scared, always preparing for something to happen. What if they come for Billy?'

'Who exactly do you mean?'

I shrug.

'Fear is a normal reaction, Freya – especially given your history. Do you feel that you do enough as a mother for Billy?'

'Yes. Of course, I do,' I say, keeping my voice neutral.

'You went through a lot. Sometimes very good, very kind people make mistakes and sometimes these mistakes hurt others. That doesn't mean something bad is going to happen to you.'

I often wonder if she thinks I deliberately hurt Aspen. I don't push back on the point. 'I know. The last few days I've had this feeling, though. I have a sense that something is going to happen. I feel like someone is watching me.'

'Do you think part of this is about Henrik Masters?'

If I am honest, the answer is yes. I've been waiting almost twenty years for him to come out, knowing it was always going to happen.

'Maybe.'

'What else is happening around you when you get this feeling?'

'I'm alone, or with Rocky.'

'Right. So maybe it's born out of fear of the unknown? Of being away from Billy?'

'Yeah. But it's not just that. I noticed a van parked near my house. Just up the road. A *van*, Olivia.' I let my eyes settle on her face.

'A van,' she repeats.

'And there was a strange couple hanging out by the river on my property.'

'Do you feel as if things you can normally count on and control have changed? For instance, having full privacy and isolation at home?'

I lean back and suck my teeth. It's more than that. I have always been controlling – I like control, I *need* control – but it is so much more.

'I worry about bushfires. What if they accidentally start a fire?'

Olivia gives a knowing nod, makes a thoughtful noise at the back of her throat.

This is not the real fear, we have the fire bunker and a solid escape plan. I can't say what I am truly afraid of. My eyes roam the carpet chequered with squares of light passing through the window.

'Perhaps it would be good to have a change of scene. Have you considered a short holiday?' Olivia shuffles in her seat, adjusting her legs, one knee over the other.

'I'm thinking about getting a panic button installed.'

'That could help. But let's focus on the exact nature of the dangers you are perceiving and why they stimulate this acute threat response.'

I sigh, sinking through the couch, the floor, into the hot dark soil. 'It's Henrik. I'm at home thinking about Henrik. And now Wayne is back.'

'Oh,' Olivia says. She touches her glasses. 'Right.'

I can see her processing this, that sharp little mind springing into action now that she is faced with a real problem with potentially serious consequences. 'Where?'

'Where?'

'Where did you see Wayne?'

'At the grocer. I heard him.'

'You heard him? You didn't see him?'

'That's right.'

She looks sceptical.

'I know his voice,' I insist.

'Perhaps you still blame him for the loss of Aspen – which is a completely natural feeling to have. If you had a friend in the position you are in, what would your advice be to them?'

I think about it. It's a good question, a way to rationalise the situation with an alternative perspective.

Then I understand what I would say. 'I would tell them to run.'

— Amy's journal —

Three facts about my mother:

1. She is the reincarnation of Jesus Christ.
2. She will do anything to protect her family.
3. She believes education and discipline are the most necessary virtues when preparing for the new age.

That's what our six school days of the week are designed around: education and discipline.

This is what normally happens:

6.00:   Wash, clean teeth, make beds.

6.25:   Put tracksuits on.

6.30:   Hatha yoga and meditation.

7.30:   Listen to one of Adrienne's sermons.

7.45:   Chanting, then meditation.

8.00:   Sprints to the front gate and back (short bursts of exercise are healthier than endurance exercise).

8.15:   Breakfast (usually a piece of fruit or a single slice of bread).

8.35:   Get changed again, this time into our regular clothes. (If outsiders are coming to the Clearing, we wear our best clothes: matching dresses for us girls and matching shirts and pants for the boys.)

8.40:   Set up our classroom at the back of the Great Hall.

8.55:   First bell, school begins.

10.45: Recess.

11.00: Schoolwork.

12.15:   *Exercise. (Badminton, usually, or foot races. Occasionally we are instructed on self-defence with rubber knives or rubber bats. Or sometimes Adam hangs wallaby carcasses up for us to practise with real knives.)*

12.30:   *Lunch.*

1.00:   *Schoolwork.*

2.30:   *Recess.*

2.45:   *Schoolwork.*

4.00:   *Pack up classroom, tidy Great Hall for dinner, sweep bedrooms, clean showers and bathroom.*

5.00:   *Meditation. (Each day a different child will meditate alone in the blue room – a small alcove off the Great Hall, where the walls are painted sky blue and a single image of Adrienne's face hangs to the west. We are not allowed to close our eyes but must stare at Adrienne's face.)*

5.15:   *The servers for the day begin cooking dinner while the rest of us do chores such as chopping wood, collecting eggs from the chickens or working in the vegetable garden.*

6.00:   *Dinner. Portions are determined according to our weight. Younger children receive much smaller meals than us teenagers.*

6.30:   *Clean teeth, occasionally listen to a sermon from Adrienne.*

AMY

THIS MORNING ADAM was away and the minders were in charge. We complete our morning meditations and exercise. We unstack the desks and line them up before beginning school. Asha is there, weeping silently as Jonathan hands out our reading for the day. The books are ancient, the corners tattered and torn with threads showing through the hard covers.

I open the first page and begin reading the dense text. We are going to be tested on comprehension; I need to understand and annotate the book. I raise my hand.

'Yes, Amy?'

'Could I have my notebook, please?'

'Certainly. Would anyone else like their notebook?' Jonathan asks. Most of my brothers and sisters raise their hands. He goes through our individual steel drawers one by one, making his way to the end. My drawer is last. I see him rifle through it for my notebook. I have a feeling inside, I know something bad is about to happen. The notebooks he is carrying in one arm slip, clattering to the floor. Everyone looks up to see Jonathan's hand fly to his mouth. He turns to stare at me, his eyes wide, as he draws out a piece of paper. My chest feels heavy as though wrapped tightly in worry. *What have I done?*

'Amy,' he says. 'Come with me.'

I stand up and he leads me through the Great Hall to the top of the steps outside. He closes the door behind us. Then stops and turns back to me. My fears are confirmed when I see what is in his hand. The sketch of Jermaine Boethe.

'When did you draw this?'

I can't bear to look at it. I'm so scared they're going to punish me that I can't speak. I can only see the image in my mind of water sloshing in the Cooler. I keep my eyes down and shake my head.

He makes a clicking sound with his tongue. 'Wait here,' he says. I hear the rhythmic whoosh of his pants as he strides off towards the minders' quarters, still clutching my drawing in his fist.

It's hard to know what the teachers think and how they are going to behave. Our music teacher, Ian, once sat for over an hour listening to me playing Chopin's *Nocturne in F minor, Opus 55*. Adrienne wants me to develop as a pianist. Each time I dropped a note, I felt the hard edge of a ruler crack against my knuckles. After the first few times through I was able to play it without the music in front of me, and soon I could get through it without dropping a note. Music can be fun. Playing with all my brothers and sisters, singing together in harmony. Sometimes Ian and Adam play together, taking the guitars and harmonicas. The memory distracts me only for a moment. When I finally look up, Jonathan has reached the minders' quarters. Tamsin and Indigo are sitting out the front on the grass. The teacher raises his fist, holding the sketch out before them. The minders look over at me then back at the picture. My cheeks glow. I brace myself but for what I don't know.

FREYA

Three days to go

BACK IN THE car, as I head out of town towards Mum's place, I call Corazzo. He doesn't pick up, so I try again. Sometimes I feel homesick for a place and a time I never really had, and that's when I turn to Corazzo. He is also just a good friend to have. He still has contacts in the police from before he retired. He was there for me first with Henrik, then after Wayne. He fought for me when everyone blamed me for what happened to Aspen. He is *good* – as good as a man like him can be. He's objective and honest. He will be the first to help you move to a new house, and he'll be the first to visit you in hospital. He knows most of my secrets except the one that only Mum and I share.

'G'day, Freya.'

'You weren't answering a moment ago.'

'Sorry, I've been in the garden. This dry weather has done a real number on my veggies.'

'You need a new hobby,' I say. 'Or a wife.'

I hear him laugh down the line. 'I used to have one of those, didn't end well as you may recall. But if you know anyone looking for a grumpy old husband, let me know.'

'I'll keep my eyes peeled.'

'So what can I do you for?'

'I just wanted to chat.'

'Since when have you ever wanted to chat? This wouldn't happen to be about Henrik?'

'Henrik, yes,' I say. 'And something else. There's a van parked down the road from me. It's been there a while. I'm a bit suspicious.'

'Suspicious? That doesn't sound like you.'

'Ha-ha,' I deadpan. 'If I get you the plates, is there any way you can check them out?'

'I can organise that for you, sure.'

'I'll text you.'

'No worries. Come out and see me soon, okay?'

I hang up and turn the radio on. I think about what Olivia said about taking a holiday. A holiday is the last thing on my mind, but it might be a good idea to disappear for a while, just until Wayne clears out. The advice to my imaginary friend was *run* but I know it's not as simple as that. We could stay with Mum if she's got room. Or maybe not. Me and Billy going incognito in a retirement village – not my best idea. Perhaps we could head up to Jonas's place while he's away. He owns fifty barren acres up in a dustbowl near the border. He's going off the grid, he told me. Solar panels, a dam (dry at the moment), a vegetable garden the size of the CBD. Jonas is the type to rub sage under his arms instead of deodorant, and he's fashioned a brazier out of an old washing machine drum. I get the feeling he's setting himself up to be some kind of survivalist. On second thought, heading all the way up to Jonas's probably isn't a good idea either. I don't want to leave civilisation behind altogether.

It takes over an hour to drive out to Mum's from Tullawarra. She's been in the home for eight months. For two decades before that she lived in a five-bedroom house by herself, and now she's in a two-bedroom unit with a nursing station nearby and twice daily visits from a carer. As her condition worsens, she will have to be moved again into full-time care. Jonas is resisting the idea, he thinks she's doing fine, but it's inevitable. In the last few months she has deteriorated rapidly. It's a question of weeks now; Jonas will just have to accept it.

I roll up into the hills. The road's edge is lined with native brush, bleached by the harsh dry summer. I turn off down a country road, and soon I'm driving through a dusty township. A milk bar, a fish-and-chip shop, an old-timey service station. I pull the Disco in. I duck down to pull the lever to open the gas flap, and when I look up again my heart leaps and lodges in my throat. An old man with grease-stained cheeks and blue overalls is bending to look in through my passenger window. *Jesus Christ*, I think, *It's like* The Hills Have Eyes *out here.* 'Hi,' I say, lowering the window.

'Ninety-one?' he says.

'Sorry?'

'What petrol you want? Will ninety-one do you?'

'Yeah,' I say. 'Fill it up, please.'

'Want me to check your oil?'

'Sure.'

'Pop the bonnet.'

I do, then head inside to pay. There's a woman behind the counter wearing a large dress that might have once been a tablecloth. She's sitting on a stool watching a YouTube video on an old desktop computer.

'Hi,' I say. 'Just the fuel.'

She pauses the video and turns to me. 'He's still pumping.'

'Right.'

'Where you heading?'

'Eucalyptus Acres.'

'Oh yeah,' she says, studying my face for a moment. I glance away and find myself looking at the paper on the counter, the front-page story about the missing girl.

'You got a mum or dad out there?'

'Mum,' I say.

The bell tinkles as the door opens and the man enters.

'Oil's good, topped your water up too.'

'Thanks,' I say.

I pay on my card and quickly walk back to the Disco. As I'm driving away, I see the man standing out on the forecourt watching me, one hand cupped over his eyes.

Soon the sign appears on the left, lichen-chewed but the words still legible: *Eucalyptus Acres.* I turn between the pale trees and drive along the gravel track. The reception building looks deserted, but a nurse walking between the units raises her hand at me as I pass. I wonder if Mum remembers that Henrik is coming out. I wonder if she remembers what Henrik did.

I park near reception, then walk past other units, all detached, all brick walls and steel roofs with their own tiny yards and parking spots. I walk all the way to Mum's unit hidden at the edge of the village and knock on her door, she doesn't answer. I knock again, louder, then I hear her call from inside.

'It's open,' she calls in her prim voice.

'Mum,' I say, stepping into the room. 'It's me.'

She's in a chair at the dining table and swivels her head towards me. 'Oh, hello. I didn't know you were coming today.'

I look around the sitting room. It opens into the kitchen where the dining table is. Reminders are scrawled on a whiteboard on her fridge. I see her art on the walls; even here she manages to show off her extraordinary privilege. Her jewellery is laid out on a cabinet, her crystal on display. Nurses don't make a lot of money. It's probably not a good idea to leave this stuff lying around.

She has that vague look in her eyes.

'I brought you croissants,' I tell her, raising the paper bag. For years I've done this dance, treating her tenderly, showing her the love a daughter is supposed to.

'Oh,' she says, looking uncertain. 'Croissants. Thank you. Is your brother here with you?'

'No, Mum. He's away at the moment. He's overseas.'

'Overseas? I thought he was coming today.'

'No,' I say. 'He'll be back in a couple of weeks.' I sit down across from her at the table. 'Do you want it heated up?'

'What?'

'The croissant?'

'Oh, um, yes. Just warm, please.'

'Here,' I say, opening Facebook and handing her my phone. 'Look at Jonas's travel photos.'

I rise and place both the croissants on a plate and put the plate in the microwave.

'It looks nice there, doesn't it?' she says.

'Mum, did you know Henrik is coming out?' I say, turning back to face her.

She closes her eyes, either in pain or trying to recall something long forgotten.

'Mum?'

She opens her eyes. 'He's coming out of where?'

'Prison.'

'Oh yes, of course.'

'He hasn't tried to get in touch with you, has he? He hasn't tried to find out where I am?'

'Is he still in prison?'

I let my breath out. It's exhausting trying to get sense out of her. This woman whose sarcasm could once draw blood can now barely follow a simple conversation. What was I thinking? Of course she doesn't know about Henrik. Last time I visited her here, she caught me going through her drawers. She'd taken my hands in hers and pulled them away. 'Don't do that, please,' she said. I wonder if she told Jonas.

I carry the croissants to the table and begin tearing them apart. Mum just watches me. I wonder what she is thinking? Or more importantly, what does she think I'm thinking?

'Could we maybe look at some photos together, some photos from the past?' I say.

Her gaze seems to sharpen, but she merely reaches out and takes a piece of croissant. We eat for a moment in silence.

'What photos?'

'I was wondering if you had any photos from when we were younger? Photos from my childhood. Where would they be? I can get them so we can look at them together.'

'No,' she says. 'No photos here.'

I turn away. How many times have I visited? How many times have I searched for the old photos? They must be somewhere. She can't have just thrown them out. I think about Billy. I look up at the clock above the door. School is out in a little over an hour. I'd better get moving.

AMY

ADRIENNE WAS GONE last night and when a dark car with black windows turns up in the morning, I rush out with all my brothers and sisters to see her. Adam arrives first, and Adrienne gently embraces him. Then we all gather around and take turns hugging her, touching her, being close to her.

One night without her and I missed her so much. She wears big sunglasses and when she removes them, her eyes fall on Asha, the new girl. Adrienne looks at her with such love that I feel a stitch of jealousy.

'Asha,' she says. 'You, my daughter, are settling in and don't you look so beautiful.' Asha lets her eyes drop to the long pale grass of the Clearing. She is still adjusting. She doesn't know that it is rude to look away from Adrienne when she is speaking to you. 'My new angel, welcome to Eden.' Adrienne reaches down and tugs a loose thread from Asha's dress, snapping it between her long manicured nails, before she sets off towards the Great Hall.

Adrienne seems to float as we follow in her wake. She turns back to Anton, who is lumbering along behind her.

'I can see Annabelle's roots, and Alex is scratching like a leper. Can you check the bunks for lice?' Anton simply nods.

The minders – Tamsin, skinny and sweating, and Indigo, her wrists folded against her hips – stand near Adrienne in quiet reverence. Jonathan is there too.

She turns to me. 'Amy,' she says. My name from her lips warms me. 'Look at your cheeks, so tanned. You are looking healthy, child. But you must protect your skin. And your dress is far too short. Lower that hem – do it today.' I wonder if she knows about the sketch. I still haven't been punished, no one has even mentioned it.

My face flushes with heat. 'Yes, Mother.' I must have grown. I should have thought about how my clothes would change as my body did. 'I'm sorry.'

'Don't apologise. Just don't act like a little whore,' she says to me. Then she stops walking at the foot of the steps up to the Great Hall and turns back to the entire group. 'As you know, we have been searching for your brother, one more child to make up our perfect twelve.' She smiles. 'And I believe that we have found him.'

Clouds of tiny flies.
The sting of the sun where my hair parts.
Shreds of eucalyptus bark.
Hard dusty earth.

This is what I think of when I think of the bush. We were out there today.
    A low branch opened a red scratch across my cheek. It still stings.
Adam wanted us to witness a miracle, and we did.
    We all wore our brown boots. It was even hotter in the bush. Adam
says the humidity makes the air thicker, like you're wading through
it, and that's what it felt like to me. I could feel all the crawling bugs
and spiders. I can still feel the dust clinging to my calves.
    Adam was talking about the natural world. He talked about
our pure blood and God's slow vibration of energy. He talked about
Adrienne and how she can control the energy.
    My earliest memory is from before my brothers and sisters arrived,
when it was just me, Anton and Adrienne. I was nude in the shallows;
Adrienne's hands were holding my hips, keeping me afloat. I remember
cucumber sandwiches and my hat with the neck flap. I remember the
path through the bush. I've walked it so many times over the years.
I know it like the back of my hand. I know the trees and the rocks, I know
the parts where you can find blackberries and other edible plants.
    Mind where you tread. Snakes don't care for your boots and
they might snap at your ankles. *That was what Adam told us.*
    He had these big yellow rings of sweat under his arms, and his shirt
had faded and stained like an old sail. His blue jeans were cinched with
a brown leather belt. He must be so different from when he was a doctor.

We reached a fork in the track; a big gum tree divided the path. We stopped for a moment to drink from the canteen. Then we continued up an incline. It's all sticky and crusty out there. My foot sunk into a rotten tree trunk and filled my sock with wood crumbs. The heat got into my clothes and settled against my skin like a warm hug.

Adam had warned us so many times about snakes. Every summer we see a few of them at the Clearing, weaving between the diamonds of the chain fences or up our windows. If they ever get too close Adam or Anton crush the snakes' heads with the back of the axe or a spade. Today Adam wanted me to show leadership. He told me there was a snake that had been killing the chickens and we were going to find it.

We hadn't walked far when, near the path, a snake rose, S-shaped and hissing.

Adrienne says sometimes our bodies do things our mind doesn't want them to do. She says we meditate to understand and control this better. I know at that moment I lost control of my body, just for a second. I froze dead still, and even though I wanted to move I couldn't.

'Children,' Adam said, his voice even, 'that is an eastern brown.' He said that if the snake bites someone their kidneys will fail and they will die within hours.

The snake watched me, tongue flicking.

Why was I so scared? Adrienne would protect me, I knew. Adrienne can control all the snakes and all the spiders. But still I was scared, staring the snake in the eye. I felt something pushed into my hand and looked down to see Adam had handed me the machete.

I said, 'No.'

I said, 'Please, no.'

Adam stepped in behind me, holding me in place. I could have cried, but I knew it wouldn't help.

He asked if I trusted him, except he whispered it all breathy in my ear.

I was so nervous that my jaw was shaking, I could barely speak. 'Yes,' *I said.* 'Yes, I do.'

'Kill it,' *he said.*

There is a line in the Bible about how, when the snake deceives Eve, God punishes all snakes.

The Lord God said to the serpent, 'Because you have done this, Cursed are you more than all cattle, And more than every beast of the field; On your belly you will go, And dust you will eat all the days of your life.'

I've been thinking about that line a lot. Whenever one person does something bad at the Clearing, we are all punished. If I disobeyed Adam now, not only I but all my brothers and sisters would be punished.

The snake coiled tighter. Adam pushed me towards it. The snake reared back. I saw its fangs. I held the machete. Then it struck.

My breath was trapped in my throat but as the snake lunged towards me I swung the machete. The blade went through it, cutting it clean in two. It fell to the ground and I could see all the pink inside its head. It twitched on the path right in front of us. The trapped breath inside of me came out and I was shaking all over. I had done it. I was so proud and still so scared of the dead snake. Asha was there close by, and on the way back I walked with my arm around her.

Then Adam came up to me. This is what he said, right into my ear: 'Now do you see how it feels to have that power over another creature?'

FREYA

Three days to go

BILLY'S BOWL CUT frizzes out in the heat and his nails are crusted with dirt. I remember when he was a baby I would bite his nails down so he wouldn't scratch himself.

'What happened at school today?'

'Me and Eric found an ants' nest.'

'Be careful – some ants can bite and it is very painful.'

As we drive towards home, I pull in at the bottom of the road near the drain. The van is still there. I type the number plate into a text message to Corazzo and send it off.

Back at the house, Billy drags his easel out. I find the brochure that had been stuffed in my letterbox a while ago advertising home security and call the number. Billy squirts some paint out; it misses his palette and splatters on the floor.

'Billy, watch what you're doing,' I say, taking my phone to my ear. While it rings, I switch it to my left hand and reach down with a paper towel to scrape up the paint.

'Good afternoon, Edinson Security.'

'Yes, hi. I'm hoping to have an emergency button installed at my property.' I drop the paper towel in the bin. 'If you can do it today, I'm happy to pay extra.'

•

At around five a man arrives in a white truck. Billy retreats to his room. I order Rocky to stay where he is. He sits up, ears pricked, watching with curiosity. I let the man in. He wears shorts, revealing thick calves, and a cap with the company's logo emblazoned on it. Though brown hair sprouts from beneath the cap, I can imagine a bald spot underneath.

'Hi,' he says, offering his hand. His tanned arms are dark with swirling tattoos.

I shake, discreetly wiping his sweat on the hip of my jeans.

'Where do you want it?' he says with a little side-mouthed smile, his eyes tiny and dark.

Rocky watches him intently.

On my instruction, the man drills a red button into the wall of my bedroom.

'You want another one?'

'How many can you do?' I ask.

'As many as you like.'

'One in the kitchen and one in my son's room, just through here,' I say, crossing the lounge and pushing Billy's door. It doesn't budge. 'He's a bit shy,' I say, turning back to the man. 'Billy, will you open up, please?' I can hear him breathing behind the door, pressed up against it. 'Billy?'

The man makes a clicking sound with his tongue. Billy doesn't like strangers – something else he inherited from his mum.

'How about I start with the kitchen,' the man says, stepping away.

I push the door again, but it still doesn't open. Frustrated, I push harder. It's for the best; Billy needs the button more than me. I shove with all my weight and the door swings half a foot then stops with a thump. Billy howls.

I turn back to see the man watching me. I roll my eyes, give him a smile.

Billy is sobbing now. I step into the room and pick him up, holding him against me.

'It's okay, where does it hurt?'

'My eyeeeeee.' He drags the word into a wail. His chest quivers against me. *Well, if you listened to Mama, this wouldn't have happened, would it?* I could squeeze the life out of him. I paste a *kids, huh?* expression over the embarrassment and carry Billy away, out onto the back porch.

'You're okay,' I say, over the din of the drill. 'You're such a brave boy. That must have hurt. Let me see.' I pull his hand away from his eye. I don't show my concern, but I can see his cheek is already swelling.

Back inside, I lay Billy on the couch and find an icepack to hold against his eye. While I press it to the skin, I run my hand through his thin corn-silk hair to soothe his crying. Rocky comes over and licks Billy's face. Billy pushes him away.

'Silly to try to lock Mama out, wasn't it, Billy?'

The man goes into Billy's room and I hear the drill start up again. I cringe at the sight of the red button shining in the wood of the kitchen, right beside the fridge. It's ugly, but it's necessary. What point is a beautiful home without the comfort of knowing you're safe within it?

The man goes outside to install a receiver near the fuse box, with a battery locked inside and black aerials poking out.

He tests the buttons with his mobile phone in one hand and his eyes fixed on the screen.

'Yep, they're all set.' He looks about him. 'Mind if I have a drink of water?' Sweat is running into his eyes.

'Sure.' I lower the temperature of the air-conditioning and pour him a glass of water.

Billy is still lying on the couch.

'Always better to go with private companies for this – faster response time than the police in most cases out here. Plus, it's a silent alarm.'

'Great,' I say.

'Where's your phone?'

'My phone?'

'Yeah, do you want me to set up the app? Just another measure. You can choose who the panic button connects you with; you can go direct to the police or us. You can also use it outside of the home.'

'Right.'

'Make sure location services are on, so if you're in trouble we can find you.'

I unlock my phone and hand it to him then watch as he downloads an app and configures it.

'All done,' he says at last.

'So, what happens when I press one of the buttons?'

'If you press it once, we'll come out. If you hold it down, the police will come. I'll just take a picture of you and your son to keep on file so our security guys will recognise you if they're called out. Anyone who is not supposed to be here will be escorted from the property.'

'Between the buttons and the dog, I think we have all bases covered,' I remark.

The man looks towards Rocky. 'Sure.'

'He might seem friendly now, but he's trained to attack.'

Rocky hears the word and rises, eyes alert.

'Oh, I don't doubt it.'

'Lie down,' I say.

Rocky lowers himself back to the floor, still tense, with his ears pricked. He doesn't like the man.

'Can you stand one at a time in front of this wall?' I pick Billy up off the couch and carry him over. The man takes a photo of each of our faces with his phone. I try to shape my mouth into a pleasant smile when it's my turn. 'Alright, I'll send that off. Now, did you want me to quickly do a free security check before I go?'

I glance at Billy who is back on the couch now and let my breath out. 'How long will it take?'

The man gulps down the last of his glass of water then picks up the drill. 'Oh, five minutes. You can read and sign the paperwork while I do it, if you like.'

He wanders down the hall while I vacuum the wood chips left by the drilling. I sign the paperwork. His broad shape moves about, room to room. I hear him tapping on the windows and doors, the roller shutters winding up and down. He even gives the steel security door a firm pull, staring closely at the hinges. I brace myself for the upsell . . .

'Everything is actually really secure here.' *Well, that's a pleasant surprise.* 'You get many break-ins out this far?'

'No,' I say, smiling. 'It's very safe around here.'

'Worried about an ex or something?'

I sigh just loudly enough for him to notice and get the message. 'I'd rather not talk about it.' I'm smiling as I say it. He looks shy for a moment, his eyes darting away.

'Oh right, sorry. I, um, I just wanted to make sure you're all covered, that's all. Most of our work is domestic stuff, you know. I don't normally say this, but if anything this place is probably *too* secure. Your roller shutters are on the main power not batteries, so they won't work in a power outage. If they're down, and there's a fire or a blackout, you could be trapped inside.'

'Right,' I say. 'Well, I leave them up mostly.'

'You don't want to have everything latched up this time of year when the fire risk is so high. Is it just you here?'

'Me, the kid, the dog.'

'Sure,' the man says, a single tear of sweat running down from his left temple. 'Well, I mean, I can give you my card. You know, if you're ever feeling worried about something . . .'

Jesus, he fancies me. *No, thanks.* 'I'm fine – I have the buttons now,' I say, adequately blunt. 'Thanks, anyway.'

'Okay, Freya.' He's big. Even his head is big, squeezed into the cap. 'Well, just in case you ever want to call me for anything else, I'll leave my card.'

I glance over at Billy, who is standing on the couch, cheeks still damp with tears.

I sweep a strand of hair away from my face and turn back to the man. It's easy to feel flattered.

'I'll keep that in mind . . .' I look at the card '. . . Jock.'

I walk him to the door.

Outside kookaburras are perched in the high branches of the paperbark tree near the house – five of them, pointed beaks, chest feathers the colour of damp hay and dark wings tipped with iridescent blue. One begins that long jerking cackle and the others join in.

Koo-koo-kah-kah-kah. The chorus grows as Jock drives away.

I go to the bureau in my study and pull open the third drawer. I lift out my passport, Billy's passport – unused – and fish for the small blue folder I keep tucked underneath. Sliding the rubber band from around the folder, I open it and look down at the documents I've assembled. I can't tell you exactly why I first decided to keep them. Wayne's driver's licence. Wayne's old passport. Bank statements, utility bills. Photographs of his home. Photographs of Aspen as a three-year-old, a five-year-old, a seven-year-old. Wayne's medical records. I began actively collecting this stuff a few years after he left. I had no idea where he'd gone, Mum didn't help much but eventually a private investigator found out where he lived. After that I made frequent trips up to Queensland to watch his house. He steered clear of all social media so it was the only way to keep tabs on him.

Then he contacted me out of the blue. I thought the game was up. I thought he must have realised that some of his mail had gone missing, someone had been watching his house. It turned out he just wanted to sell the car I had bought him, the one that was still in my name.

I hoped he had changed his mind about Aspen, so I agreed to meet him. When we saw each other I knew what would happen; the moment he stepped into the bar and his eyes fell on me. I felt it: the longing that drew us together the first time. It was back, stronger now than ever. We both knew it was inevitable. I had spent seven years hating him and it was all wiped out in a moment. We shared a bottle of wine. *I can't love you again, Freya, but I miss you.* He kissed me. It was one weekend together, before he disappeared again.

When I saw those two lines on the pregnancy test, that's when I stopped thinking about Aspen and Wayne. That's when I stopped making those trips to Queensland to watch his house. Suddenly the stakes had risen, and I remembered what Wayne was capable of.

I won't lose Billy the way I lost Aspen. I won't go through it again.

When I check my phone in the kitchen, I see I've got a missed call on WhatsApp from Jonas. I check Instagram. He's posted more photos. He's in the jungle feeding a monkey a piece of banana, tagged in a place called 'Monkey Forrest Ubud'. Then he's on the back of a scooter, swaying palms in the background. *He's in Bali.* I go back to my study and call him back.

'Jonas,' I say. 'Sorry I missed you earlier.'

'It's fine,' he says. 'How are you?'

'Stressed.'

'It's a stressful time for everyone. Just make sure you're meditating lots.' A long pause. 'So how is Billy?'

'He's good.'

'You keep him leashed to you at all times still?' There's laughter in his voice.

'He's a sensitive boy.'

'You need to cut the apron strings sooner or later. Let him be his own person.'

'I'm not that bad,' I say, making myself laugh.

'Have you been keeping yourself busy?'

'Same old. Trying to swim more and exercise. I saw a couple hanging around the river near my place.'

'A couple?'

'Yeah, they're young and a bit strange.' It's been a couple of hours and I still haven't heard back from Corazzo about the van.

'Nothing wrong with a bit strange.'

'I'm paranoid. I guess I'm feeling a bit anxious about Henrik's release,' I say. *That's because you're the one who put him away.*

'Sure, but remember: Henrik can't hurt you. Mum doesn't think there is anything to worry about.'

I let out a small huff of laughter. 'She doesn't think so?'

'What's that supposed to mean?' There's an edge to his voice now. And we were having such a nice normal conversation.

'I think you know what it means. It means Mum isn't herself, is she?' I'm careful with my words. My brother still hasn't really accepted what Mum is going through.

'What are you saying?'

'I'm worried about her. She's got no idea who she is. How can you not see that, Jonas?'

He's quiet for a moment so I try to steer the conversation away from Mum. 'How's Bali? It must be hot there.'

He doesn't accept the peace offering. 'She's much more with it than you give her credit for.'

'Right,' I say, reading his tone, knowing this won't end well if I push it any further. 'Sure.'

'She's been so supportive, don't forget that.'

'I know,' I say. *But what did she do to help with Aspen?* I ask silently. *Where was she then?*

'Have you been visiting?'

'I was out there this afternoon.'

'Did you take Billy?'

'He was at school.'

When the call ends, I realise Billy is standing at the door of my study. 'Mum, who was that?'

'Your bloody uncle,' I say, tossing the phone on the desk. I stand up and head towards my bedroom. 'He wants you to see Grandma.' Jonas was pissed; he's got a temper.

Billy follows me.

'Grandma is sick,' I explain. 'Sometimes she forgets things. But we have to pretend that she is the same.'

•

Later, when Billy is asleep in bed, I step out into the night, leaving Rocky inside and locking the house behind me. I walk down towards the river. There's a fork in the path: one way leads back up along the river to the road, where the van is parked; the other way leads to my swimming spot. I steel my nerves and turn up the track leading to the road. Even though the evening is cooler, I can feel the prickle of sweat on my chest, the breeze whispering on my neck.

At the road, the van takes shape in front of me, a beaten-up old thing. As I approach it, the gravel crackling beneath my boots, I wish that I had a torch to blast the path before me. I don't know what I'm expecting to see when I peer through the window, but the sight makes my heart catch. In the back of the van I can make out the shape of two bodies. I can see dark nipples, curls of pubic hair. They are so still, like drowned things trawled up from the deep. I don't move. I'm nailed to the spot. Then I realise the man's eyes are open. He's staring back at me.

I stumble backwards, my eyes still fixed on the van, expecting the door to fling open, the man to rush at me.

Could I have imagined his eyes open? No, I know what I saw.

I turn and sprint back down the path. Within minutes I'm home, jamming the key in the lock. Inside I lean against the door for several seconds, waiting for my pulse to stop racing. When I'm calm again, I walk down the hall to check in on Billy, still sleeping in his room. Then I check all the doors are locked. It's going to be one of those nights: sleep coming in gasps and the morning coming too soon.

THE WATCHER

I SEE YOU. There in that big house of yours where *anyone* could be hiding. You think you escaped unscathed. You think your lies will go unpunished. You get up in the morning, you meditate then prepare breakfast. You take the child to school and trust the teachers to protect him while you go about taking yoga classes, shopping, reading, walking that big dog down to the river.

Then, in the afternoon, you collect the boy. Almost always you arrive early, before all those other women. You think you are protecting him, but you are selfish, you are suffocating him. You think you are giving him a better childhood than your own. You imagine him growing up as a creative, happy and engaging member of the community. Maybe one day he will move into politics – the kind you agree with, the selfless planet savers, the suitless men and women who once strapped themselves to trees. You don't believe he has violence in him, but you can't nurture out those darker traits embedded deep within.

At night you can't sleep. You sense something is wrong. Your hair is knotted and split like spun wool. You have chewed your nails down and not even that shrink with the pinched eyes and pencil skirt can make you believe it's all in your head. You *know* it's not all in your head, because you have been through this before. You went through it with your first son. You knew disaster was rippling towards you; you couldn't stop it then, and you can't stop it now.

If something happened to you, the boy would have no one in the world to look after him. I could raise the child, you know that. Maybe I will take him away. It's just a matter of showing him what you really are and what I can give him.

You sense my presence. You've almost caught me in the act – you'll never know where I have been, what I have been organising for you. Yes, *Freya*, I have something very special in mind for you. It won't be long now. All it will take is one slip-up. This is what happens to liars. You think you know pain? You know nothing.

FREYA

Three days to go

'I HAD A NIGHTMARE,' Billy says, the words fraying at the edges.

He was sound asleep when I got back inside, but now he is in the doorway of his room, eyes heavy-lidded, dragging his teddy bear Bun-Bun by the arm. Some nights he doesn't sleep at all. What causes these nightmares? Can a child inherit memories? He comes over to me on the couch and I lift him onto my lap.

'Aw,' I say softly, rocking from side to side, stroking his hair. 'It's okay. I've got you now. The nightmare is over.'

'It was one of your paintings,' he says. 'A man climbed out of the picture and grabbed me. I couldn't breathe.'

I can feel my face changing, the mask slipping. A drop of the brow, a shift of the mouth. Billy has seen my paintings before the final coat. He has seen what the black square covers. I stopped painting because I didn't want to scare him. I think about the couple out there in the van, how close they are right now.

'Ow,' Billy says. His eyes are wet and sleepy. I realise my fingers are knotted in his hair, squeezing. 'Mama, stop.' I release my grip.

My gaze settles on the darkness beyond the windows. On the nights when Billy can't sleep, I take his red glowing alarm clock from his room so he is not reminded of how late it is.

I take Billy and put him in my bed, trying not to think of how the last time I let him sleep in my bed I woke up with a dampness pooling beneath me, soaking into the mattress. I tuck him under the covers then go into the bathroom to brush my teeth, staring at myself in the mirror.

In bed, I shuffle in against Billy and breathe in the scent of his shampooed hair. I squeeze him hard against me.

'Don't, Mama,' he mutters, irritated. 'It hurts.'

The roller shutters are up. Outside the window the ghostly paperbark sways. There's a breeze and it's going to be thirty plus all through the night. The country is a stick of dynamite. The fire bunker is a twenty-metre dash from the house. It's stocked with provisions but it also houses all my unsold paintings, I can hardly bear to look at them for all the memories attached. The paintings are about a time I've tried so hard to forget. If a fire came and I couldn't escape, I'd carry Billy out there to the bunker.

People often leave their pets behind when fleeing bushfires. They find them later, scorched, pink, skinless. Volunteers move silently among the charred trees with rifles, finishing off those shrivelled wallabies, dying wombats, cats, dogs, horses. If a fire did sweep through here I'd make sure Billy was safe, then Rocky, then myself. The best thing I can do for now is be prepared.

Two days to go

In the morning I drag the lawnmower in a ring around the house. The grass is white and dry as chalk.

Out in the yard the heat brings sweat out between my shoulder blades. I work my way down towards the fire bunker. It's the largest one they could build. First they dug a huge hole in the hillside, then they deposited a concrete box into it about the same size as my lounge room.

You couldn't design a more ideal storage facility for my art – a consistent low temperature, airtight, not a single photon of sunlight coming in. I keep a few bottles of wine in there too. The handle is dusty in my palm. Inside, I hit the light and see my bubble-wrapped paintings leaning against one another in the corner. I see the wine, the bottles of water, the tinned food. It's all set up.

Back at the house, I realise we are running late. 'Shit,' I say. 'Sorry, Billy, we'd better rush. Can you get your own breakfast while I have a quick shower?' Billy woke with a bruise the colour of an eggplant around his eye from where the doorhandle had hit him.

When I get out of the shower and head back into the lounge, a magpie is strutting along the balustrade with its chest out. Billy is at the table, a piece of toast in his hand. The peanut butter is still on the bench. I can't stop staring at his bruised eye, it's not a good look.

'Come on,' I say. 'Let's get you to school.'

•

After I've dropped Billy off – only five minutes late – and returned home, I sit down with my acai bowl. The sense that I am being watched comes over me again. Scopaesthesia. Gaze detection. There are countless names and explanations for this feeling, but I just *know* that someone is watching me right now. Someone is fucking with me – trying to distract me, to peel the skin of Freya Heywood away.

I open the newspaper on the kitchen bench, the missing girl has already slipped from the first page but I find a new story about her a couple of pages in. She still hasn't been found. The police are searching for a van. *O-U-P*, I think. Could it be related? I call Corazzo.

'Freya,' he says. 'Sorry I didn't get back to you. Seem to be busier in retirement than I was when I worked.'

I realise I'm holding my breath. 'So, did you find anything?'

'Well, nothing noteworthy. Van is registered to a twenty-four-year-old from Brunswick, Liam Moore. Works at a gardening store. He had a parking fine in June 2019, which has been paid, other than that not a mark against his name.'

Liam Moore. It doesn't ring a bell. 'Anything else you can tell me?'

'Nothing sticks out really. Clean as a whistle. Harmless, I'm sure, but I can ask someone to drive out and send them on their way if you're still worried?'

'That would be good, if you can,' I say.

•

I collect Billy from school. Back at the house, Billy watches me as I tug my shoes off beside the door. There is a mouse beneath his eye from the doorhandle. What must the teachers think?

'How come you don't have five toes, Mama?'

'Well,' I begin, dropping my shoes by the door and walking to the kitchen, 'when I was a little baby, a thread of hair got wrapped around my toe.'

Billy squats down and fingers the gap where the toe is missing. I reach out and put the kettle on.

'And the hair got tighter and tighter as the toe swelled more and more. I was a fat baby so I could barely move. Eventually the hair around Mama's toe got so tight that the toe swelled up, and then it got unhealthy because the blood was trapped inside and so a doctor' – I pause for a moment, dropping tea into the teapot – 'well, they removed it.'

'Removed it?'

'Very carefully. They surgically removed it, so it wouldn't hurt Mama.'

The kettle screams. I kill the burner and fill the teapot. Billy is lingering; there is something on his mind. 'What is it, Billy?' I ask.

'The man,' he says. 'The man scared me.'

I place the cup on the table, frowning at my son. Melodramatic little prince – he was scared of Jock, the security guy. 'He was just here to help us,' I assure him. 'To put the buttons on the wall.'

'No, not *that* man.'

A cold hand drags its fingers down my spine. 'What man, Billy?'

'The man at school.' He shuffles his bottom lip over his top in concentration.

'Billy, look at me,' I say, taking his chin in my palm. 'Tell me: what man you are talking about?'

Billy shrugs his face free from my grip. I can feel my pulse; I can hear it as if it's the only sound.

'The man at school, near the back fence. We were looking at the ants.'

'What did he do?' I can barely control my voice. 'What did the man do?'

'Nothing.'

Billy tries to move towards the couch, but I snap him back by his wrist.

'Ouch,' he says, grabbing his shoulder.

'Billy,' I say.

Billy looks down then slowly raises his eyes back to mine. 'It hurts – let go.' He tries to pull free, but I tighten my grasp.

'Tell me. What did he do?'

He takes one finger and places it over his lips.

'The man did that?' I say. I put a finger to my own lips. 'Like this?'

Billy nods.

'Did anyone else see?'

Billy shrugs.

'Was he looking at you?'

He twists, turning back to the couch. 'I don't know,' he murmurs. I can't remember.'

I grab his shoulders. 'Speak up,' I say, more harshly than I intended.

'I don't know. He was far away.'

'But you are sure it was a man? You are sure you saw him?'

'I think so.'

'Okay,' I say, before clearing my throat. I wrangle my features into something approximating a neutral expression, pushing back against the fear and anger, pushing it out of my head. *I* am in control, not him. 'If you *ever* see this man again, I want you to tell the teachers. Show them where he was.'

He nods.

'Was he about Mama's age?'

'You're scaring me.'

A long breath escapes. I take my phone and leave the room. Stepping out into the heat on the back deck, I hold it to my ear, finding the school phone number in my contacts. It's after four, but someone should still be there.

The phone rings and rings until finally it goes to voicemail. I hang up and dial again. Still no answer.

Could the man be Wayne?

'Billy, come here.'

He trudges over, reluctant; cartoons are on the TV.

'What did the man look like?'

He shrugs. He's on the edge of tears.

I screw my palms into my eye sockets. 'Sorry, Billy,' I say. 'Just tell me: what did the man look like? Was he tall?'

Billy nods.

'Did he have dark hair?'

Billy nods again.

I think back to those days. The years of love, Wayne's big yellow Datsun sliding on the gravel. The afternoons of sex, of laughing against his collarbone. I think of Aspen trapped in the hot car, the smashed window. The people staring as I calmly sat down on the footpath and watched the ambulance zipping away. Then I remember Wayne, all the lies he told, and the truths he exaggerated. I think about everything he told the lawyers and the judge.

Rocky's wet nose touches my fingertips. I look down into those soft brown eyes, then to Billy.

'Tell me if you see that strange man again, please.'

Billy just stares. I remember the manic look in Wayne's eyes as he screamed at me. I remember thinking, *This is how it ends*.

PART THREE
THESE VIOLENT DELIGHTS

For God knows that in the day you eat from it your eyes will
be opened, and you will be like God, knowing good and evil.

Genesis 3:5

FREYA

One day to go

WHEN I DREAM, I am at the river. I see Billy floating facedown on the surface, but for some reason I am not alarmed. Instead I feel calm; in fact, I feel a rising euphoria. Then I hear a voice. I turn and Wayne is there, sitting on the bank. I don't know why I think it is Wayne – where his face should be there is nothing but skin – but I know it in the same way I know it is Billy in the water. And someone else is there: Henrik. He's talking so quickly I can't understand what he's saying, but it's clear he's instructing the faceless Wayne.

Wayne stands. He rushes towards me with his hands outstretched. I laugh, it is all a game. He grips my neck and we both fall back into the water. I don't resist. I let it happen. *Why did you do it?* I know I can't die, he won't let me drown. Despite how much he hates me, he will never stop loving me, so I just lie there as his grip tightens and tightens. But he doesn't let go. I can't breathe. I kick out, fight back, but he is too strong.

When I wake I am breathless, clutching at my throat to peel away the fingers that aren't around my neck. I reach for the familiar kink of my nose and remember the day I almost died. The day I got the scar at my waist.

Your body senses something is wrong before your brain. That's how it was with Aspen. I knew I was doing something wrong, I could feel it. It was a mistake. I just wanted a break. A moment away at the park. He had too much energy, wouldn't stop screaming. I locked him in the car. I didn't know what it would cost me. I didn't know that it would almost kill him. I didn't know that they would all blame me.

The nights back then were long. I expressed during the day when Aspen wouldn't feed, then he would wake me up at all hours while Wayne was out working. Wayne didn't need to work. I had enough money. He didn't need to drive himself into the ground, growing more and more stressed, more and more sleepless. We fought. Well, not so much fought; rather, Wayne got angry and I kept control most of the time. He made me feel like a bad mother. I have regrets, of course, but I was *not* a bad mother.

He was collecting debts to make money. He didn't know how close I was to breaking down, how the stress was grinding my bones, how my skin was wearing thin and how more and more that woman inside was breaking through.

I squeeze Billy who again is sleeping in my bed; the sky is dark outside of the windows and the twiggy branches of the paperbark tree dice up the crescent moon.

I picture Aspen as a baby, the occasional smile, a single nib of white beginning to break through his bottom gum. At twenty-two I was too young to be a mother; I was still a girl, really.

I cannot reside in the next memory for too long without the acid of grief washing away the calm veneer I've built up. I recall *the* moment. There is a pause before the pain, just enough time to know, to understand there is nothing you can do. When I looked up and saw the gun, I knew what was coming. I recall waking up between the crisp sheets. A small sterile room. Waxed halls, nurses in squelching white shoes. Looking up and seeing a solemn, suited man watching over me.

Reaching for the nightstand, I find my glass of water and take a long sip. Rocky, at the foot of the bed, snorts, and stretches before going back to sleep.

I roll out of bed, careful not to wake Billy, and creep into the lounge, where I turn on the TV and lie back on the couch. A fortune teller is accepting calls at $4.90 per minute to read people's fortunes live on air with cards and crystals. A scarf is twisted about her hair, and each eye shines beneath a substantial ellipse of purple eye shadow. I change the channel. An old movie comes on, a Christmas thriller. Probably a bit much for my heart to take after that dream. I change the channel again, this time settling on the early-morning news. So long as there are no new abductions, no infanticides, I'll be okay. The news doesn't help. In my mind I revisit the past and think of the future. I think of how much it hurt to lose Aspen. With no one around, no one watching, I let myself cry and it all comes in a flood.

I take my phone off the charger. Back on the couch, I find I have two missed calls from around midnight. I stare at the ten numbers as if deciphering a code. I type a message.

Whose number is this?

I hit send and watch as instantly the three dots appear on the screen. Whoever it is, they're typing a response. My heart tumbles about my body. Instinctively I look out into the night. Is he here now? Is he coming for me? The panic button is within reach, if I need it. But he couldn't know where I live. Last time he was in town we stayed at a hotel.

You're awake early.

My hands shake. I look up at the TV, thinking for a moment.

Wayne?

Good guess. I'm looking for my son, Freya.

My breath catches. I eye the panic button. Billy.

What are you talking about? I type rapidly.

Let's not make this difficult. I need to take him home.

Are you watching me? Are you here?

I'm not leaving without him.

You've lost your mind.

I'll be seeing you soon.

Again I feel that tugging feeling of the invisible cord between me and Billy. I head back to my room and fall into bed beside him with my phone in hand.

Leave me alone, Wayne. I have no idea what you are talking about.

My heart is kicking at my sternum. I need a distraction. I go to Facebook, and scroll. I scroll through the lives of the few people I know. Jonas has more photos up from Bali. I search Wayne Phillips. I flick down through all the suggestions, but I already know I won't find his account. He's as good at hiding as I am. I was naive to think I could ever have a normal life. It was always going to turn to shit again.

•

I drop Billy at school in the morning and sit there tracking him with my eyes until he is safely inside. Then I scan the faces of the parents and people walking along the footpath outside the school gate. There is no sign of Wayne. I turn the car for home.

The van is still parked near the dip in the road.

As soon as I get to the house, I put Rocky on the leash and head down through the yard towards the river. The world around me is a riot of birds, cicadas, the crackle of dehydrated flora beneath my boots. The human eye detects movement before all else; I read that somewhere. Before we think, before we can understand what we are seeing, we identify a threat and our body is already reacting to it. Hairs rise. Eyes widen, blink less. Breathing quickens. Our pulse soars.

Near the back gate, I notice an opening in the fence wide enough to pass a soccer ball through. I squat down beside Rocky, who sniffs at the foot of the fence. Something has chewed it. I'll have to lace it up with wire. I imagine sluggish wombats, or foxes, or wallabies. Or could it be the same person who opened the gate, making a new entry point now that the gate is padlocked?

When we reach the river I don't swim. I stand at shin depth, hurling stones for Rocky to chase. Occasionally he dunks his head in after them and brings them back up in his mouth. The heat quickly saps any energy I had.

'Come on, Rocky,' I call, 'let's get back.'

Inside the house, I pause for a moment. It's completely still. I go to the sink, turn on the tap, and water rushes over my hands. I feel rather than see a shadow pass before the open back door. Is someone there? It was just a flash in my peripheral vision. A swooping bird, perhaps? I twist about, my body stiff and electric.

'Rocky,' I call. He trots to my side. Without turning from the back door I reach for my phone and call Olivia.

•

In the psychologist's office, I sit holding my face in my hands. She cancelled her lunch to make time for me.

'Everyone understands what he put you through, Freya. No one will judge you. Do you believe that?'

'He's coming for my son.'

'What do you mean?'

'He sent me a text message. He said he won't leave without Billy.'

Olivia shifts in her seat. 'Well, that could be construed as a threat. How would you feel about contacting the police?'

'No,' I say. 'No.'

'He has caused you a lot of pain.' Olivia's eyes narrow, hawk-like behind square-framed glasses. 'Do you blame him for losing Aspen?'

'We each played our part.'

'What do you mean, Freya?'

'I don't know. I wasn't trying to hurt Aspen. I was just tired, and I didn't know any better.'

Olivia closes her notebook. One eyebrow arcs over her glasses as she waits for me to speak. The silence game, a favourite among psychologists. Except I'm immune to social awkwardness, I don't leap to fill the silence with my thoughts the way others might. Olivia breaks first.

'We've been through this, Freya. *No one* blames you—'

'I know. It's not that. Wayne didn't hurt Aspen, but he wasn't there for me. *He* blames me. He told them I was hurting Aspen, that I almost drowned him in the bath before the car incident.'

She pinches the bridge of her nose, turns her wrist to see her watch. 'You can make the choice to continue to exclude him from your life. You haven't seen him in years and he's got no right to take Billy.'

'But what if he takes him anyway?'

'You should contact the police. It would be irresponsible of me to encourage you to do otherwise.'

I sit for a moment, thinking. Olivia knows the real me – well, she knows *about* the real me, which is an important distinction. She knows I harbour the real me deep inside. She knows I won't trust the police after what happened with Aspen.

'Do you believe that you are in danger?' Olivia asks.

'Yes.'

'When was the last time you heard from him?'

I haven't told her about the night I spent with him. 'Not since he took Aspen. He blocked me out.'

'You haven't heard from him in fourteen years?'

'No.'

'But you're certain it's him contacting you now?'

'Yes. It has to be.'

'And you've never had messages like this before?'

I think back. He seemed so loving and kind when we were together. He had hidden behind doors sometimes to give me a fright, or he would reach into the bathroom when I was in the shower and flick out the lights, but it was all for a laugh. And he always got one from me.

'No,' I say. 'No, never.' I remember him making blueberry pancakes in the nude, bringing them to me in bed. I remember the way he nestled Aspen against his shoulder with such tenderness I thought I might cry. It seems like so long ago now, and in a way it is. But then I remember the violence he held inside, how quickly he turned away, how the force of his fear for what I might do to Aspen overwhelmed his love for me.

•

I go straight from my appointment with Olivia to my class, getting there early. Milly is at reception, she greets me with *Namaste* and I go straight into the studio. I use the time to meditate, my hands curled over my knees, eyes closed, feeling gravity pull me down, feeling the blood in my veins, and air rushing in and out of my lungs.

I become calm. People drift into the room. I am aware of them quietly unrolling their mats. I open my eyes and rise to a standing position, placing my hands together as in prayer at my belly button. I shape my mouth into a smile and greet them all as they enter.

I start out by synchronising the collective breath. It is here, in this position standing at the front of the class, that I notice a face through the window at reception. He is sitting down, looking at something in his hands. Dark eyebrows, hair combed back, mouth bracketed with lines. Swipe of grey at the temples. My breath quickens and the calm of my meditation evaporates. He looks too familiar. I fight to contain myself within the skin of Freya Heywood; I fight to maintain my calm. *Wayne is waiting in reception.*

AMY

I WAKE IN the night and everything is still and dark. Tonight, Adrienne gave us children a sermon and I was proud that Asha was sitting up the front, her head tilted back, her eyes wide. Anton gave her an entire carrot for her good behaviour and the other children watched with envy as she chewed it.

Now, lying in bed, I can see the stars outside the window. The room is hot; it is too hot to sleep. I think about the snake, the way its head fell to the dirt. I feel eyes watching me from the bottom bunk across the room. I stare into the darkness and realise Asha is staring back. She is awake.

I wonder if I woke her or if she has been awake all along. Even in the darkness I can see her fear. I can see the shine of tears. I climb from my bed and cross the room to lie beside her, grazing my hand down the buttons of her spine. She looks into my eyes, the fear replaced with hope.

'Can I please go home now?'

My heart twists. She doesn't understand how lucky she is. He could hear her if she speaks too loudly. I place my finger over my lips and shush her, knowing that I should report her, knowing I could be punished for protecting her.

'Asha,' I say, 'you *are* home, so don't ever say anything like that again because he will hurt you if he finds out.'

She tucks in against me. Her face, warm and damp with tears, presses against my chest. She wraps her tiny arms around my neck. I squeeze her. It's been almost a week since she arrived, and she has gotten skinnier. Her face has thinned. She looks completely different.

'It's going to be okay. Keep going. Protect the Queen.'

I feel her grip tighten, then she speaks. 'I hate it here. I want to go home.'

'This is your home now, Asha. You are safe here. We will never make you go back to that man who hurt you.'

'No one hurt me, never. Not until you brought me here.' She says the word *you* with force. I feel afraid, not for myself but her.

'That's not true.'

Asha trembles against me. I can tell she is crying again as a sob escapes and soon her tears soak through the shoulder of my nightgown.

'I'm sorry, Asha,' I say. I don't know why I say it but it's out now. In my heart, I know we saved her, I know I have nothing to apologise for. 'What was it like out there in the world?'

'It's different. I have friends at school. Laura is my best friend and she misses me.' She is speaking fast now. 'I eat dinner and breakfast, proper food. I used to have roll-ups and cheese sandwiches for lunch. My poppa . . .' She lets out a tiny whimper. 'I miss my poppa. He'll be looking for me.'

'No,' I whisper. 'You're confused. He hurt you. You are with God now, Asha.'

'My name is *Sara*!'

I slap my hand against her mouth and snatch her head back by her hair so she is forced to meet my eyes. Our noses are almost touching. Someone moves in a bunk nearby. I can't risk her waking anyone else.

I swallow, lean forwards and kiss her head. Her entire body tenses. The air is damp and sticky.

'Adrienne has a plan for us all,' I whisper close to her ear. I slide my hand from her mouth. 'Just be good and it will get better, I promise. Our mother will show you the light.'

'She is not my mother,' Asha says. 'My mum died. Don't call her my mother.'

Once she has fallen asleep again, I slip my hand under my mattress and pull out my journal. I steal away to the bathroom to think. Perhaps she needs another dose of medicine to help her see, to bring her into the light.

Why would she say her mother had died, though? Her mother is Adrienne. We are, all of us, Adrienne's children. I just hope it gets better for her here soon. She doesn't understand what will happen if she resists.

— Amy's journal —

I am back in my own bed now but I still can't sleep. Adam had come for me in the night, careful not to wake the others. He gently nudged my shoulder. Come.

He led me out across the Clearing. I walked without my shoes, half expecting a bull ant to light a fire on the underside of my foot.

He turned to me and instructed me to stick out my tongue, dropping a little of the magic bullet on it.

'Once a caterpillar becomes a butterfly, there is no turning back,' he said, looking up. 'You're beautiful, Amy. And you are only going to get more beautiful as you get older.'

No one had ever said anything like that to me before. I followed his gaze up to the stars. They looked brighter than ever.

'Come on,' he said. 'I'm going to show you one of life's great pleasures. I'm going to help you purge the feelings you've been developing inside.'

As we approached the Great Hall my heart rose in my chest. I looked across the Clearing to the squat wooden shacks where the minders live.

I climbed up the ladder to the loft. Adam followed.

'If we are all going to die, Amy, what would be the problem with hastening another's death?' The question caught me off guard.

'I don't know.'

'If someone is suffering, let's say, what then?'

'It depends.'

'Right and wrong are not fixed points on a compass. Sometimes we do things just because they are necessary. Do you understand?'

'Yes.'

I felt his hands on the front of my nightgown.

'It is important that you do not tell anyone what we are about to do, not even Adrienne. She can never find out. She would hurt us both.'

A candle spilled cooling wax onto the wooden boards. The flame made the spiders' shadows huge.

'Stay still, Amy,' Adam said. 'Stay still, child.'

He unbuttoned the front of my nightgown, and it fell from my shoulders. Next he unthreaded my underwear – carefully, so his hands did not touch my skin. The cotton slid against my legs, prickling the hairs. His breath was thick and loud. I stepped from my underwear, leaving it pooled on the wooden boards.

'Just like that,' he said. 'Be still.' His face was inches from the dark hair that has begun to sprout between my legs. His breath changed, not concentrated but flowing like warm water. 'This is natural,' he said. 'To purge.'

I drew in a breath, he leaned forwards and, wet and warm, his mouth touched me.

FREYA

Twenty-two hours to go

I DON'T LOOK up again. I can feel my pulse thudding in my chest.

'One moment, sorry,' I say to the class. Wayne is here. He has cornered me in the one place I must stay composed, this room full of yoga mums, and Milly sitting out there in reception. Is he talking to her? Does she know why he is here? 'Hold that pose,' I say, taking a sip from my water bottle then starting the music.

I look at the potted ficus tree in the corner of the room, forcing myself into a state of calm. I run my gaze over the pale wooden walls, smiling, but inside I am screaming. There is a second exit through the back room. My class finishes at 3 pm and the school bell rings at 3:10. I should leave now and pull Billy from class. Otherwise it will all happen again. He will take Billy away.

'Okay,' I say. My face still wears a warm smile. 'Now stretch upwards, drawing a deep breath.'

He is tanned, with a mass of black hair cinched back in a ponytail. He always kept it short when he was younger, only letting it grow after we'd been together for some time. Men of his age with a full head of hair tend to show it off. Deeper dimples, shining blue eyes. His nose still kinked from a particularly brutal break. He glances up; our eyes meet.

He could be a charter pilot or an author. You would never know by looking at him how violent, how dangerous and manipulative he really is.

I begin moving the class through more challenging poses. The panic is humming inside me; I'm ready to run. The ambient sounds continue: the Balinese chimes, the falling rain, the gentle shimmering cymbals.

I find myself pushing the class into the deepest poses, stretching the fibres of my tendons until the pain threatens to morph into a cramp. The burn is so deep in my thighs and calves I think I will buckle, and when I look up the entire class is making small adjustments, bending backs and knees, turning hips to complete the poses without causing an injury.

Practising yoga is about moving the body while stilling the mind, but my mind is racing. As I urge the class to sit in preparation for the final meditation, I keep my body and face relaxed and entirely still, but inside I am plotting my escape. The music keeps playing. Piano and panpipes now.

I roll up my mat and collect my drink bottle. I would usually linger and make conversation. Today I simply stride towards the back room. Jupiter, one of the regulars, whom I sometimes have chai with, cranes her head out to chat as I pass, but I carry on briskly without meeting her eye.

I push through the back door and emerge into the alley beside the car park. I can see the Disco at the far side, but I make my way towards the road and speed walk to the school gate.

'Hello, can I help you?' the pretty young woman at the desk says as I rush into the reception area.

'Hi,' I say. 'I'm Billy Heywood's mother. He's in year three with Mr Holden.'

'Oh, hello, Mrs Heywood.'

Mrs. I don't correct her.

'I need to pull Billy out of school a bit early today. Can I go find him in class?'

'Oh,' she says, looking back to the computer screen. 'School finishes in six minutes, if you want to wait?'

'No,' I say. 'I need him now.'

'Okay. Is everything alright?'

'No,' I say, with a sad smile. 'We've got a family issue.'

'I see. Well, I'd better call him over.' She picks up the phone and presses a few buttons. 'Yes, hi, Mrs Heywood is here to collect her son Billy. Could you bring him over to reception? Thanks.' She hangs up. 'He won't be a minute.'

I sit down in the too-small seat near the door. The woman turns back to her computer.

'Hot out, isn't it?' she says. She does that thing doctors do when they talk to you without turning away from the computer screen, scrolling down through your notes, asking you questions.

'Yes,' I say. 'Very.'

Minutes later Billy is there, dragging his backpack along behind him.

'Mama,' he says. Does he intuit something is wrong?

'We've got to go, son.'

Outside other parents are arriving, milling near the gate. I stroll past casually, avoiding eye contact. Then I pull Billy across the road, towards the car park.

I'm fishing for the keys in my handbag as we approach the Disco.

'Freya!' a voice calls. It's hostile, aggressive. 'Stop. Right now.'

I hear footsteps pounding across the pavement behind me. I fumble for the keys.

Feeling a hand on my shoulder, I swing around, the key lodged between my fingers. I tuck Billy behind me.

'Get away from him!' I say, my voice so harsh it hurts my throat. I can see yoga mums standing in a clutch with Milly, across the car park. Their faces turned towards me. I look up at Wayne, his scowling face, his blue eyes sharpening on me.

'Where is he, Freya?'

I can feel Billy's hands clutching the hem of my yoga top.

'What are you talking about?'

'Don't play dumb, Freya. I know you're involved.' Wayne's gaze slides from my face. I look down, see Billy's head poking out from behind me.

'Get away,' I say. 'Get back right now – I'm warning you, Wayne.'

'Just tell me where he is and I'll go. That's all I'm here for. *Tell me where he is.*'

'Where who is?' I say, puzzled. He has seen Billy.

'Aspen,' he says, exasperated.

Aspen?

'I have no idea what you are talking about!' I snap.

His eyes bore into me. 'He disappeared three weeks ago. I know it was you, Freya. I've seen the messages.'

Messages? What messages?

'No, Wayne. You've got it wrong. I've had no contact with Aspen in years. I swear.' Aspen would be seventeen now. Could he have run away from his controlling father?

'I just want to take him home,' he says. There is real desperation written all over his face. Wayne is incapable of subterfuge. 'I don't want to involve the police, but I will if I have to.'

'Wayne,' I say, staring him down, aware of others watching us, 'I have no idea what you are talking about. I really don't.'

He still looks sceptical, his brow pleated.

'Look,' I say. 'I've got to go . . .'

'No. I want the truth. I'm not leaving until you tell me.' He inches closer still.

I glance across the car park again. Our body language suggests a confrontation. I round my shoulders, soften my expression.

'Okay,' I say, reaching out and gently touching his arm to show the yoga mums that it's just an everyday exchange between friends. 'We can talk, but not here.'

Wayne brushes my hand away. 'Where then?'

Out on the street there is a small cafe. It will be quiet at this time of day. Can I risk it? I study his face. *Is this all a ruse, Wayne? Do you know you have another son?*

'Come on,' I say. 'This way.'

Twenty-one hours to go

In the shade of the cafe's awning there are only a few people, but inside, with the air-conditioning, it's busier. At the entrance, I scan the patrons inside to see if I recognise anyone. A baby screams in her father's arms as he steps past me outside, bending his knees in that rocking dance all parents know. He pats her back to soothe her, his face resolute.

No familiar faces, but I don't want to risk it. 'Let's sit outside. I've got five minutes,' I say, leading Wayne to the most isolated table.

Wayne keeps shooting glances at Billy. He is so close; it is like holding your child over a pit of snakes. Billy looks down, fiddling with the salt shaker.

Sunlight leans across the table. A waitress approaches, holding menus against her chest. I sit with my arms folded, showing mild impatience. Wayne smiles at the waitress.

'Just a drink,' I say.

The waitress bends to scoop up the cutlery on the table. 'Great, I'll get these out of the way. Almond milk chai latte?'

'Yes, please.' My voice sounds as though I haven't used it in weeks. 'And a chocolate milkshake.'

'Sure.' She turns to Wayne. 'And for you?'

Now Wayne turns on his megawatt smile. 'Black coffee.'

In the twenty-plus years since I met him he has shed twenty kilograms of muscle and half an inch of hair at his temples. Aging has been less kind to me. Parts of my body have sagged; things I didn't expect, like my calf muscles, my shoulder blades. He's got the same shape to him. Gravity and time will come for his looks eventually, one can hope anyway.

He is staring at Billy. I feel sweat on my chest. Maybe he is just curious about the black eye. I also notice now, the island chain of bruises on Billy's forearm where I had grabbed him. It's possible that Wayne is registering Billy's features and reconciling them with his own. Billy has his chin, and the full lips.

That night with Wayne comes back to me: wine and beer, then negronis. Then bed, his body pressed hard to mine. It was so much more exciting; we were almost like strangers.

'So,' he begins when the waitress has been and gone, dropping our drinks off. 'Are you going to introduce me to the kid?'

'This is Billy. But you're not here to talk about him, so let's get this over with.'

'If you've got nothing to do with Aspen disappearing, why are you so hostile? What did I do?'

I breathe deeply through my nose before I speak. 'Because you ambushed me at my yoga class, and you've been sending me messages in the middle of the night, and who knows what else.' A shuffling of his features: embarrassment, regret, fear? 'Let's not forget the lies you told about me.'

Wayne's knee jogs up and down, rocking the table. My chai wobbles and a tongue of foam spills down the side of the cup over my knuckle. Billy is holding his milkshake in both hands.

Wayne raises his own cup to his lips. He is the opposite to me. He wears his emotions like a strong cologne.

'Lies?' He swallows. 'Freya, I never lied. I just told it how I saw it.'

I shake my head. He still won't admit it.

'So you haven't seen Aspen at all? You didn't organise to pick him up three weeks ago? You haven't been messaging him for months?'

'No,' I say. 'No, of course not. He's seventeen. Maybe he got sick of you. Did that cross your mind?'

'So you're telling me you haven't been contacting him online?'

'No, I haven't, Wayne.'

'Well, the messages came from your email address.'

'What email address?'

He reaches into his pocket and removes his phone. He shows me a screenshot. I see my old email address: *freyaheywood@ausnet.com.* I read the message.

I'll pick you up at 12 pm on Friday.

I'm leaning closer, my stomach sinking. I had changed everything from the past: I had a new bank account, new address, new email account. But had I closed my former email address or had I just stopped using it?

I hand his phone back. 'It's not me.'

'Really?'

'What did the other emails say?'

'I don't know. They were all deleted except for that one and another from a couple of years ago telling him you were his mother and you wanted to talk on the phone. But you know that already, right?'

'Wayne, I haven't used that email address in at least a decade. I don't even know the password anymore.'

'This is bullshit, Freya. Where is he?'

I glance towards Billy then back to Wayne. I clear my throat – *Keep control, Freya* – and say politely, 'Please don't speak like that in front of him.'

His eyes narrow on me and I feel the twist in my chest. I reach for my necklace through my shirt, the copper ring hanging from it, the one Wayne gave me all those years ago. I rub my thumb over it, like running my tongue over a capped tooth. Those almost forgotten feelings come rushing back.

Wayne finishes his coffee, and abruptly turns to Billy. His voice softens. 'How old are you, mate?'

Billy looks up. 'I'm seven.'

A lump gathers at the back of my throat.

Wayne smiles, but only his lips move. There's a tremor near his right eye, a faint twitch. 'Seven,' he repeats quietly.

My pulse slams at my temples; I fear I might be sick.

I rise suddenly and my chair tips back, clatters against the concrete. People are watching. People from yoga. I flatten my top, place a hand on my chest as if surprised by my clumsiness. Then I speak softly, so that no one else can hear me. 'You stay the hell away from us, Wayne. Don't come anywhere near me or Billy again.'

'I've come here to find my son. That's all I want. Give him back and I'll go home.'

'If you keep this up, Wayne, you'll get hurt.'

The waitress comes back through the door to collect our now-empty cups. She stands, mouth slightly agape, eyes moving from Wayne to me and back again. I take Billy by the wrist and pull him away from the table. Wayne signals for the bill and the waitress gives a small urgent nod then heads back inside. The other diners outside are watching, and some are looking on through the window from inside. The violence, or threat of it, is just a small fissure, a seam that closes a moment later. I know I have the potential to be cruel, the potential to hurt others.

I take Billy's hand and turn and stride across the car park towards the Disco. I have lost one son to Wayne; I will not lose another. I will do anything to keep Billy safe. *Anything*.

AMY

ALL DAY WE sweep and dust. We do our daily clean of the floors and surfaces but also the windows, even the high ones, which Anton has to climb a ladder to reach. We sweep the dry leaves in the Clearing and cut the grass. Adam rakes the stones on the driveway. Annette collects bouquets of wildflowers and jams them into vases. When we are done the Clearing looks like a different place. It's beautiful. It's Eden.

A van sweeps down towards the Great Hall with food wrapped up in plastic. There are tiny pies, sausage rolls, tarts, sweets. My mouth waters as I help to carry them inside. I notice Asha is not helping us. She must be locked in the Shed or still in the Burrow.

There is a box with the word *Champagne* marked on the side. The bottles come out one at a time and are put into a steel bucket that looks exactly like the rusty old Cooler, but instead of muddy water this bucket is brimming with chunks of ice.

We have had gatherings at the Clearing before, where all of the members from the outside world come together. Adrienne says it's important for everyone to see the good work we are doing with the children, so they can see how we are preparing for the new age.

Tonight we wear our best clothes. Stiff dresses, pressed shirts and pants. Our hair is freshly bleached, washed and combed flat to our skulls.

Tamsin takes us to the Burrow just before the guests arrive. Her shadow flares out behind her in the sun streaming through the window. She examines us closely. Her dark eyes and gaunt face look strange with blue eyeliner and pinked cheeks.

'Not a single foot wrong, children. Tonight you will be perfect.' She comes closer to me. Our eyes are level and I notice a spot of sweat cutting a path through her make-up. 'You will make sure they stay in line.'

Her words tie my stomach into a knot. 'Yes,' I force out.

•

I recognise some of the guests rolling down into the Clearing in black cars. They are not dressed like princesses, like I was expecting; they wear jeans and shirts, they wear cotton dresses and flat shoes.

We take up the trays of food and champagne and weave through the growing crowd inside the Great Hall, just like we have practised. Trestle tables lined with burning candles and silver platters are covered in dips and bread. I move about with my back straight and my hand flat beneath the tray.

'Good evening, sir,' I say, approaching a man with a curled grey moustache. 'Would you care for a glass of champagne?' I say it just how we were taught. *Sham-pain*. Isn't it strange how some words seem to leave a taste in your mouth?

'Goodness, you children are well behaved, aren't you?' the man says, reaching out to stroke my cheek with a finger. His finger feels dirty but I simply smile.

'And for you, madam?'

The woman next to him takes a glass and I feel the tray wobble a little in my hand.

'Thank you,' she says. When she sips, she leaves a crescent of lipstick the colour of blood on the glass.

Jermaine Boethe is there with his scraggly hair and sharp leering eyes. It's the first time I've seen him since I sketched him, for some reason I thought he wouldn't be here. He watches me from across the room. There are others I've never met, like the man with tiny silver spectacles and a long arc of tanned forehead, who rests his hand on my bottom for a moment as I pass. Turning to look at him, I make myself smile.

Soon a tall man in a cowboy hat mounts the stage. He taps his glass with a butter knife that winks in the candlelight.

'Ladies and gentlemen,' the man begins. He has a strange voice that makes me imagine him floating across the sea in a boat. 'I have come all the way from Minnesota to be with you here tonight.'

Silently, I say the word to myself: *Minna-soda.*

He smiles broadly. 'I have been head of psychology at an Ivy League college and spent seven years travelling the world, studying anthropology. I revived some of the more contested debates regarding phrenology and the hereditability of intelligence. Then I began to shift my focus towards higher consciousness.' He adjusts his hat and turns to fix an adoring gaze on Adrienne, standing at the edge of the stage. 'I meditated for two years in a cave in the Himalayas and have met many spiritual leaders. *Then* I met Adrienne. We all have a story. For some she has cured your illness. Others she may have rescued from dark and damaging relationships. One thing we all know is this: Adrienne understands us better than we understand ourselves. She can tap into the wisdom of the divine. She will usher in the new age. We must always protect the Queen.' The crowd murmurs. 'We must be one and keep going, despite what comes our way. Despite the evil forces on this planet conspiring against her. She is the head and we are the body.'

When Adrienne takes the stage, the crowd explodes with cheering and whistles. It goes on for so long I begin to think it won't stop. Then Adrienne raises both her hands and all the sound drains from the room. That is our cue. We make our way to the edge of the stage and stand in two rows, girls and boys, shortest to tallest. She gazes out at the people gathered, her blue eyes intent. She is so beautiful, so perfect in every way.

'My family,' she begins, 'tonight we celebrate, but we also plan. What is mine, this gift, it is yours too. I am simply God's tool, a beacon for him to communicate his wisdom with you. We have no use for our worldly possessions when the new age comes about.' She pauses, looking towards us children. 'So we need to combine our resources. Give everything over to me and I will make sure that you can live without fear, that you can all walk tall and proud, knowing you are part of something bigger than this world. We have eleven of the twelve now. We are just one child away.'

'My family.' Her head tilts to one side, a smile spills across her lips. 'And now: where is our newest child, the eleventh?'

The door at the back of the room swings inwards and Asha steps into the hall. She seems different. Her hair is cut into a bob like ours but her eyes are faded, as if someone has sucked her personality out of her head. She stumbles forwards into the room.

'Asha,' Adrienne says.

The crowd parts to clear a path for her.

'Come here, sweetie.' Adrienne crouches and beckons to the girl. 'Come to Mother.'

Asha walks towards her, ushered along by the hands of the crowd.

'She's a little shy,' Adrienne says, as palms push Asha up the steps to the stage.

The girl stumbles into Adrienne's arms then begins to push away, but Adrienne holds tight. Her smile slips for just a moment. An awkward laugh rolls through the crowd.

Standing at the back of the room, I see Adam. He is the only person who doesn't smile. His arms are folded across his chest. Adrienne and Asha step down from the stage and I hold Asha against me.

The next woman to take the stage describes how Adrienne contacted her out of the blue and warned her to abandon a holiday she had planned in Barcelona. She didn't know why, but she listened; she cancelled her plans, and the plane she was scheduled to fly on disappeared somewhere in the Pacific. After a few more have shared their stories, Adrienne moves about the room, touching people gently on the forehead. Their bodies all tremble, they catch their breath, they feel her power.

Adrienne ascends the stage once more. 'Now, we have one last matter to deal with,' she says. 'It pains me to bring you this news, but we have a defector in our midst.'

The room stills, grows tense, a mood of anger permeating.

'Someone in this room has turned against us. One person in this room is a traitor and has defiled one of our children.' I can sense movement towards the back of the hall. 'He exposed himself to her in the vilest manner.' Adrienne starts to chant now. 'Protect the Queen, be one, keep going . . .'

As the chant rises up, someone is dragged forwards. It is Jermaine Boethe.

'Bring that man to me.'

All the people gathered handle him, shoving him. A leaf on an irresistible current.

PROTECT THE QUEEN, BE ONE, KEEP GOING . . .

'No,' he says. 'No! What is this?'

That's when I notice Tamsin carrying the axe towards the stage and Indigo beside her carrying the chopping block.

PROTECT THE QUEEN, BE ONE, KEEP GOING . . .

They wrangle him to the stage and release him at Adrienne's feet. She looks down upon him as a man wraps a rag around his mouth and pulls it back until it rips between his lips. He tries to rise again but he can't as a boot presses his spine.

Anton heaves the scarred chopping block on the stage beside Jermaine Boethe and Adrienne places my sketch on it.

She turns to me. 'Take the axe, Amy.'

I hesitate.

'NOW!'

I step forwards and pick it up. My breathing is thick and fast.

'Crush his fingers.'

Jermaine Boethe begins to struggle. I can hear him whimpering through the gag.

'I . . .'

'You will do as you are told. Do it with the blunt side of the axe. If you refuse, your brother will do it and he will use the sharp side.'

I look down at the fingers curling into a fist to protect themselves. A man is holding his arm in place by the wrist.

PROTECT THE QUEEN, BE ONE, KEEP GOING . . .

I think about the lustful look in the art teacher's eyes as I sketched, the way his body bucked as he touched himself. I knew it was wrong at the time, I knew he was a bad man. The axe feels good now, I feel the power of it. I draw it back, raising it up over my shoulder. I look over the heads of the crowd as my mother urges me on. I meet Adam's eyes where he stands near the door and for the first time I see fear, real fear. It feels good. The power. Energy surges. I smile. Then, with all my strength, I bring it down.

PROTECT THE QUEEN, BE ONE, KEEP GOING . . .

FREYA

Twenty hours to go

I CHOKE THE steering wheel in my fists. I saw the way Wayne looked at Billy; if he doesn't know the entire truth, he at least suspects it.

Despite being younger than me, when we met Wayne stood half a foot taller and already had thick stubble. We were at the gym. I was undergoing physiotherapy and when I was struggling to add iron plates to the leg press machine Wayne came over and helped me. From then on, whenever I was struggling with something at the gym, I asked Wayne for help. That's how it started: he was my own personal trainer. I saw the spider web tattoo on the back of his hand, the muscles bulging beneath his t-shirt, and thought he was older than he was.

'You're different,' he said on our first date.

A few dates later, I realised that dating someone made me normal. Normal girls had boyfriends, normal girls felt attracted to other people. It was another way for me to fit in. I felt protective of him. I felt compelled to spend more time with him. He was my first – and, in truth, my only – boyfriend.

I still lived in the flat Mum owned in Carlton near the city when Wayne began staying over, slowly moving himself in. I was working at one of Mum's friend's galleries near the university. I didn't need the money, but I needed the *normal*. The routine. I spent my days meeting other artists and art enthusiasts, and I was painting more and more, up all night sitting before the canvas. Wayne only worked Friday and Saturday nights.

Trust is a precious flower. Squeeze it a little and it wilts. Pick it and study it beneath a microscope and it will die. Or, like Wayne, you can just crush it beneath your boot. I would only break someone's trust if it was completely necessary. You draw attention to yourself by being untrustworthy. People watch you with a critical eye and they talk about you.

When my trust in Wayne died – after too many unexplained absences, too many marks and bruises on his body that he couldn't account for convincingly – I decided to follow him. I sat in my car by the side of the road near his house for several Friday nights in a row, until one night I saw him coming.

The Datsun roared along in a yellow streak. I flicked my lights on and carefully merged into the traffic. I stayed a few car lengths back as we rolled down through Melbourne city. On the docks, cranes reached out over the water. Cutting through Footscray towards the western suburbs, the roads were quiet and empty except for the occasional car or truck.

At times I almost lost him. It was a little after 10 pm when his car pulled in beside a McDonald's half an hour outside of the city. I parked further along and watched him in the mirror. I wasn't going to lose him.

Wayne climbed out and waited as another man crossed the car park towards him. The second man wore a tight woollen cap and black leather gloves. He punched one hand into the palm of the other as he approached Wayne. When the two men met, they shook hands, slapped backs.

My throat closed. It was clearly not another woman and yet somehow this was more of a betrayal.

•

At the house, I put the air-conditioning on low and settle on the couch in my dressing gown beside Billy. I sit there with my phone in my hand thinking about Corazzo. I wonder if he could help clear Wayne off. What if Wayne is telling the truth about my old email address? What if someone was impersonating me, luring Aspen away? I notice a drop of blood on the front of my dressing gown. I plug my nostrils with my thumb and finger and rush to the bathroom for tissues. When I remove my fingers, blood rushes from my nose as though I've struck oil.

Back in the lounge room, nose plugged with tissues, I drop the roller shutters, blocking out the buzzing, squirming life in the yard. We are in our own controlled little terrarium. Rocky is on his side near the back door.

When evening falls and Billy complains that he is hungry, I cook one of the emergency pizzas that I keep in the freezer. You won't find *Antioxidant-rich*, *FODMAP friendly* or *Superfood* stamped on the box. In fact, frozen pizzas sit at absolute zero on the nutritional scale. But nothing placates Billy more than fast food and I just can't muster the energy to cook something from scratch. I smear organic tamarillo relish on a slice and eat it standing at the kitchen bench, the previous morning's newspaper open in front of me. I scan the words of the article again. *Abducted less than one hundred metres from her front gate.* In the photo accompanying the article I see a child. I know she has perfect blue eyes, and long blonde hair but the image is black and white.

'Billy.'

He looks up from the television, a string of cheese looping down from his mouth to his slice of pizza.

'Come here a moment.'

'Why?' he asks, scooping up the cheese. His eyes are now fixed on the screen, where *The Simpsons* has been replaced by *Family Guy.*

'I said so, that's why.'

When he opens his mouth to cram the cheese in I see the gap from his missing tooth, a tiny point of white already coming through to fill it. His eye is less swollen now, but the convex bruise is the colour of a plum. He has been wiggling another tooth; it'll come out soon enough. A mini businessman, that's what I'm raising. I still feel guilty about hurting him.

'And for dessert, maybe we can have ice cream?'

He looks up with a sudden smile, a struck match, and nods.

•

It is hot and claustrophobic in the Disco. I lower the windows as we pull out, dust rising in our wake. The van is still there . . . that's three days now. *O-U-P.* Corazzo said the owner was harmless, but how does he know? He works at a gardening store, which seems innocuous but I know most serial killers have normal lives and jobs, they look normal from the outside. Jeffrey Dahmer worked at a chocolate factory, Ted Bundy worked at a suicide crisis hotline.

We get ice creams, then on the way back at the lights in town, I stop, and check my phone. There are messages from Wayne and a couple of missed calls. I ignore them all. If Wayne took me to court, would he win custody of Billy? What view would the legal system take of me keeping Billy's existence a secret from Wayne all these years?

We are mostly silent on the twenty-minute drive back home. As I ease down the driveway, the headlights rake over the front door, and that's when I see them. Flowers. A spray of yellow wattle, just like before.

My breath catches. I sit up straight. I'm shaking.

'Mama?' Billy says. 'What's wrong?'

People commonly talk about the 'fight or flight' response when a threat is perceived; few mention the third response: 'freeze'. I can't seem to think clearly. The flowers were not there when we left, I'm sure of it. That means someone has been here. Someone was watching us, waiting for us to go out.

I study the house for movement. I take my phone and open the panic button app. My thumb hovers over the call button as I open the door and step out.

'Stay in here,' I say to Billy, locking the door behind me.

My senses are electric, my eyes wide and heart thumping. I reach the door and look down. This time there is a note with the flowers.

29/02/2020
Matthew 19:14

I'm still shaking. *Are you watching me now? Are you here some-where, hiding out in the bush?* I rush back to the car, gather Billy in my arms and freight him back to the couch. I lock the door behind us and go from room to room, lowering the roller shutters.

'Mama, I'm scared,' Billy says.

'It's okay,' I say. 'It's okay, son.'

The twenty-ninth of February. I think of the flyers posted up on a noticeboard at the town hall beside the yoga studio advertising an apocalyptic party on the leap day.

I type the Bible verse into Google.

Let the little children come to me and do not hinder them, for
to such belongs the kingdom of heaven.

Then I feel . . . oddly calm. This is all designed to scare me, whoever is doing this is trying to make me afraid, put me on the defence. If someone wanted to hurt me or my son they wouldn't give this warning, they wouldn't give me a chance at all. I draw a breath and force myself to smile down at Billy.

'Don't be scared,' I say. 'There's nothing to worry about.' Wayne, Henrik or the man at the river – someone is playing games. Someone wants to make me run away, so that's the last thing I'm going to do.

Twelve hours to go

I would have preferred to hear it from some card-wielding mystic at a fair. That way I could disregard it completely, but the message with the flowers is much more . . . grim. It might as well have been a black crow crashing through my window, carrying a note written in blood. I know it's *designed* to let me know someone is watching, the sender is near; they must have been to be able to drop the flowers off in the time we were out.

Later that night, I'm sitting on the couch when my phone rings. It's Wayne. I silence it before it can wake Billy, who is asleep in my arms. An old movie runs on TV. Our discarded ice cream sticks lay chewed up and abandoned by Rocky near his rug. It's ten past eleven; why would Wayne be calling now?

The phone rings again.

'What?' I stage whisper.

'You answered.'

'You've got ten seconds, Wayne.'

'He looks like me,' he says. 'He looks like Aspen, too.'

'Fuck off, Wayne. You're delusional.'

'I just want Aspen. That's all. I think he's in trouble, Freya. If it really wasn't you contacting him, then someone else was pretending to be you. Someone has stolen him away.'

I swallow hard. I try to calm myself. The phone has grown warm in my hand.

'You took him away from me,' I remind him. 'You said you wanted to protect him, but now he has disappeared.'

Wayne sighs down the line. 'What if it happens again?' he asks. 'What if you hurt Billy like you hurt Aspen? Couldn't help but notice the shiner.'

Is he threatening me?

'B-Billy is fine,' I stutter down the line, struggling to speak. 'I think we should just leave it at that.'

'I'm sure he is. I'm sure you've got a big ole dog up there keeping him safe.'

'How did you know that? How did you know I have a dog?'

Billy shifts against me. He is waking.

'I know what you're like. I know how calculating you are, and how you always need to be in control.'

'Have you been spying on me, Wayne?'

'Of course not.'

'You've been following me, haven't you?'

I imagine him smiling as he says, 'You're losing it.'

'Look, Wayne.' I'm speaking slowly now. 'This stops tonight. I haven't seen Aspen in almost fifteen years, I've never contacted him, and I don't know where he is.'

When the call ends I close my eyes. Every cell in my body is trembling, electric with pain.

When I open my eyes again, Billy is watching me.

'Who was it, Mama?'

'No one, Billy. Go back to sleep.' I drag my fingers through his hair, then wrap my arms tightly around him. Some snakes kill in this way, simply by squeezing; some snakes don't bite at all.

I think about the secret Wayne kept from me. I had a secret of my own swelling in my belly the night I followed him. Our first child. I had stopped my contraception and let it happen.

After he got into the other man's car that night in the McDonald's car park, they headed back towards the city and I trailed them beneath the yellow glow of streetlights as they travelled out along the industrial stretch near the port, pulling to a halt outside a warehouse. Cars lined the street outside. I found a park between a beaten-up old ute and a slick black BMW and killed the headlights. Knots of people milled about in twos and threes, men with their coat collars turned up against the cold, gradually trickling through the lone door of the building. I waited, sitting in my car. An hour passed, maybe more, before I could bring myself to move.

I stepped out into the night air and started along the footpath to the warehouse, my shoes crunching over broken glass. When I reached the door, it was closed. There was no doorhandle, so I knocked twice as hard as I could.

After a few minutes, the door opened to reveal a man with a shaved skull and the telling kink of a brawler's nose. Beyond him I could make out a crowd of men – thirty or forty of them – arranged in a circle in a big open space. I couldn't see what was in the centre of the crowd, but I could hear the meaty thump of flesh being struck.

'Wrong door to knock on, sweetie.'

I was surprised to hear an Australian accent. What had I been expecting?

As the man began to push the door closed, I stepped up and put my shoulder into it.

'I'm here for the fights,' I said without thinking.

'No you're not. No women.' The man looked annoyed now. He pushed the door so hard that I stumbled back. I pounded on it, but it wasn't opened again.

I returned to my car and sat there waiting, watching the exit for Wayne. But when people started to stream from the building at around 3 am, there was no sign of him. I must have missed him in the crowd, I realised. I stayed until the last car had gone before returning to the McDonald's where he'd left his car. It was no longer there.

We'd both kept secrets but this was big. Confronting Wayne wasn't easy; I knew I needed to stay calm. As he began to deny it, I said, 'Just let me watch. I want to watch you fight.'

'You really are fucked up, aren't you?'

He was a criminal, there was no other way of putting it. He was part of a world I didn't know or understand. Oh, I knew about crime – I had been dragged through the legal system when I was a kid – but Wayne's crime was different. This was before professional fighting became a legal and popular sport. This wasn't nearly as safe. If he'd started fighting a decade later, he could have made a lot more money than he did. I didn't want the father of my child being routinely beaten to a pulp and excluding me from a large part of his life. I decided to give him an ultimatum.

Leaning against the kitchen bench in our house, I stroked my belly, watching first the shock then the scepticism flit across his face.

'No,' he said. 'You . . . you're not . . .' He was staring at my belly.

At that point Aspen was only a collection of cells forming inside of me, but he would change everything.

'I'm pregnant, Wayne. You're going to be a dad.'

'How?'

'I don't know, I guess it just happened.' Then I let my mask slip for the first time in front of Wayne. The sudden anger made my voice low and grating. My eyes grew wide, unblinking, fixed on his. 'No more fighting. And if you *ever* lie to me again, it's the last you'll see of me or the baby.'

AMY

JERMAINE BOETHE IS in my head. His fingers bloody, swelling, black as burnt sausages. His body writhing in throes of pain. Anton and Tamsin dragging him off the stage, his screams muffled against the gag while everyone continued their chanting.

It felt good, having that power. It felt good to please my mother.

When I wake, I cannot remember falling asleep. One moment I was staring at Asha, her arms wrapped around her legs, rocking on her bunk with her jaw trembling, and the next the birds are chirping and a seam of daylight is passing beneath the door and Asha is asleep.

Then the bell begins to ring. It's too early for the bell, I think, but it doesn't stop. I can hear something else over the sound of it. A distant thumping. *A helicopter?* The bell keeps ringing and I realise that this is not a drill.

I leap up – we all do, except Asha, who Anton drags from her bed by the arm. We quickly pull on our tracksuits then hurry into the bathroom. I push through the false panel in the wall at the far end of the bathroom and lead the others along the low, dark corridor. When I reach the end, I lift a panel from the floor to reveal a ladder that disappears down into the Hole.

I stand beside it and count off my brothers and sisters as they descend the ladder one by one into the oil-slick blackness. Tamsin comes through, bringing up the rear, and Anton stays above with her as I follow the rest into the Hole. Anton slides the panel back into place and darkness swallows us. I start down the ladder, the heat from the earth pressing against me, my hands and feet become my eyes, feeling for each rung until I reach the bottom. The Hole is thick and damp with breath.

I wonder what has happened to make it necessary for us to hide. Perhaps rapists and murderers are even now descending on our sanctuary, just as Adrienne has described: those evil men in blue who would set us alight and send us all to hell. Are they out there now, desecrating our home?

'It's too hot,' someone murmurs.

'Shh,' I hiss. 'Silence.'

For a while there is no sound but our breathing, then I hear a creak. It's the ladder. Someone is climbing. I move quickly towards the sound, bumping between bodies, and reach out. My hand finds an ankle. Grabbing it, I pull back hard. A foot slams against my face, catching me right in the mouth. I feel the hot rush of blood from a split lip and my eyes water. I straighten, push through the pain, and begin to clamber up the ladder. 'Stop,' I hiss.

I feel a foot on the rung above me, grab it and pull hard, but whoever it is holds fast. I move quickly, climbing over the child above until I'm able to reach up and peel the tiny hands away from the rung.

We both fall, twisting in the air. There is no time to brace for the impact. The air thumps from me.

'Stay here,' I say, my voice hoarse and breathless. My mouth is bubbling with blood. I hold the small body against my own in the dirt, waiting.

'HELP!' A high voice shatters the silence. Asha. 'HEL—'

I cover the child's mouth and slam a fist into her body. Doesn't she understand what will happen if they find us? She is putting us all at risk, and it's my job to correct her behaviour. I thump her again. It feels good, punishing her, knowing I am doing it for my mother.

'Stop it right now. Stop or I will hurt you. You cannot leave.'

Others are moving in the darkness. I feel more hands reaching in, helping to hold her down.

Seconds stretch into minutes; the minutes stretch on and on in silence. No one moves or speaks. I lie with my body pressed against the squirming child. The smell of piss fills the Hole.

Eventually the bell tolls for us to leave and suddenly the darkness swarms with bodies desperately moving towards the ladder. The panel slides open and I gaze up into the light.

Tamsin is visible at the entrance to the Hole, Anton behind her. 'You can come up now,' she says.

She counts aloud as we ascend one by one. Tamsin's forehead creases when I emerge. 'What happened to you?'

I recall the sickening crack when Asha's foot struck my mouth.

'I bumped my face climbing down,' I lie. Another deceit to protect Asha.

She frowns. Anton stares at me. Then Tamsin says, 'You're number nine. That means someone is still down there.'

I climb back through the open panel; the light is limited to what passes down the hall from the bathroom and through the opening into the Hole. I take the ladder carefully, one rung at a time, my heart fluttering.

My hands tremble with fatigue as I descend. In the trace of light seeping in, the Hole feels somehow both smaller and larger than I imagined. In the dim light I see the body on its side. One arm is flung over his face. The earth is soft and damp around him from where he pissed.

'It's Alex,' I call up to Tamsin and Anton. 'I think he's fainted.'

Anton descends, and together we manoeuvre the boy slowly up the ladder. We carry him by the arms and legs back to the bunkroom and place him on his bed.

'I'll sit with him,' I say to Anton, who is preparing for school. His huge frame lumbers towards the door. I fetch a glass of water and hold it in my hand, waiting for the boy to wake. My eyes roam around the room, searching for distraction. I notice something silver glinting in the seam between the mattress and the frame of Asha's bed. I put the glass of water down on the floor near him and rush across the room. Thrusting my hand in under her mattress, I pull out a knife.

I stare at it. It's one of the vegetable knives from the kitchen, small and sharp enough to break skin. Why would Asha have this? To hurt someone? I am stashing it beneath my own mattress when I hear Adam's voice behind me.

'He awake yet?'

I spring up and turn to see him enter the room and stride towards the unconscious child.

'Not yet.'

Adam gives the boy a small slap. He takes the glass of water and splashes a little of it on Alex's face. His eyes seem to move beneath their lids. A slight flutter. Then they slowly blink open.

'You're back with us,' Adam says.

Tamsin appears at the entrance of the Burrow, leaning in the doorway. They'll probably want him out with the other children as soon as possible but he won't be ready just yet. When you faint from dehydration or heat, you wake up dizzy and with a dusty mouth and sore throat. If you faint from pain, you wake as if from a nightmare. You're still dizzy but your mind screams awake. I think about the knife beneath my bed, I think about the Cooler, the way it feels like your skull is compressing around your brain the longer they hold you under.

'He's going to be groggy for a while,' Adam says, and I feel grateful for it. 'Sit with him, feed him water while he recovers.'

I do as I'm told, but after a short while instead of watching Alex I let my gaze travel through the window to the other side of the Clearing, where Adam gently swings in the hammock. He is picking a tune from his guitar with Asha nestled in beside him. The tune drifts across the Clearing towards me. The other children are in class.

The sun slants down between the trees and Alex stirs behind me.

Beat a dog with one hand, offer it a treat with the other. Keep it obedient and make it love you. But Asha is not broken. She stole the knife. She kicked me in the face. She is always awake in the evening, so maybe she is planning something. Maybe she is planning to hurt someone or herself?

•

In the early afternoon, Adam, Anton and Adrienne get in the van and leave the Clearing. It's just us children, with Jonathan, Tamsin and Indigo. From the classroom, I can hear the boards squeak every time Indigo moves about in the kitchen.

After our silent reading time, we head out to sit beneath the Great Tree for half an hour of silent meditation. But my mind wanders; I can't seem to clear the thoughts from my head. I wonder about something Asha said about the outside world. How her friends miss her, how much she used to eat, how happy she was. I can't escape the idea that maybe she was happier out there. It's a deviant thought, but I can't seem to push it out of my mind.

Adrienne says that if you leave a light on inside first one moth will come, then another, then many will come, just as they swarm the lantern swinging from the entrance of the Great Hall at night. That's how deviant thoughts work too. It's best to simply turn the light off, forget everything, block all those distractions that worm their way into your brain. But I can't. I open my eyes for a moment and that's when I notice a gap in the circle of children. Someone is missing. I look around, and see something moving at the far side of the Clearing. It's a child, I realise. It's Asha, and she is scaling the fence.

FREYA

Six hours to go

I WAKE EARLY. Early for a Saturday, anyway. No school or yoga, nothing to be up for. The flowers have failed to scare me away but I was awake most of the night thinking about them, and in the morning they're the first thing I think of. The second thing is Billy. I leave Rocky dozing on my bed and go to Billy's room, gently opening the door and peering in on him sleeping. Then I walk out into the yard. While the sun fingers its way through the trees, I sit down in the grass, watching the snake-like head of a blue-tongue lizard bob out from under a shrub. I lean back and rest my head against the grass, reassured. Blue-tongues are a good omen. I need a little luck to come my way. I've had a lot of bad luck and it's making me think more and more about the past.

Aspen was in the hot car.

My baby boy had almost died. If he'd been in there any longer, he would have. The police wanted to charge me with attempted murder. They had a strong case and it cost a lot of money to fight it, but my lawyer managed to keep me out of prison. I had a breakdown, she explained, presenting a psychologist's report which suggested that I had completely disassociated. The judge said no one could deny that it was a deliberate act to leave Aspen in the hot car. He said with all of the witness testimony of ongoing abuse he had no choice but to exclude me from Aspen's life. Witness testimony. Wayne's testimony. The things he said I had done. Statements from the neighbours. The cards were stacked.

No serious conviction was recorded. The judge determined that with the help of a psychologist I could live a normal life. That's why the story of the missing girl causes me to ache. I know it's different, but I can appreciate what her parents must be going through. That gut-sinking feeling of loss; it feels like an illness. The newspaper article said the police are looking for a van in connection with the girl's disappearance. Like the van on my street and the couple within. *Could they be related to it?* Would the police investigate them with all the strange things that have happened? The flowers, the gate being unlocked? Corazzo had already checked the van out, there wasn't a mark against it.

I return inside and do my push-ups then grab a nectarine from the fruit bowl and check on Billy. He's still sleeping.

I lock the house, leaving Rocky inside, and walk down to the river. I swim out into the brown water and turn to float on my back. I close my eyes and just drift for a moment. Then I suck in a breath, curl into a ball and sink like a flesh-coloured stone. I stay there at the bottom and count to ninety seconds.

When I surface, I see stars shifting at the edges of my vision. I look across to the other side of the river. Something zips by. It is fleeting in the early sunlight. Through a gap in the trees I see the flash of skin. The skin of a child. Then the child is gone. A girl – it looked like a girl – should not be running around out here alone. Could it be *the* girl? The day is heating up, drawing the snakes out; one wrong step could be the end of her. Of course, it could have been a trick of the light, not a girl. Heat shimmering on the bank looking like movement. But it looked so real.

I wade further down the river, searching the opposite bank for another glimpse of movement. There is no sign of anyone, no sound, nothing. *It's in your mind. You're seeing things.* Maybe it's an echo of the news stories. A projection. Déjà vu.

Back at the house, I put the TV on and gulp down a glass of kombucha. Distracted by Wayne's voice at the grocer, I forgot to grab a new bottle. This one tastes a little sweeter than usual; maybe it's still fermenting. I can feel it working on me like an elixir. Healing from the inside out. I pour Billy a small glass and take it into his room, setting it beside his bed. I rub his hair gently; he's been up late the last couple of nights.

I return to the lounge to lie with Rocky on the couch. Hyper vigilance is more fatiguing than any exercise I have ever done. The last few days of nervous strain are catching up with me; I feel like I could drop off to sleep. Instead I switch the channel and listen to the news. They are talking about the drought; there have been fires over on the other side of the city, out to the west. They've come close enough to the outer suburbs to warrant evacuations. No rain is forecast until next week. *The fire risk remains severe,* a deep authoritative voice intones, *with other regional fire crews on standby should the situation worsen.* My body is feeling slow and heavy now and I'm struggling to resist the fatigue. Deciding not to fight it – after all, I haven't had a good sleep in over a week – I reach for my phone to set my alarm. Then sleep fells me like a bullet to the chest. I descend deep, deep, deep into the darkness of the earth.

•

I wake a few minutes later, my mouth is bone dry. I bring my phone before my eyes, blinking away the haze of sleep. 12.03.

Shit. I fly from the couch as if it were suddenly alight and race towards Billy's room.

'Billy!' I call. *'Billy!'*

The TV is still on, only now infomercials are running. Rocky rises slowly from his spot near the kitchen, his mouth stretching in a yawn. I throw the door to Billy's bedroom open. He's not there. I reach for the panic button, hold it down.

Then I call them to make sure they are coming. 'My son is missing,' I say. 'I think he has been taken.' I give them the address, as I rush about the house. I feel sick with panic. 'Please hurry,' I say before I hang up.

At my heels, Rocky is more alert now, his ears pricked. 'Billy!' I scream across my yard. I sprint down to the river and scan the surrounds. Where is he?

I sprint along the path back to the road, my body electrified. Rocks and sticks sting my bare feet but I don't stop. Rocky is by my side, growling as he runs.

'Billy!' I scream into the void of the bush. 'Billy!'

I get to the road and feel my heart stop. Cement sets in my stomach. The earth opens up and swallows me whole.

The van is gone.

— Amy's journal —

Which is worse?

A – Keeping a secret from your mother.
B – Looking away when someone does something wrong.
C – Causing pain to another human and enjoying it.
D – Doing something horrible because someone told you to.
E – All of the above.

No one noticed Asha missing at first. She was there when we started the meditation and gone when we finished, but it wasn't until we were doing chores that Indigo realised that there were only ten children. Asha was supposed to collect the eggs and then help in the garden, but there was no sign of her.

Indigo rang the bell and we formed two lines out the front of the Great Hall. Jonathan came over from the minders' quarters. Indigo counted us off then asked Jonathan if he recalled Asha being in class. He did. I did too. We all remembered her at the beginning of the meditation. We were talking about it when we heard the sound of the van returning. Adam climbed out, all smiles at first, but when Tamsin approached him and told him what had happened he stormed over towards us.

'Where is she?' he screamed at me.

I told him I didn't know.

He struck my cheek, so swift and hard it almost knocked me over. He asked me again. 'Where is she?'

'She must have run away,' I said.

He turned to Indigo. 'Have you checked everywhere? The Hole? The Shed? The minders' quarters?'

She nodded. I could see a vein pulsing in Adam's temple. I was so scared. I knew he was going to hurt us all.

The cicadas screamed. The sun was so hot I could feel it burning my arms but he made us stand there.

'Why is it no one noticed Asha was missing?' Adam demanded.

Silence.

'Someone knows. One of you let evil invade your brain. Your thoughts are evil and Adrienne will be very disappointed. I'm going to find out who let this happen, but we don't have time now – first we have to find Asha.'

Adam made us crawl under the Great Hall and the minders' quarters. He made us check the perimeter of the Clearing.

By the time we had finished searching, trucks had rolled down into the Clearing with dogs in their trays. Tamsin and Indigo were there along with others – men I had seen before.

Adam pointed at me and Anton. He told us that we were the eldest and were responsible for our brothers and sisters. He gave us three hours in which to find her. For every hour beyond that, he said, we would spend a day in the Shed being realigned. I couldn't suppress a gasp. A single day in the Shed is enough to break anyone. When we are locked in that room with him it's as close to hell as anyone will find on earth.

Adam took his keys from his belt. He placed the inch-long knife between his fingers and held it up. I braced for the blow to the ribs, but it didn't come.

'Three hours,' he said.

As the men with the trucks unloaded their dogs, Adam told us all that the Devil had our sister now. The Devil is everywhere that God is not. The Devil had entered her mind and he was controlling her.

We filed into the bush following Adam in the lead, tracking Asha's boot prints through the scrub. Then we spread out in a line; we must never lose sight of those to our left and right, Adam told us. Indigo was close to me, a white dog pulling her along as though it was stronger than her, even though Indigo is bigger than Adam and almost as big as my brother Anton. I could see that the dog made her nervous. She was watching it, rather than looking out into the bush like the rest of us.

We lost the trail early on, but then the dogs caught hold of Asha's scent and they led us deeper into the bush until we found more boot prints.

I scanned the bush desperately; I wanted to be the one to find her. Maybe I could protect her from Adam. Maybe I could stop what was coming.

Before he found Adrienne, Adam was a surgeon, a powerful doctor with incredible healing powers. Adrienne showed us a newspaper clipping about him once; about how he'd saved a girl. He was the first doctor in Australia to successfully transplant a liver in a child. Then he left his job and went travelling, and he started to take the magic bullets. When he returned, he was different. He met Adrienne, his spiritual leader. Together they were touched by God and they learnt their gifts. They learnt of their mission on earth.

I wonder what it would be like to be a surgeon; to cut someone open, repair them, then sew them back together again, healed.

We walked for hours. After a while out there, everything always ends up looking the same, but there are small landmarks that make it easier to remember where you are. Like the river.

It's all brown and low right now, but sometimes when it has rained a lot it grows stronger and higher. I could hear it trickling. I looked down below the rock face, through the trees, to the opposite riverbank. I wondered what was over there. Then I saw something. A building. A house.

A house . . . just like the one Asha once lived in. A house across the river, out there in the bush. I thought about the story from the Bible about Eve's apple. How she plucked it. The original sin.

In the Bible, God is crafty, he tests people, he surprises them, he changes his mind. That house could be my test. I could fixate on it or block it out, pretend I didn't see it.

Adam yelled and it ripped through the bush. The noise startled a flock of galahs into flight. It almost sounded like he was in pain, like he was being attacked.

I knew then that someone had found her. We ran, drawing together around her. God had returned the child. The punishment was yet to come. A washy grey feeling filled my chest.

I was angry like the other children at what Asha had put us through. It was her fault we had spent hours out there in the bush, in the heat. Part of me wanted to hurt her. That meanness inside was swelling, all angry red and full of pus. The meanness was hot in my chest.

One of the men carried Asha back to the Clearing. She was hardly moving at all.

Annabelle told me Asha had been caught because God plucked her up and turned her around. She was walking the wrong way. She was walking back towards us.

As the sun began to set they took Asha directly to the Shed while the rest of us lined up. I could barely stand and my mouth was as dry as dust. When we heard the splash come from the steps of the Great Hall, we all knew what was coming.

Question: If the world outside is so awful, why was Asha trying to return to it?

A – The Devil had her, and the Devil was using her to fool me.
B – She was sent to bring about our end.
C – It's not so bad out there.

The Cooler floated between Indigo and Tamsin towards us. They set it down, water splashing over the edge.

Anton moved closer, so our shoulders touched. He was scared, I think. He was always so tall and strong, so brave, but now he seemed fearful. A scream came from the Shed. Cockatoos rose from a tree, first just one beating across the Clearing, crying out like it was on fire, then two, three, four others flew over us. They looked like white petals floating in the sea.

Blisters had filled my boots with sticky pus. My head was all hot and my face was burnt from the sun. I had insect bites up my arms and on my legs.

The men left with the dogs. Then Adam brought Asha out. She was kicking like a demon.

He set her down right in front of the Cooler. It was clear the Devil had her by the way she kicked and screamed. Adam told us that we had let this happen, so we must be the ones to exorcise her.

The younger children were excused, and they went back to the Great Hall. There were just five of us left.

Adam pointed at Alice and then at Asha, kneeling in front of the Cooler with Tamsin and Indigo holding her in place.

Alice stepped forwards, as stiff as the scarecrow in our garden.

This part hurts the most to remember. This part is hardest for me to write.

'Now,' Adam said.

Alice pressed Asha's face into the water. Asha squirmed and twisted her head. Alice was not pressing firmly enough.

Adam told her to press harder.

Alice bit her lip then pushed until Asha's head was under the water. I could see that Alice was crying, but she didn't stop.

At first Asha became still. She was faking unconsciousness. Then she began to fight. Water churning, splashing. The girl's head slamming against the steel base of the Cooler.

'Enough,' Adam said.

Alice released her grip. Asha sucked in a few long breaths then collapsed in the hard dirt.

'Thank you, Alice, for doing God's work,' Adam said. 'Dry off and go to class now. Alex, you're next.'

Alex is pale and small-boned. He had recovered from fainting but looked exhausted. He swallowed and did not lift his eyes up from the dirt as he walked over to the Cooler. He was always the fastest at morning sprints. He also once had his hand crushed in a doorframe for disobedience but it has mostly healed now.

Asha lay wet and still on the ground. Adam gave the command and Alex did not hesitate. Cathy and Indigo lifted Asha into place and he pushed her head under.

As the realignment continued, Adam changed. He seemed happier. He was in control. He stood up tall and proud like a soldier. By the time it was Anton's turn, Asha was exhausted. Anton stepped forwards, but instead of squatting down and putting his big hands on the back of the girl's head, he dropped to his knees.

Adam's voice was as hard and sharp as a broken bottle. He asked what Anton was doing. Anton just rolled up his sleeves, held his arms behind his back and lowered his face to the water.

'Adrienne would not want this; this is not her teaching,' Anton said.

Adam strode over, drew his foot back and swung it so hard his boot hit the side of Anton's head with a crack that echoed across the Clearing. Anton fell, knocking over the Cooler, and the water ran out.

Indigo rushed off to refill it. While she was gone Adam kept kicking Anton, in the chest, the stomach, the back.

This was the first time I had seen someone openly defy Adam. I was scared for Anton. I knew it would be bad. I didn't know if I should be angry or proud or scared. I know what he did was wrong, but it was also brave. It was brave to stand up to Adam.

Indigo returned.

The three minders positioned Anton's head over the water, with his arms behind his back. Anton was drowsy now; strings of blood and snot hung from his face. Adam plunged Anton's head into the water with both hands. Anton revived briefly, but there was no point in fighting. Four adults held him in place.

When they were done, they dragged Anton off to the Shed for further realignment.

On their return, the minders hauled Asha back into place over the Cooler. It was my turn.

My stomach was turning inside me and my arms and legs felt numb with fatigue. I couldn't do it. I knew I couldn't. But Adam was watching closely. It was either me or her.

How had they found Asha?

How did they know she was one of us?

If she was sent by God, why did she want to leave?

Deviant thoughts flooded me. I stepped closer. Then I did what he told me to do. It felt righteous. It felt necessary. But, still, it hurt to do. I pressed her under. Then, when Adam told me to stop, I stepped back so he could come forwards and dunk her again. She had no time to catch her breath. He made me watch as he dunked her again and again until she stopped moving altogether.

So, back to my question: which is worse?

A – Keeping a secret from your mother.
B – Looking away when someone does something wrong.
C – Causing pain to another human and enjoying it.
D – Doing something horrible because someone told you to.

I've done them all in the last few weeks. But at least I can make one right. I can tell Adrienne what Adam did to me that night. Has he purged any of my sisters? I think about Asha again now.

What would have happened if we didn't find her in the bush? Would she have ended up at the house? I wonder who lives there. I wonder if they know how close we are.

PART FOUR
MISSING

FREYA

Thirty-two minutes missing

'WE HAVE A report of a missing child,' says the stout policeman with a curved nose like a beak.

'He's not missing,' I say, my voice frantic. 'He's been abducted. Someone has taken him.'

My child is gone; history repeats. The officer had introduced himself as Sergeant Corbett, and with him, the other officer with the small black eyes is Constable Trioli. Everything goes slower than it should. The police want to ask me questions. That's all they've done since they arrived. They don't fly off after the kidnapper, they don't set up a perimeter, checkpoints, order a helicopter to perform an aerial search. They simply sit me down and fire questions at me.

'So when was the last time you know you saw Billy?'

'It was earlier today. This morning, before I dozed off. He was still asleep in bed.'

'Any idea what time that was?'

'I don't know. I think it was after seven, around seven fifteen.'

I'm sitting at the kitchen table, resisting the urge to stand up and run outside to continue searching myself.

'And Billy is seven years old, correct?'

'Yes, he turned seven in November.'

'And does he have any hiding spots or anywhere he goes outside?'

My eyes are damp, my mouth sour. 'Someone took him. He's gone.'

'We have phoned it in,' says Trioli. He has the unappealing trace of a moustache. 'The best thing we can do now is narrow down the possibilities and consider every option, so it's important for us to know about Billy. You last saw your son roughly four hours ago, correct? But you noticed him missing around noon?'

My mind is whirring. Corbett has stepped outside now and is holding his radio close to his mouth.

'Yes,' I say. I stare at the notepad before him, the way his hand dances across the page as he writes down my words. They're assuming Billy will turn up at any moment; they're assuming this is all some misunderstanding. I have a physical reaction to him, an anger burns in my chest. I eye the revolver hanging from the officer's belt.

'Have you got people looking for him?' I ask.

'We have sent out an alert, and cars are currently patrolling parks, playgrounds, main roads nearby. We must assess risk factors closely, but in situations such as this, when we have limited information, it's best to collect information and make a plan. Billy is, after all, only seven years old. He can't have gotten too far.'

I clear my throat, turn my gaze away. He's right; Billy is only seven. A young seven. A defenceless seven.

I know this man Trioli – or I know his type, at least. A boy from the outer suburbs, not clever enough for uni so joined the cops. He has been instructed to take complaints seriously and investigate properly, but he has been in the job long enough to know that in situations such as this it is almost always a mix-up: a child at a friend's house, divorced parents getting their wires crossed, a kid going off exploring. He doesn't know what I know. He doesn't know my history. He couldn't possibly understand that his calculations have failed to take in one big and important factor: I am not who he thinks I am.

Corbett, I see now as he re-enters the room, has a receding hairline to go with his parrot's nose. He's *smiling*. What has he got to be happy about?

Rocky sniffs his reluctant hand.

'Would you gentleman like a glass of water? Kombucha? Tea?'

'We're fine.' Corbett lowers himself into the seat beside Trioli at the dining table.

'Nice house,' he says. He appears slightly older, is probably the alpha of the pair.

'Thanks.' I stand, flick the kettle on and lean against the bench.

'If Billy has wandered off, we'll want to get a search party out into the bush as soon as possible.'

'That's a good idea,' I say, knowing that whoever has taken him will be far away by now.

'Got one of those panic buttons, huh?' he says, pointing at the red button on the wall near my wrist. I follow Corbett's gaze. Trioli is clearly keen to push on with the procedural stuff, crossing t's and dotting i's, but Corbett is prepared to let the conversation wander.

'Yes.' *And how is that related?*

'Had trouble out here?' he asks.

'You can never be too careful,' I say.

Trioli looks to Corbett, but Corbett doesn't take his eyes off me.

'Ms Heywood, is there someone in your family that might have picked him up?'

I scratch the back of my neck. Jonas is away. Mum can barely dress herself let alone drive a car.

'No, but I have a fair idea who might be involved. I think he has been taken by my ex.'

'Alright,' Trioli says. 'That's a good start.'

'Wayne,' I say. 'It's got to be him.'

'Surname?'

'Sorry?'

'What is Wayne's surname?' he annunciates each syllable without looking up from his pad.

'Oh, ah, it's Phillips.'

Trioli's mouth moves as he scribbles. 'Have you got a phone number or an address for him?'

'On my phone,' I say. I go to the bedroom to fetch it. When I return with my phone in my hand, I see that Rocky is resting his head on Corbett's lap while the cop scratches between Rocky's eyes. *Turncoat.*

I make my hands tremble slightly as I place the phone down before them and I make sure I'm wearing the most desperate expression I can muster.

Trioli scratches the number onto his pad.

'I'm so scared for Billy,' I say. 'He wouldn't just wander off. I know he wouldn't.'

'Why do you believe this man is involved?' A current of accusation in Corbett's voice.

'Well,' I begin, dragging a hand over my eyes, 'I haven't seen him in years and he turned up a few days ago.'

The two cops stiffen, sitting up. 'I see,' Trioli says.

'And did he do or say anything to make you suspicious of him?' Corbett again.

'He thinks he is Billy's father, but he's not.' A lie, but there is no way these two could know that.

Corbett rises, grabbing at his walkie-talkie. He steps away from the table, calls in this latest piece of information.

Trioli sets his meaty hands on the table and hunches forwards. 'And why would he think that?'

'I'm sorry?'

'Why would Wayne believe that Billy is his son?'

I can feel myself scowling, my fingers tingling, so close to the panic button. I rearrange my face into an expression of concern, as if thinking. 'Because, well, we spent a night together years after we broke up. We both agreed it was a mistake. But Billy wasn't conceived that night. I didn't become pregnant till a few months later.'

'Right,' says Trioli, sitting back in his chair. 'And Billy's biological father – is he in the picture?'

'No,' I say. 'It was a sperm donor.' The lies are racking up now. Could they fact check this somehow?

'Can you think of anyone else who might have picked Billy up? A friend's parents, for instance?'

'No, but there was a van parked down the road for a few nights, and now it's gone. I've got the licence plate number here on my phone.' I show him.

Trioli dutifully records it in his notebook. 'We'll check it out.'

I recall the flowers that were left outside my house. I'm tempted to mention them, and the open gate, but I know it will only distract them from Wayne. I must keep in control of the situation and keep them focused on Wayne. It has to be him.

I check my phone again; no missed calls, no text messages, no emails.

Corbett has returned to the table by now. 'Would Billy have any reason to run away?' he asks.

'Sorry?'

'Has he ever shown signs that he might want to run away?'

'He's seven.'

'Does he spend much time in the national park or near the river?'

'Yeah, I guess. But always with me. I don't often let him out of my sight.'

'And he's never run away before?'

'No. He wanders about the property sometimes, but like I said he's never far from me.'

'What about the neighbours?'

'I only have one. Derek. I checked in with him. He's not seen Billy.'

'We'll head there and speak to him ourselves.'

The police continue with their questioning. They ask me for photographs of Billy and make notes of his height, and hair and eye colour. They inspect his room closely. I know family are always the first suspects, that they're just doing their job, but it means they're not looking where they should be. They're still expecting Billy to turn up.

'And you say he was wearing his pyjamas? What do they look like?'

I feel lots of things – distress, anger, frustration at myself – but these emotions sit below the surface. I have to make myself cry to show them how upset I am. I give it a few moments before speaking through the tears. 'His pyjama top is yellow with a red dinosaur on it and his pyjama bottoms are red.'

'A yellow shirt with a red dinosaur. And he was definitely wearing it this morning?'

'Definitely,' I say, scrubbing at the tears with my sleeve. 'Please, just bring him back.'

'We'll do our best,' Trioli says.

Corbett takes over again. 'So you sat for a moment in your yard at approximately six thirty am, then you went for a swim in the river, and when you came back inside you checked in on Billy and he was still asleep. You lay on the couch at approximately seven fifteen and woke up at . . .' he glances at his pad to check the time '. . . approximately twelve o'clock and got up straight away to check on Billy. You then discovered his bed was empty and you have not seen him since.'

'That's right.'

They walk through the house and check every room, as though he might be hiding.

'That's everywhere?' Trioli asks.

I think about the fire bunker, all those paintings. 'Yes,' I say. I don't want to waste any more time. 'That's it.'

'Well, Ms Heywood, the good news is we have some very solid leads to pursue. I'm more than confident that we will have Billy back to you in no time. We have officers and a small search party on their way now to help us search the bush if he has wandered out there and got lost.' They place their caps back upon their heads and make their way to the door. 'Is there someone you should be with now?'

'No,' I say, without hesitation. Does this look bad? Does this suggest some guilt? But there's no one I'd want to call. Jonas would take control like he always did. I could call Mum, but most days she struggles to remember my name, so there's no telling if she'd remember Billy. Those friends I had before moving from the city are now just mere acquaintances, and the same with the people from yoga. The sad truth is, I don't have anyone to call other than Corazzo, who I plan to contact the moment these two leave. 'I mean, I'll probably head out and search.'

'Well, we're going to continue looking around the area. Please don't go into your son's room, and if you should discover anything suspicious, don't touch it but contact me immediately.' He holds out a card.

'I will.'

'We'll start out in the yard. The searchers will be here shortly.'

They go out the back door and are soon walking across the yard towards the river.

The cord between me and Billy tugs so hard on my heart that I feel it could snap in two. I stand by the back door with my phone in my hand. Is it really possible Billy simply wandered off? But why wouldn't he have answered when I called? I'd been all over the property, even out to the road where the van had been parked; he hadn't been anywhere. The van . . .

All problems out here in the country begin and end with dodgy vehicles parked on quiet streets. The van was there and now it's gone. I'm smarter than this, I can figure this all out. I've been so busy trying to keep up the facade that I stopped concentrating, I saw the stars when I should have been focusing on the constellations. I squeeze my molars. *Think Freya, you bitch, think.* The van, that man and his girlfriend, Wayne, the missing girl and now Billy – it is all connected, somehow.

AMY

I CAN FEEL the cockroach wandering around my empty stomach. When I ate it, I couldn't bring myself to chew, I simply swallowed. We've been in the Hole for hours, all sitting close together down on the dirt. We didn't eat last night or this morning; the minders and Adrienne are on edge and everyone is talking about the Blue Devils. Adrienne pulled me aside after we punished Asha. She said that only I can save the Clearing, she said she has a plan for me and Adam.

Tamsin said the Blue Devils were up at the road. She said they have been spying on us, that's why we are in the Hole now. My legs are too tired to stand so I sit thinking about Asha and about Adrienne's plan. I imagine the world Asha came from.

I think about the house I saw out in the bush. I wonder who lives there. Are they kind or scary?

Finally the bell sounds. We all climb from the Hole and head straight to our beds. My stomach squeezes like a fist. I am so hungry. Outside the window, clouds have blocked out the moon and it's cooler now. I curl up in my bed and stare at Asha's empty bunk across the room. I reach for my journal beneath the mattress.

FREYA

Two hours missing

'FREYA,' CORAZZO ANSWERS. 'What's going on?'

'It's Billy,' I say. 'Someone has taken him.'

A long pause. 'What do you mean?'

'I mean he's disappeared. He was here this morning, then he wasn't.'

'He hasn't wandered off? Not hiding somewhere?'

'No,' I say. 'The police have been out here.'

'Shit,' he says. I can hear him sucking in a breath. 'What'd they say?'

'They think he will turn up. They didn't really take it that seriously. I don't know what to do.' I need his help; I need him to understand.

'So talk me through your day. When did you notice he wasn't there?'

I repeat what I told the police.

'I had a run in with Wayne,' I say. 'He thinks Billy is his kid – and he told me that Aspen has disappeared.' I think about the email address again. Wayne said someone was impersonating me, but was that all a lie?

'That's not good. You think Wayne's involved?'

'It seems like too much of a coincidence, him turning up suddenly.'

'Have you called him?'

'Yeah, there was no answer. The police have his details too.'

'Alright,' he says. 'I'll jump in my car and head out your way. Should be there in an hour or so.'

'You don't need to do that.'

'I'm coming. I want to help search, just to be sure he's not hiding there somewhere.'

I call Wayne again but it goes straight to voicemail. I try again; voicemail once more. It must have been his plan when he turned up, distract me, keep me up all night then swoop in. I send a text instead.

Where the fuck is he? Where is Billy?

•

I sit at the table for a few minutes, turning the phone in my hands. Then I go to Billy's room. Opening the window, I test the bolt. I check under his bed and open his drawers. I find the coin I had placed under his pillow, still there. I push his blankets and sheets onto the ground.

I hear a tap on the back door and then Trioli's voice. 'Ms Heywood,' he calls.

I hear his footsteps coming through the lounge and move out to meet him.

'What are you doing?' He looks over my shoulder.

'I was trying to work out how someone could have got in here,' I explain.

He frowns and steps past me towards Billy's room. He reaches for the doorhandle with his latex-gloved hand and closes the door.

'I asked you not to go in there. I asked you to stay where you were.' He leads me back to the kitchen.

'I'm sorry. I forgot.'

'You forgot?'

I look away. 'I'm not thinking straight. I'm sorry. My son has disappeared.'

He shakes his head then says, 'I was coming to let you know that we're heading off now. The search team will get to work as soon as they arrive. Don't go back in that room, leave the door closed. I'll be in touch soon.'

•

When they've gone I call Wayne again. I hate his nauseatingly bland voicemail message. *Wayne's phone, leave a message.* I'm sitting at the table searching news sites on my phone, refreshing every few minutes to see if there is anything online about us yet, when I hear a knock at the door. I rise, hoping for good news but fearing the worst.

Opening the door, I see the bushy eyebrows, the Stalin-thick moustache, the shoulders you could serve a buffet on.

'Corazzo,' I say, then he pulls me against him, holding my head to his chest.

'We'll find him,' he says. 'He can't have got too far.'

I make him tea and we sit down at the table. The former cop eases himself into his chair slowly, his hands on his knees.

'Can't move as well as I used to,' he says with a smile. 'It's a race to see which goes first: my heart or my knee.'

'You're alright,' I say, placing a cup before him.

'I passed the roadblock near town and saw a couple of cops down at the park,' he says. 'They're taking it seriously, despite what the first two on the scene thought. They'll have searchers out here soon enough.'

'He's not in the bush. He wouldn't just wander off.'

'They've got to follow every lead,' he says, taking a sip of the tea. I notice the way tiny beads of it stick to the bristles of his moustache. He's got grease near his collar and creases at the elbows of his shirt.

'I know you think it's Wayne, and you might be right. But the former detective in me is saying it's best to check every avenue.'

'What does that mean?'

'We should take a walk out there, try calling him. At the very least it will show the cops you're searching for him. They're suspicious pricks at the best of times.'

'They know how desperate I am,' I say.

'Come on,' he says, draining the last of his tea. 'A walk will do you some good.'

We take Rocky on his leash out the back gate and up the path. It's hot and dry still but low clouds are sweeping in from the east.

Corazzo is walking ahead, scanning for footprints or tracks. Every so often he stops, squats down and studies something on the dusty path.

'They ask about your history?' he says, as we reach the fork in the path.

'No,' I say. 'I guess they don't know. They'll figure it out soon enough. I don't want to give them any reason to suspect me of anything.'

'Billy,' Corazzo calls. 'Billy!'

I know it is no use, but it can't hurt. We go back the long way, via the road.

'What will happen now?' I ask as we walk down the driveway towards the house.

'Well, they'll keep searching.'

'And when they don't find him?'

'*If* he doesn't turn up by tonight, I'd say they'll issue an alert to the media with his image and start reviewing any CCTV footage from surrounding roads. It'll become a full criminal investigation. They'll look much more closely at people like Wayne, they'll go see your mum and any other family members.'

'When they find Wayne, they'll find Billy,' I say. 'You didn't see the look he gave him. He took Aspen away, and now he has taken my other son.'

He studies me for a moment, then turns away to gaze over the back lawn.

•

The afternoon wears on into dusk without word from the police. I don't see any sign of a search party, and I haven't heard a thing from Wayne. The police think it's a domestic tiff, I realise. They don't know what Wayne and I are capable of.

Corazzo makes pasta. I just sit, sipping a glass of wine to settle my nerves.

'You better eat something, Freya.'

'I can't,' I say. I wait for him to insist.

'You've got to eat. Go on just a few bites.'

My stomach clenches in anticipation. 'Okay,' I say. 'I'll try.'

'I can stay out here tonight,' he adds. 'Happy to.'

'No,' I say. 'No, that's okay. I'll be fine.'

After dinner, he presses his big palms into his knees to rise. 'I'll hear from you in the morning then. Don't worry – he'll turn up. If you're thinking of doing anything crazy, call me first.'

I know I shouldn't drink, it won't help in the end, but when Corazzo has gone I pour another glass of wine. It tastes sour and the hangover will compound all the awful feelings I have inside, but if I don't drink I won't sleep. I will feel that needling fear. I will feel the motion sickness of loss. I will overthink everything, analysing and interrogating all the moments of the week leading up to Billy's disappearance. I check Google Maps, looking at the roads leading towards my home. I zoom in and out of the national park, becoming more familiar with the shape of it, its enormity. All that green on the map, with the blue river snaking through it, from Mum's village all the way to me and then on down towards the city. It will take them months to search the park, and even then they could never be sure. They will focus their efforts and attention on the wrong place.

Aspen has also disappeared, according to Wayne. My mind drifts back to the day I left my son in the car. What was I thinking? Why did I do it? I realise I have no answer; I have blocked it out. Sometimes I hide the truth even from myself.

— Amy's journal —

This will be short.

I am going tonight. I will step out to discover the world outside. I want to go to that house in the woods to peer inside and see what Asha saw before we brought her home to the Clearing. I'm taking my journal, to document what I find. I need to know, I need to see for myself. Asha hated Adam, she loved the world outside.

Adam's punishments and cruelty have increased in frequency and severity. He is hurting us for fun now. He blames me for what happened with Asha and if I don't leave I'm worried he might take it too far.

Even Adrienne seems afraid of him now. She hasn't been at the Clearing much but I know she only wants us to be safe and happy and she can't control him.

It's getting dark outside and I plan on waiting until everyone is sleeping before I go. I know I need to be brave. I can always come back before dawn if I change my mind. I'm so scared and excited that my hand is shaking. I know there is a chance I will encounter the Blue Devils.

I know not to trust them.

They hate us.

They were sent by the Devil to stop Adrienne's plans.

They will kill me if they get a chance.

But if I can somehow stop Adam from hurting us, then it will be worth it.

FREYA

Nine hours missing

I CONTINUE TO down glasses of wine and stare out into the darkness.

When the phone vibrates on the table I stare at the number. I don't recognise it. Putting my wineglass down, I bring the phone to my ear.

'Hello?'

'Freya Heywood?'

'Yes, it's me.'

'Detective Sergeant Jennifer McVeigh, Victoria Police. Do you have a moment to speak?'

'Yes. Yes, please, what is it?' My voice is small and tentative. Thank God it's not Trioli or, worse still, Corbett. Hopefully this Jennifer McVeigh is a little more competent.

'Well,' she begins, her voice steady and authoritative, 'there's no good news yet, but we are making progress.'

I make my breath shaky, it sounds like I'm on the edge of tears.

'Someone at a neighbouring property has confirmed that he saw a vehicle depart from your road shortly after ten this morning.'

'What does that mean?'

'Nothing at this stage, but were you anticipating any visitors?'

'No.'

'Wayne Phillips was scheduled to fly back to Coolangatta from Tullamarine airport this evening at six-forty, but he was not on that flight. His rental car was due for return shortly before then and he has not returned it; we have the plates and car make and model. We have also been in contact with his wife. She hasn't heard from him. We haven't been able to locate him as yet, but we should be able to pinpoint his whereabouts based on activity from cellular towers.'

I clear my throat. 'So, it's definitely him? He took Billy?'

'I can't confirm that. He's on the list of people we are interested in speaking with.'

'I see. Can I ask who else is on that list?'

'I can't disclose that, I'm afraid. But please rest assured we are pursuing every avenue. We've had a search team out in the national park this afternoon and they'll be back at first light.'

'Well, thanks, I guess. Please bring him home. I just want him back.'

'I'll keep you up to date as the investigation progresses.'

'Thank you.'

The call ends.

Wayne, you prick. I tip back the last mouthful of wine then pour myself another glass. Was there any way I could have foreseen what Wayne was planning?

After a while, I rise, leaving Rocky snoring on his side on the kitchen floor. I don't take the torch or my phone as I set out across the lawn, using only the moonlight to see by. I make my way towards the river. Shadows move among the trees, but it's only the breeze. *There is nothing to fear*, I tell myself, *be brave*, even as another voice in my head reminds me: *Blind bravery comes from ignorance of the real threat.* Bravery will not bring Billy home, I need to be smart.

Through the trees the river's surface is jewelled with the moon's light. I just stand and breathe in the darkness, my body tingling with adrenaline. I hear someone or something moving in the trees. Could it be the wind? No, someone is near. I feel it. I turn and rush back to the house. Inside, I turn off all the lights and lock the doors. Alert and bristling, I move to my room. I make myself still, sitting there on the edge of the bed. Who is out there? Could it be Billy? Or one of the searchers?

I hear a sound close to the house. The crunch of footsteps. A twig cracking. I feel every muscle in my body beat in time with my heart. Someone is in the yard.

AMY

I STEP THROUGH the back door of the Burrow and fly across the Clearing like a ghost. I can hear and feel everything so intensely. I climb the back gate and run out into the bush, my heart thumping and legs tight. It is a perfect night to go; the moon is out and it's cooler than the last few nights, but I am still so scared.

In some parts of the bush it's so thick and so black that I have to use my hands to feel my way along. Branches scratch my face and roots trip me at every turn, but I keep going, heading in the direction we took when we found Asha, moving towards the river.

At times I follow my ears, listening carefully for the trickle of water. I pass the huge rock I'd seen when we were searching for Asha and know I am getting closer. I feel hot and full of energy under my skin. As planned, I have my journal with me, tucked into my waistband.

I climb a ridge and the trickling grows louder. Then I see it, there across the river. The house.

I start to work my way down the bank on my hands and knees, gripping the shrubs and stones. But then a rock loosens beneath my fingers and I slip, sliding down the hard rock face and into the water. I'm wet up to my thighs, but fortunately my journal wasn't submerged. I stand and wade through the water, which is still and cool. I lose one boot, but I don't stop, I can't stop now.

The fear of the dark, of snakes and Blue Devils grabs me like the hand of God and shakes me. I feel sick inside, but I know that I've got to keep going. I recall something Adrienne said to me this afternoon and I realise I have nothing to be afraid of now.

The rain is coming; I can feel it inside. I reach the other bank. The house is close now.

I walk quickly before my nerves overwhelm me. The building looms larger. I run.

Something crunches my nose. Black, red. The taste of blood at the back of my throat. The pain is sudden. I've run straight into a fence and I think my nose is broken. My eyes water but I don't stop. I can't stop now that I am so close. I climb the fence with blood on my tongue.

I creep in silence towards the house. I knew I would end up here; I knew it from the first time I saw it.

I think of something Adrienne had once said: *Eve stood, stark and beautiful. Her hand paused an inch from the apple, just a heartbeat of hesitation. There was doubt. There was fear, a dark coiling energy in her bowels. But she stared at the rich ruby fruit, then plucked it.*

I am missing a boot and the grass is hard and crackles with each step. There is a gentle breeze pulling through the trees. I climb up the back steps. The house is completely dark. I imagine a family inside a lot like my own. I imagine twelve children. I take my journal from my waistband, holding it in both hands. And . . . is that a face I see there beyond the glass? Breathe in and breathe out. *Keep going, girl.*

I say the words to myself: *Protect the Queen.* Someone is staring back out at me. And then the door swings open.

FREYA

Eleven hours missing

IN THE KITCHEN, I press and hold the panic button for the police then reach beneath the sink for my toolbox. No one should be lurking around my house at this time of night.

I find the largest spanner. I go to the back door, steady my breathing to relax my heart. *I'll get you, you bastard.* Rocky follows me, his ears pricked. This is what we trained for.

I stare out across the lawn into the darkness. I blink hard, squinting to make out the shape. I see a pale figure. I won't hit the lights until the bastard is close, close enough for Rocky to catch. My heart stops as something slides across the bleached grass. I can't turn away, I can't blink – I'm entranced. The apparition drifts closer, like smoke. Maybe it is smoke. I sniff the air, shielding my eyes to get a better look. The apparition fades. It was nothing but an illusion. Just shadows, a trick of the moonlight, my breath fogging the glass. Then, before me in the darkness of night, I see the shape again, a girl so young and fearless. She is so real, so tangible, but I have seen this before . . . so many times before. Like the child I thought I saw at the river, I know she is not there. Time collapses. I'm not looking at a ghost but a memory. I'm looking at myself. The moment I escaped and met the world . . .

PART FIVE

THE ESCAPED, THE TAKEN

Then the Lord God said to the woman, 'What
is this you have done?' And the woman said,
'The serpent deceived me, and I ate.'

Genesis 3:13

AMY

BEADS OF SWEAT leap out all over my skin. A man is looking through the window. Bright light leaps into the night. I block it with my hand and, before I can think, the door swings out, sending me stumbling back.

'No,' I say, my voice trembling. 'Please don't hurt me.' I begin to weep. 'Please don't hurt me. I will go home. I will be good.'

A hand tightens around my arm and a face hovers above me. Small dark eyes blinking rapidly. I can't form words. My journal tumbles to the ground.

The man is dragging me inside. He puts something in my hand. A glass of water. I am shaking so hard that it knocks against my teeth when I try to drink.

As my eyes adjust to the light I take in a man with a grizzled beard and torn t-shirt. He turns away from my gaze and walks up a hall into the darkness of the house. 'May,' he calls. 'May. Wake up, May.'

I look around. Bare bulbs hang from the ceiling, casting light upon the brown walls. I move closer, tilting my head to get a better look.

'May,' the man says again. 'Get out here now.'

'I'm coming, I'm coming,' a woman's voice responds.

The world outside blinks bright white; less than a second later I hear the crack of thunder. My heart is racing.

'Looks like we finally got rain,' she says as her heavy steps come up the hall.

'May, someone's turned up,' says the man.

A woman steps into the light, pushing a pair of glasses up her nose.

I look outside. I could run, I think. *Be brave.*

Her nose crinkles as she stares at me. 'Who is it then, Bruce?'

'I don't know. She turned up all bloody in the backyard there.'

I touch my nose, feel the stickiness.

I can see a knife block, pots and pans hanging down from the ceiling.

'What are you going to do to me?' I ask. 'Please, just let me go.'

'She's missing a toe,' says the woman.

Bruce frowns; he looks worried. He rakes his brow with his sleeve.

'Please don't hurt me,' I say.

The man shakes his head like a dog snapping the neck of the idea. 'I'm not going to hurt you. No one's going to hurt you.'

Rain is drilling down now.

'Better make a call,' he says to the woman.

I block them out, pressing my fingertips into my eyes. I can feel the room closing in. I feel like something foreign, trapped in a damp lung as it compresses. The woman touches my shoulder gently, pressing something to my nose: a damp cloth to soak up the blood.

'What's your name?' she asks.

I clear my throat and stare into May's eyes. 'Amy.'

'Amy?' She says it like a question. 'You know, someone could have sent her in here,' May says to Bruce. 'They could have sent her to case the house.'

'Nonsense.' Bruce sits down at the table.

'How far off are they?' May says.

He looks over to her. 'I don't know. I've only called them five minutes ago.' He takes another draw of smoke and turns his gaze to me.

I know what I've got to do. I know why I am here. 'He hurt her,' I say. 'He held her head under. He hurts us all.'

The man looks at me like I've slapped him. 'What'd you say?'

'Adam . . . he held her under. He will come for me.'

He looks out into the yard, squinting. He thumbs his bottom lip. I can see him thinking, two stones clashing together making sparks in his mind.

'Get the rifle,' May says.

'Quiet!'

'I won't stand here waiting,' the woman says. She leaves the room.

Lightning flashes, illuminating the yard, followed by the drum of thunder a second later.

I try to stand but Bruce rises, blocking my path to the door.

'No,' he says. 'You're not going anywhere.'

There's a sharp-knuckled knock at the door.

The man looks at me then at the door. May returns, carrying a rifle. My heart leaps. This isn't going to plan, I should run now. Bruce takes the gun and points it at the floor.

Three more knocks.

I see his finger near the trigger. I'm trembling now, watching as he reaches for the doorhandle. It could be anyone behind the door.

He turns the handle. I cower behind May. The door swings in and catches on the chain. Bruce aims the gun outside into the darkness.

FREYA

Eleven hours missing

THE GIRL WHO escaped, that's what the newspapers called me. The miracle child. The photos of me in hospital were all over the newspapers. The first year on the outside I grew twelve centimetres and my body took shape, like something long compressed rapidly expanding. I was fostered out for three years, until I was eighteen, then I moved out on my own.

When people learn about my past, they look at me differently. *How can a child growing up in that environment be normal?* The police, the lawyers, youth workers, family services . . . Adrienne always told me about the woman, Freya, who lived in the woods. She was alone but not lonely. The solitude, the distance – I always liked the idea of it. So that's who I became. Not many children get to start from scratch, choose their own name, choose who they want to be.

I didn't know how to ride a bike, how to open a bank account or even how to cross a road. I didn't know how to have a normal conversation, so I had to learn what most people take for granted.

I learnt to be normal, I learnt how others acted and learnt to wear this mask and be like them. I knew I would always be burdened with the past and Adrienne would always have control over me.

I've seen the statistics. I've read the studies about the way violence cascades from one generation to the next. I have it in me; violence and obedience is all I knew. I act because I don't want anyone to know where I come from and what I've done.

I hear another sound outside. I squeeze the spanner in my hand, scanning the backyard for movement. Rocky unleashes a volley of loud warning barks, but he is not looking out into the yard; he is looking at the front door.

I turn and march towards it. It could be Billy for all I know. I throw the door open and a gust of hot night air rushes in. No one is there. Rocky pushes himself out between my left leg and the door. He sniffs.

Another bouquet lies on my doormat. Yellow wattle again, identical to the last two. Rocky is baying, growling. I can remember every time in my life I have been truly spontaneous, every moment I have done something without careful consideration. Now is one of those moments. I say one word. 'Attack.'

Rocky looks up, alert, as if he has misheard.

'Attack!'

In a flash of black and brown, he flies into the darkness. I hear someone say, 'Shit! What the fuck?' I hear slow steps become sprinting steps. I don't hear barking, just the growl then snap of Rocky latching on. I hear a man scream. Calmly, I walk out into the night.

'Rocky, stop!' I call. Rocky steps back, his mass still pointed close to the man dragging himself away across the gravel. 'Stay right there,' I say. 'If you run, I won't stop him.'

'He attacked me.' The man's voice wavers. I think I detect an accent.

'Get up,' I say. The adrenaline is surging in my limbs.

The man lifts himself slowly.

'Walk towards the house.'

'I'm sorry, you weren't supposed to see me.'

'What does that mean?' I demand, squeezing the spanner.

'I'm sorry,' he says. Are there tears in his voice?

'Do you know where my son is?' I ask, my voice calm and steady.

'Your son?'

'Where is he?'

'I don't know. I don't know what you are talking about.'

He stumbles towards the house without taking his eyes from Rocky. I follow. Rocky growls, matching me step for step.

'Your dog bit me.'

'He'll do it again if you don't do exactly what I say. Go on, inside.'

Stepping over the bouquet, the man walks through the open door and into the light. I can see him properly now. Blood drips from his fingers. He is thin, wiry. Younger than I thought.

'Turn around.'

The man turns to me. I study his face. Acne scars on his cheeks, a wispy beard, deep pouched eyes, cracked lips. His greasy hair hangs down over his ears. I don't recognise him.

'Who are you?'

'Can I sit?'

I nod towards the table. The man pulls out a chair and sits down. Rocky is still growling. The man's chest rises and falls in quick huffs.

'Don't look him in the eye.'

'What?'

'My dog. Don't look at him.'

He drags his eyes away, watching Rocky without looking at him, his jaw clenched.

'So, who are you? Why have you been leaving those flowers on my mat?'

'I'm just doing a job.'

'A job? You mean your job is to deliver flowers in the middle of the night?'

I think about the wattle blooming in a yellow haze about the Clearing.

'Would you mind tying your dog up?'

'Not yet.' I step closer. 'Not until you answer my question.'

He just sucks his lips.

'Oh well, you can tell it to the police. They shouldn't be far off.'

'You called the police?' His eyes grow wide. 'I've got to leave.' He stands. I step between the man and the door. I raise the spanner as if to hit him. 'You're not going anywhere. Sit down.'

He lowers himself into the chair. He is gaunt beneath his sweat-stained t-shirt.

'Please, I have to go. Someone wanted to send you flowers and I delivered them. That's all. I won't complain about the bite. I need to leave.' It's only when he mentions the bite that I notice how much blood is seeping out between the fingers gripping his forearm. I imagine a jagged flap of skin beneath.

'Why?' I ask. This can't be a coincidence. Could Henrik be sending these flowers from prison? Or is Wayne taunting me? 'Do you know where my son is? If you tell me, maybe I'll send the police away.'

'I don't, I promise. I'm just a Taskie. This job was paying well. I'm not supposed to be working over here. Please, if you report me to the police I will lose my visa.'

'What the fuck is a Taskie?'

'Taskie is a website. People list jobs and offer a price. I saw this listed and it sounded easy.'

'What were the instructions?'

'To place a bunch of flowers on your doorstep between eleven and one am. That's all. Someone dropped the flowers off at my hostel.'

'How many times have you done it?'

'Taskies?'

'Delivered the flowers.'

'Just once. This is the first time.'

I run my palm down my face, letting my breath out. I sense he is lying. The police should be able to trace the jobs he's done through the website and work it out.

'Who hired you?'

'I don't know. Users are anonymous. They just have usernames.'

'What is the username?'

When he takes his hand away from the bite to retrieve his phone from his pocket, I see the blood pulsing. It's dripping all over the floor tiles. Rocky got him a lot worse than I thought. I fetch a tea towel while the man stares down at his phone. He shies away when I step close to him.

'Don't move an inch,' I warn. I wrap the tea towel around his arm and tie it off tight. It's the best I can do. A dark ring of blood rises through it immediately. I use masking tape to compress it.

I can hear the police pulling into the driveway.

'Here,' he says, holding up the screen of the phone to show me.

> VDVM (LAST LOGGED IN: ONLINE NOW)
>
> MARK TASK AS COMPLETE?

'Mark it as complete,' I say. Whoever it is, I don't want them to know I caught their guy. The man touches the screen of his phone.

'Done,' he says. 'Now, please, will you let me go?' Surely immigration would not deport him for this . . . he must be worried about something else. Maybe he has a criminal record. Maybe this is all an elaborate ruse and he really is involved in Billy's disappearance.

'No,' I say. I can't risk it. 'You're staying.'

'My dad is going to kill me if I am sent home,' he says, harsh Eastern European notes rising through his voice. 'He paid for my flights and I've only been here for a month.'

'Bad luck,' I say.

The man stands as if to run. Rocky bristles.

'Stay right there.'

Car doors open.

'How much did you earn for this?'

He looks at me, defeated, then looks away as he answers. 'Good money.'

'How much?'

'Fifty screet.'

'Screet?'

'It's a cryptocurrency.'

I roll my eyes. Whoever hired him, they've gone to a lot of trouble to conceal their identity. I can feel the hope that this might lead me to Billy slipping between my fingers.

Two police officers enter through the open front door. I see their eyes widen at the trail of blood.

'So,' says the closest one, a short woman with black hair. 'We've had an emergency reported.'

I nod towards the man. 'This guy was trespassing – delivering flowers in the middle of the night.' I point to the flowers near the cops' feet.

They turn back and look down.

'My son went missing today, so it's not a great time to be delivering flowers.'

AMY

'PUT THE GUN down!' The voice comes from behind the door.

Bruce leans the rifle up against the wall before pushing the door closed to unchain it. I step further back into the kitchen, reaching behind me for a weapon. My body feels weak.

Bruce opens the door again and steps aside. 'She's over there,' he says with a tilt of his head.

I step out from behind May into the light. I see a man in a blue uniform with a flat-topped cap. My heart leaps into my throat. A Blue Devil! Standing beside him is a man with a bushy moustache wearing a long grey coat. The vague annoyance slips from their faces when they see me. Their mouths are both slightly open.

'Crikey,' the man with the moustache says. 'Are you alright?'

I slowly step back from the kitchen into the living room, my heart pedalling. I don't take my eyes off the Blue Devil. Everything I've heard about Blue Devils comes rushing to my mind. That if they found us children at the Clearing they would beat us. That they were intent on stopping Adrienne from carrying out her plan. It wasn't supposed to go like this.

'Put that down,' the Blue Devil says, his words hard-edged.

I look down at the long steel kitchen knife grasped in my fist.

His hand moves to his side, fingers lingering by his belt as he steps closer.

'It's okay,' the man in the coat tells me. 'It's going to be okay.'

They both move towards me. I back up, brandishing the knife. The door is close. I think of what I was taught to do if I should encounter a Blue Devil. *Don't let them touch you; turn and run. If you are cornered, fight back. Always whip the blade out in a teardrop motion so they can't snatch your wrist.*

'Now, now, sweetheart, you're safe here,' the man with the moustache says, his voice soft and soothing. The doorknob to the back door digs into my spine. I reach back and in one deft movement fling it open and hurl myself through. I sprint down the stairs, into the dark sheets of rain. I feel the absence of my journal.

They're behind me, calling after me, but I keep running. I can't help but fear them, I can't help but panic. I skid and fall, hitting the grass hard. The knife slips from my grip. Footsteps thunder towards me, louder than the crack of the storm, the drill of the rain.

'Stop right now!' The voice is close. I reach for the knife; it's my only hope of defence. I rise again and take off at a sprint. They're still close behind. A hand grips my shoulder. I twist, swiping out blindly. The blade tears through. The sudden suck of breath. That feeling I remember from practising on the animals strung up from the Great Tree in the centre of the Clearing. Steel splitting skin and flesh. It's the Blue Devil. He's clutching his left side. Through the rain I see a black flow melting down over its fingers.

'She cut me!' He stumbles back, eyes on me.

I look down at the knife. I draw my arm back; this time I will aim for his chest. But the Blue Devil is grabbing something from his belt, aiming it at me. There's a flat low pop. It hits like a punch to my lower gut. I'm hurled to the ground and my vision blurs as I look up, then down. My brain throbs. The pain sears my hip. I feel numb and hot and I can't move. The gun is still pointed at me. I'm fading now. I close my eyes.

FREYA

Twelve hours missing

THE POLICE TOOK their time, writing out my statement, taking photos, eventually hauling the man and the flowers away. It's around 2 am by the time they've gone, and I am left with blood-streaked tiles to clean and a sleepless night ahead.

I tidy up, then put the TV on and sit on the couch with the infomercials running. I check social media and the news sites. There are murmurs online. A few news stories about a missing boy somewhere near North Tullawarra National Park but none suggest he was kidnapped. It's only a matter of time before the media dive deeper and uncover my history. Aspen in the car. And my childhood, who my mother is. Olivia always says no one blames me for my childhood, she says people understand I never chose to grow up in the Clearing, but everyone blamed me for Aspen and now everyone will blame me for Billy's disappearance. It won't stop until they find him, until they find Wayne. Even then, there will be the theories and lingering doubts. The trolls.

I can already feel a hangover brewing but I shove it back; I can't afford to be hungover. I need to stay alert. Dropping to the tiles, I pump out my morning push-ups.

At around five, that pink, pre-dawn hour, I hear traffic on the road, the low groan of a diesel engine. Then, as the first birds are beginning their morning chorus and the sky is glowing at the tree line, I hear the rumble of more cars arriving. I hear voices. The search party.

Soon people are moving at the fringes of my property, walking in a line down near the river's edge. Shortly, I'll go out there to help. It's useless, but it's expected of me. My phone rings.

'Jennifer McVeigh from Victoria Police. Is that you, Ms Heywood?'

'Yes, hello.'

'Good morning,' she says.

I eye the clock; it's just after six. 'I guess it is morning. Not a good one though.'

'No. I understand there was an incident last night.'

'That's right.'

'I'll be speaking with the arresting officers shortly. For now, a search party is out there and we're reviewing CCTV footage from the surrounding areas. We will also be conducting a number of interviews with people who are local to the area.'

'Okay.'

'I'd like you to come in to the station to confirm a few details about your statement, and we want to discuss last night's incident with you. We are also thinking it would be best if you prepared a statement for the media; we have a media liaison officer who can help with—'

'No,' I say, cutting her off. 'No. I don't want to talk to the media.'

'A personal plea can help mobilise members of the public.'

'I don't think I can face it,' I say.

'Right, well, we can discuss that further when you arrive. I'll have someone come by soon to collect you.'

•

It's around seven when a car arrives for me. A bald man with wide-set eyes and huge shoulders is driving. He looks a little like a young Corazzo. Which reminds me – I should call Corazzo.

The cop hardly talks on the trip to the police station. It's back near the city and it takes almost an hour to get there.

At the station, I sit with my phone in my hands, waiting. Nine am comes and goes before I hear the click-clack of low, no-nonsense heels. A woman with a black bob appears, coffee in hand, neat white blouse.

'Ms Heywood, I'm Jennifer McVeigh.' She extends her hand and gives mine a firm shake.

'Hi, Mrs Mc—'

'Jennifer is fine. Thanks for coming down. I know this is a distressing time.' She leads me down the hall to an interview room. Beige walls. Steel table with plastic cups and a bottle of water. 'And I'm sorry about the wait. I wanted to make sure I had a handle on the situation before speaking to you.'

She is a quick talker and I'm too tired to keep up, but I nod along, catching the yawn building in my throat before it comes out. There's a triangular device at the centre of the table that I quickly realise is a recorder and a conspicuous camera aims down at me from one corner.

A second cop enters the room, taking the seat beside McVeigh. It's Trioli. He hands McVeigh a file which she places on the table between us.

'We are going to record this conversation,' she tells me. 'It's just for our records, so we can refer back to it as part of the investigation. Is that okay?'

I eye her for a moment. 'Sure,' I say.

Trioli reaches forwards and switches on the recording device on the table. 'Today's date is Sunday, the first of March 2020, the time is 9:16 am. Ms Heywood, could you please confirm that you are here under your own volition and you have waived your right to legal representation for the duration of this interview.'

I study his face. It is expressionless.

'Just procedure,' McVeigh assures me, but I know it's not. I know they're suspicious of me. By now, they would surely know about Aspen, and my time at the Clearing.

'Ms Heywood?' Trioli prompts.

'Okay,' I say.

'This interview is being conducted by Victoria Police as part of our ongoing investigation into the disappearance of your son, William Heywood.'

I take the cup of water set before me and sip. My hand is dead still. I want them to see that I'm not rattled. I offer a weak smile.

'I'm happy to help in any way I can.'

McVeigh takes over. 'Perhaps you could run us through the events of the day leading up to the disappearance of your son.'

'I've already given a statement,' I object.

'I know, this is just so I can confirm the details.' *Or see if my story changes.*

I run them through my day, being sure all the details are consistent with the statement I gave the day before. The swim, coming back and drinking my kombucha, putting the news on then falling asleep. Occasionally they interrupt to ask me to elaborate, picking up on any contradictions.

'When we first spoke to you, you said the back door was left open. Now you are saying you closed it?'

'I can't remember.'

'And at no point did you leave the property before 12:15 pm?'

'No, I was asleep.'

'Your neighbour believes he heard a car leaving your property prior to 12 pm. You didn't have any visitors?'

I tilt my head. 'No.'

McVeigh powers on. 'How often do you sleep during the day?'

'Never. It was a one-off. I was tired.'

'Not sleeping well?'

'No.'

'Working late, too hot, a lot on your mind?'

'I just haven't been sleeping well. Henrik Masters is being released from jail and I've been thinking about that.'

'You're worried about Henrik Masters?' They don't ask who Henrik Masters is, I note.

'I'm sure you know all about my childhood by now,' I say. Then I change tack, ask a question of my own. 'Can you tell me what happened with the man this morning?'

McVeigh and Trioli exchange glances, then McVeigh speaks. 'I've spoken to the arresting officer. I've read the statement and it all checks out. Taskie offers an on-demand freelancer service that requires almost no identification on the part of the user. Our cyber team are working with the Danish-owned company to find out who was behind the job listing, but these things don't happen quickly, unfortunately. Still, we are hoping to have some insights into the user who booked the job asap.'

'How do you know the guy who delivered the flowers wasn't involved himself? How do you know he isn't working with Wayne or Henrik?'

The police officer draws a breath, drums the table with her fingers as if entertaining the idea for the first time. 'We can't fully discount the notion, but the man who was at your house last night has an alibi; he was on another job, which was tracked via the GPS on his mobile phone, when Billy went missing. He also made a complaint against you, Freya. We're not taking it seriously, but he has puncture wounds and lacerations from the dog bite, and if he found himself a decent lawyer, he might have a case for false imprisonment.'

'That's bullshit.'

Why are we talking about false imprisonment? Why aren't they interrogating him? I draw a breath, let my eyes roam the room. I'm growing restless; I need to focus. 'What about Wayne? What are you doing to find him and Billy?'

'We are following up every lead,' begins McVeigh. 'We've still had no contact with Mr Phillips and his mobile phone has been inactive since last night. Nor have we found any trace of his car. But it's only a matter of time until we track him down. We've run his photo on the news and will continue to do so.' She pauses, breathes out. 'It's been almost twenty-four hours since the last confirmed sighting and we have determined certain risk factors that would elevate this case.' *Certain risk factors*, I presume, is a tidy euphemism for *You're a mess, your ex is an overprotective psycho and your family started a cult.* 'Getting you out there in the media and raising awareness of the missing child will enhance—'

'No,' I say, pre-empting where this conversation is going. I see disappointment sweep over her face. I glance down at the recorder. 'I don't think I will be able to keep it together in front of a camera,' I lie.

'If I may be frank, Ms Heywood, the story is already running on the morning news bulletins with no specifics except for Wayne's mugshot and a description of Billy. The media will release details about you. You can't control that after it all comes out. If you get there first, it will help. Trust me.'

'Not yet,' I say. 'I'm not ready.' If I draw attention to myself, everyone will look in the wrong direction while Wayne slips away. 'A girl went missing a week ago.'

'Yes, that was in New South Wales. It's highly unlikely that the two incidents are connected.'

'I saw on the news that they still haven't found her.' I remember seeing a flash of skin at the river; I know it was only an echo of a memory of Asha.

'There is nothing to suggest that the two incidents are connected,' she repeats with the authority of someone already on her second coffee and with years of experience assuring worried parents, husbands, wives, sons and daughters that the police are doing everything they can. 'Part of my job is also to obtain a history of recent family dynamics. Has Billy ever run away before?' *Recent family dynamics*; she's well versed in cop speak, this one. I know precisely what they are doing, but do they know *I* know?

'Why are you asking about him running away? Like I said, he's seven years old. I know he wouldn't just run away. He's not that kind of kid.'

'Sometimes kids run away if they are having trouble at home.'

'Trouble at home?'

'Have you ever hurt him, for instance?'

'Me? Wait, what is this? Why are you asking me that?' The idea is ridiculous, and I let them know. 'No, I have never deliberately hurt my child. Of course not – I'm his mother.' But according to court records, I have a history of abusing children.

Trioli gives his sly smile; he's still hardly spoken but it's clear he is enjoying this.

McVeigh continues. 'When a child turns up to school with signs of abuse, it's common practice for teachers to make a record of it.'

'I'm sorry, but I have no idea what you are talking about.'

Now Trioli opens up his notepad, flipping back a couple of pages. 'A black eye this week. Bruises on his wrists. Last year he had a broken arm.'

'He was knocked over by the dog!'

'Alright, Ms Heywood, we're not accusing you of anything – we're just exploring every avenue. If we knew he had cause to run away, that would help with the investigation. We can't rule anything out.'

'I understand,' I say, swallowing the growing anger. I paste a sad smile onto my face. 'He wasn't upset the day before yesterday; he was happy. He had no reason to run away.'

When the interview has concluded, the same officer drives me back home.

There is something about the police, the way they are talking to me, that triggers my impulse to flee. *A black eye . . . a broken arm . . .* They think there's more to these stories. It's as though they know something I don't.

Twenty-three hours missing

A gazebo has been set up in Derek's yard. Beneath it sits a table arranged with plastic cups and trays of party pies, with a half a dozen people milling around. As we approach my driveway, I see the media, swarming like flies. Two vans with satellites bolted to their roofs, photographers standing idly, reporters holding microphones. I see them before they see me sitting in the back of a police car. Other police are already there, standing at the top of the driveway, their cars half blocking the road. I see a tall figure in among the media, speaking with the cops. *Corazzo.* They part as we pull in. Corazzo strides through them, following the car down the driveway while the cops keep the media out.

'How are you holding up?' he says when I climb out of the back seat.

He puts his arm around my shoulders, propels me towards the house. He looks ridiculous in his gumboots, shorts and woollen sweater.

'Not great,' I say.

'I can imagine.'

I glance up at the media. 'They want me to talk to them.'

'You don't need to do anything you don't want to. Just ignore them.'

I don't want the police outside my house, but I can't kick them out. I don't want them coming back with a warrant and a chip on their shoulder. I know they've already fixed a target to my back.

'Search crews are working through the bush,' Corazzo tells me. 'They still haven't found anything.'

'And they won't,' I say. 'He's not out there, Corazzo. I know he's not.'

Inside, we sit at my table and I turn the TV on. The lunchtime news will be running soon.

'You'd better eat something,' Corazzo says, getting up. My home isn't small, but he seems to fill the space as he rises, moves to the kitchen. 'I'll make you something.'

'It's okay, I'm not hungry.'

'I know, but you've still got to eat.'

Corazzo makes a passable omelette on gluten-free toast and I pick at it. The truth is I'm starving and could gobble it all down, but even in front of Corazzo I need to act like I'm too sick with worry to eat. It's not that I'm *not* worried; I'm terrified. But that doesn't stop the hunger. If you grow up with almost no food, you're hardwired to be hungry for the rest of your life.

When I entered the real world, I adapted. I was always the best actress in the Clearing, the one who could act the most like the normal people outside. I'm acting now, playing the role of the distressed mother. I know I didn't hurt my son, but my reaction to this situation isn't typical. I learnt what was normal, what was expected, and right now I know I must act like a typical woman would in this situation.

I indulge myself just for a moment and take a sizeable mouthful. I look up at the contingent of reporters at the top of the driveway as I chew. I wonder if they can see me through the kitchen window.

I would make the perfect story for those vultures. My childhood in the Clearing, locking Aspen in a car, living out here near the river as an adult. And Henrik Masters. I pull my phone out and search his name.

I think of Mum and what she wanted me to be: a leader like her. I was always going to stay loyal to her, she made sure of that.

I scroll through the search results and click on a news story about Henrik.

I wanted to be Freya, the woman in the woods. I wanted to make art so I did. I continued to study art outside to help me assimilate. Art was something I could hold on to, a keepsake from my child-hood. Now all those paintings, sold through galleries and brokers, are out in the world in people's homes.

I missed the Clearing at first. The world was so big, and things moved so quickly. People often asked what was most difficult to adjust to. The answer: people. I realised you couldn't touch stran-gers. I learnt what a stranger was, that people avoided making eye contact, that people didn't speak plainly even with their friends and loved ones — *especially* with their friends and loved ones. I realised there were hidden codes and subtext to everything.

I never had a chance to be a regular artist because everything I created came with the tag 'outsider art'.

My art was often captioned: *Amy Smith-Atkins, Blackmarsh survivor.*

The black spot conceals what really happened in the Clearing.

The article has loaded. It's a couple of days old.

ADRIENNE SMITH-ATKINS ACCOMPLICE HENRIK MASTERS SET FOR PAROLE

The name Adrienne Smith-Atkins may not chill people as it once did, but for three years in the late nineties, all of Australia stared into those piercing blue eyes. Some saw a charismatic and misunderstood spiritual leader, while others saw a heartless manipulator and the mastermind of the atrocities that occurred in the Blackmarsh cult.

Smith-Atkins, according to travel records, was frequently travelling overseas and absent from the Clearing, this made it difficult for police and prosecutors to pursue the infamous leader, who is now in her late seventies. The only convictions recorded against her name were perjury and tax evasion.

Smith-Atkins' accomplice, Henrik Masters – known within the cult as 'Adam' – is set for release from prison this week after serving twenty-one years for his role in the abduction and torture of children, including Sara McFetridge.

Masters' treatment of the children in his care is considered to be one of the worst cases of child abuse in the state's history and included the starvation of children to the point of malnourishment, molestation, hose pipe beatings, routine stabbings with a penknife, asphyxiation, and water-dunking sessions. It was during one such session that Masters drowned Sara McFetridge.

Masters, who had a medical background and was once a renowned surgeon, also conducted home surgeries in the Blackmarsh cult.

Investigators gathered testimony and witness accounts, although all but two of the children, some of whom are now in their forties, were deemed too unreliable to give evidence.

One child was so traumatised he still has no memories of his first eight years of life.

Charismatic leader Smith-Atkins gained popularity in academic and medical circles through the seventies and eighties. This enabled her to acquire children. Members of Blackmarsh fixed adoption papers and fostered children. Some members themselves also gave up children to be raised in the Clearing as Smith-Atkins' own. Eventually, Masters turned to kidnapping children to fulfil Smith-Atkins' need to have a family of twelve children.

Despite progressing dementia, Smith-Atkins still maintains a vast fortune, including an international property portfolio. It's yet to be seen if Masters has remained loyal to the woman he idolised, although a reunion at this stage seems unlikely. An eleventh-hour petition to block his release has failed, however, as a condition of his parole, Masters will remain under house arrest.

•

'Reckon we should join the search party?' Corazzo says.

'I guess,' I say, glancing up from my phone.

'Don't worry about the media. It's just local guys looking for a story. It helps to have the exposure, anyway.'

We walk across my property to the river and head up to Derek's place. The gazebo is mostly deserted now, just a couple of guys lingering around. Photos of Billy are pinned up on a board beside a map of the park. The two men are talking; they haven't noticed our approach.

'We're going to have to check the river all the way down. By now he could have floated to the city or he could be caught in the rocks.'

Corazzo clears his throat and the men look over. One bows his head a little.

'You boys aren't searching,' Corazzo says.

'Heading out later in the afternoon,' one says.

Corazzo glances down at his watch.

On the table there are spare walkie-talkies, drink bottles and sandwiches cut into triangles, wilting in the sun. A fly lands on one, rubs its hind legs together, then takes flight again. I glance at the men. One closes his eyes and sprays himself in the face with mosquito spray. The other is doing everything he can to avoid my gaze – they must know I'm Billy's mother. I watch him for a while, daring him to look. I notice a bead of sweat trickle down from his temple.

Derek comes marching down from his home carrying a pot of coffee and two mugs on a tray. His forehead is shining with sweat.

When he sees me, he puts the tray on the table and rushes forwards to draw me into a hug. I'm so surprised I forget to hug him back. I hear shutters click and look up. A photographer is standing at the edge of Derek's yard, aiming his lens at us. I cling on to Derek's back and arrange my face into a sad expression. If I could squeeze out a tear I would.

'We're going to find him,' Derek says. 'Don't you worry – he'll turn up.'

I feel my phone vibrating in the pocket of my jeans.

'Sorry, Derek,' I say, freeing myself from his embrace, 'I have to take this.' I pull my phone from my pocket and look at the screen. I recognise the number instantly. *Wayne.*

AMY

FACES PEER DOWN at me. I'm in a small white room. Swinging, pulling, turning. Not a room – a corridor. I'm being wheeled on a trolley. *Am I alive?* They are taking me somewhere. Then pain. Explosions in my lower back, my hip.

'She's back with us,' the voice says. There's something in my hand. I squeeze, and it squeezes back. I try to speak but my lips won't move. *Protect the Queen.* Everything fades again.

•

The night comes back to me; the knife, the Blue Devil with the gun, someone carrying me. Light fading in and out. Panic grips me then wanes. I try to sit up but find I can't move. There's something hard across my chest: a band of leather strapping me to a bed. *Are they going to torture me?* I reach for the band but my arm stops short, restrained by a ring of steel around my wrist and a chain that disappears beneath the bed. A fishhook of pain drags through my gut with every movement, so intense it makes me cry out.

I scream and scream until a group of people in pale blue tunics and white coats flood in. They are not Blue Devils but something else. A man with silver hair and narrow eyes stands over me. He shines a flashlight into my eyes, then plugs two tubes into his ears, presses something cold against my chest.

'Relax,' he says, reaching past my head to something on the wall. 'It's okay, shh.' I feel a prick at the hinge of my elbow, just like when Adam would put us into a deep sleep. *Adam.* I see him jabbing needles into Asha, cutting her open, electrocuting her. The man leans over me, too close, so close I can't breathe. I twist and jerk. A strange feeling blooms inside me and rinses over my skin. Everything is white. I fall asleep.

I am some place completely different. I am hovering a few feet above the Clearing, my legs folded up in Padmasana. Then I fall. I'm back in a grey room. My body is heavy from sleep.

I turn my head and find a man sitting beside my bed. He smiles down at me.

Scanning the room I see more faces, more people. This is not how I expected the world outside to be.

In a voice that seems too soft for a man with such a bristly moustache, he says, 'You're back with us.' I've seen him before, I realise. He was with the Blue Devil at the house by the river. 'You've been unconscious; you had a nice long sleep.'

I remember fleeing the house by the river. Somehow, I've ended up here, chained to this bed in this room.

Adrienne had told me what I should do if I ever found myself in a situation like this. *Don't trust anyone*, she warned me. *Protect the Queen, keep going.* And, most importantly, *If they ever take you away, we will find you and bring you home one day.*

My mouth is too dry to swallow; it feels like I can't breathe. As if sensing my distress, the man reaches for a plastic cup on the nightstand beside the bed and holds it to my lips. *Don't trust anyone.* I clamp my lips shut.

'It's just water,' the man says. 'Drink up.'

I draw away from him, as far as the constraints allow. Water spills down my neck.

'Let me know if you need a sip, okay?'

I watch him. I can feel my heart thumping against the band over my chest. I can hear the blood pumping in my ears.

'Do you remember what happened?' he asks.

I don't answer. This moment is important, perhaps the most important moment of my life. I need to be careful.

'Hey,' he says, 'you're in a lot of trouble at the moment, but together you and I are going to get you out of it. I promise. You just need to talk to me.'

'Where is my father?' My voice is scratchy and unused. I know I've got to ask for Adam. I know that's what Adrienne wants.

'What was that?'

'My father. Where is he?'

'What's your father's name? I could try to find him.'

'Adam,' I say.

'As soon as I find him I'll let you know. We're just trying to piece everything together.'

I look at his face, the creases at the corners of his mouth. The dark thinning hair, combed back. 'Where am I?' I ask. 'Is this hell?'

He smiles again. 'No. You're not in hell. Not anymore.' He moves a little closer, looking down into my eyes.

'Don't touch me,' I say.

'I won't,' he promises. 'I'm not going to do anything to hurt you.'

When he turns his head, I follow his gaze. Another man is sitting in a chair at the foot of the bed. The two men give each other a look, then the older one, the one by my side, nods at the doorway. Two men and a woman, all in white coats, are lingering there, watching. Panic seizes me; their eyes seem to burn my skin. My breath becomes so loud I can barely hear the man when he says to the trio in the doorway, 'Give us a minute. Go on.' They retreat.

'The Blue Devils,' I rasp. 'Are you a Blue Devil?'

The man asks, 'You mean the police?'

'Police?'

'It will all make sense soon. But you need to help me. Can you do that? We have been waiting for you to wake.'

'The Blue Devils.'

'It's okay, they're not here,' says the man. He turns to the other man, sitting by the foot of the bed. 'You too, Mike,' he says, nodding towards the door. Mike rises, slips a notebook into his pocket and leaves, pulling the door closed behind him.

'See? Now it's just the two of us. You have nothing to fear.'

'I want my father.'

'Sure thing. I'm on your side here. I'm going to help.'

I clamp my mouth shut.

'Maybe you can go home after this. Would you like that? We can take you back to your mother.'

I nod, but I know he won't take me back. 'Please don't hurt me,' I say. He doesn't seem threatening, but I can't trust anyone; why would they bind me to the bed? I feel so vulnerable.

'No,' he says. 'No, of course I won't. I came to the house the other night to help you, remember? What's your name?'

'Amy.'

'Amy, that's a nice name. A beautiful name. And your dad's name is Adam?'

I nod. *He's not really my dad though.*

'Adam, huh? Now, can you tell me how many brothers and sisters you have?'

I look down. I don't want to answer. I'm thinking about my family down in the Clearing, I'm wondering if they miss me. I wonder if the Blue Devils have swooped in.

'Why don't I count and you nod when I get to the right number?'

'Okay.'

'One . . . two . . . three . . .' The higher he goes, the slower he counts. At ten I nod. *So close to twelve. Just one away.*

'Ten,' he says to himself. 'Wow.' He takes a notepad and a pen from his pocket and scribbles something down.

'Nine, actually,' I amend.

'Sure.'

I try to move against the restraints but the binding across my chest has no give.

'Did you have anything with you when you left?'

I shake my head.

'Really?' he says. 'Nothing?'

'My boots.'

'Anything else?'

'My journal.'

He wets his lips. 'Your journal? Where is it now?'

'I dropped it.'

He clears his throat, a flicker of something passes over his face; frustration, perhaps? 'Amy, would you mind if my friend Mike came back in? He's a good kid. A really nice man. He's just going to make a few notes while we talk. Is that okay?'

I nod.

The man walks to the door, opens it and leans out. 'Mike,' he calls.

The younger man appears in the doorway.

'She's dropped her journal somewhere. It's important that we find it as a matter of priority. Can I leave you in charge of that?'

'Sure. Any idea where?'

The older man turns back to me. 'You hurt some people when you came here. That's why you're tied down. I can loosen the strap, but only if you promise to be good and help us. Will you do that?'

'Yes,' I say. I feel like I know this man already.

'Promise?'

'I promise.'

'Alright.'

He loosens the strap across my chest and for the first time it feels like I can take a breath.

'Now, can you tell me where you dropped your journal? Was it at the house, in the bush?'

'At the house, I think.'

'Check the house first, Mike.' Mike makes a note, then the man with the moustache opens his own notebook. He places a small black box on the stand beside the bed. Adrienne had warned me this might happen. 'This will record our voices, so I can listen to it later to help me understand everything. There's nothing to worry about, okay?'

'Okay.'

'Good girl. Now tell me, did you leave your home by yourself?'

'Yes.'

'Did someone tell you to do it, or did you run away?'

'I don't know.'

'Well, did anyone tell you to go to that house?'

'No.'

'Good girl. That's good. And your ten brothers and sisters, do you all live together?'

'Yes?'

'Is it a big open space with four or five buildings?'

'The Clearing.'

'The Clearing . . . that's right. Now the, ah, the Blue Devils . . .' He moistens his top lip. 'Does your family have any plans for what to do if the Blue Devils go down there to the Clearing?'

'We'll get hurt. If we don't hide from the Blue Devils, we will get hurt.'

His eyes go wide for a second. He runs his palm over his moustache.

'We heard a helicopter once,' I offer.

'Is that right? And what did you do?'

'We stayed in the Hole.'

'The Hole? What is the Hole?'

'It's under the Burrow. In the ground. When we're hidden there, no one can hurt us.'

'Good girl, Amy. You're doing so well.' He turns back to Mike. 'Go fetch her a Big Mac or something.'

'Can she eat that?'

The man with the moustache frowns. 'Better check with the doctor.'

Mike rises and disappears through the door.

'He's tired,' the man says. His pink tongue slides between his lips and his eyes soften. 'I want you to know that you're not in any trouble, so long as you keep helping us. We will make sure you are safe, you and your brothers and sisters and your mum. Because you've had a hard life.'

I shake my head hard.

He eyes his recorder. 'It's true. You've been starved and hurt. Someone has been hurting you down there.'

'The Blue Devils.'

'Yes, the police hurt you. But you cut my colleague with a knife. You didn't mean to hurt him, I'm sure, but you did.' He sniffs, runs his fingers through his dark hair. 'Can you tell me more about the Clearing? Can you tell me about your mum?'

'I don't want to talk about Adrienne.'

I look at the black box; it's about the size of a fist with a red light flashing on its side. She wouldn't want me to talk about her, I know.

'So your mum's name is Adrienne?'

'Yes.'

'Well,' he says. 'I haven't told you my name have I? I'm Dominic.' He smiles, creating a fan of creases on either side of his dark eyes. 'But most people call me Corazzo.'

FREYA

Twenty-four hours missing

'WHERE IS HE, Wayne?' I say, my voice urgent as I step away from the volunteers.

'Freya, I've got nothing to do with this. I think I'm being set up.'

'Don't lie to me, just tell me where he is. You took Aspen and now you've taken Billy.'

'Freya, I didn't take Aspen. I was protecting him. You almost killed him. You could have denounced Adrienne and walked away, but you didn't, so stop blaming me.'

My heart is sinking. 'Aspen,' I say. 'What happened?'

'The police don't care as much when a seventeen-year-old boy goes missing, so I'm trying to find him myself.'

'You're lying, Wayne. You've taken Billy, haven't you? That's why you came back.'

'I came for Aspen and now I've been roped into this mess. I'm heading to the city now to see the police and clear this all up. My phone battery died, that's all.'

I'm silent for a moment, thinking. What if Wayne inadvertently led the kidnappers to us? 'It feels like this all started when you turned up.'

'What all started?'

'Just everything. What about Henrik? He was released this morning.'

Wayne interrupts me. 'I don't think it's him.'

'What?'

'I googled him,' he says. 'A lawyer applied for early release on the grounds of his health two times last year. He's been in and out of hospital.'

My stomach is in freefall now. 'What?'

'Yeah. He's not who he was. He's got bowel cancer.'

I pinch a handful of skin on my forehead. 'Wayne . . .' I say, focusing on controlling my voice. The scar at my waist throbs as though something is growing inside of me. 'Don't ever come near me or Billy again. Do you understand? I don't want your help, I don't want to hear from you. You may not have taken him, but you brought this on when you showed up here.'

'He's my kid too, Freya. If someone has taken Billy, I'm worried it's the same person who has Aspen.'

I hang up the phone and stride back towards my own house, leaving Corazzo in the gazebo. I find McVeigh's number in my recent calls. I need to know if Wayne has been cleared; I need to know if they're watching Henrik.

The midday news is still running on the TV.

'McVeigh.'

'Hi, it's me – Freya Heywood.'

'Freya.'

'Is it true? Wayne's coming in to the station?'

'I can't comment on that. He is a person of interest, that's all I will say.'

'What about Henrik Masters?'

'He's under surveillance at his property. He was still in prison when Billy went missing.'

On the news I see an aerial shot of the national park, then a photo of Billy's face flashes onto the screen – the one Corbett and Trioli took.

'He might have people helping him,' I point out, thinking about the van that was parked on my street. The TV is now showing a map of the area with potential routes Billy or a kidnapper may have taken highlighted in red. Billy has already risen to the top of the news agenda, climbing over all those other stories about fuel prices going up, abuse in an aged-care facility, a helicopter crash. Billy Heywood is number one now.

'We are looking closely at everyone.'

'It's been twenty-four hours,' I say. 'I read that the chances of finding a missing person drop after twenty-four hours.'

A *Breaking News* banner flashes on the TV screen.

'That's a skewed statistic. Try not to rely on what you read online.'

The screen splits in two. On one side is a photo of Billy, and on the other is a police photograph. My breath stops. The police photograph is of a small pearl of white sitting in mud, beside a yellow tab. What has this tooth got to do with Billy?

'I'm looking at a tooth on television, Jennifer. Why am I looking at a child's tooth?' I grip the phone hard.

'It doesn't mean anything. It may not even be Billy's. I'm heading out your way now; we just need to run a couple more things by you.'

It may not even be Billy's. I turn to see Corazzo filling the door-frame. His brow drops when he sees me. I touch my cheek with my finger and realise I'm crying. Losing Aspen was an amputation. Losing Billy could kill me.

AMY

I TRY HIS name out in my mouth how he said it. *Cor-art-so.*

'I'm going to look after you in the outside world,' he says. 'That's my job. To look after you, to make sure you are safe and happy. If you have any questions for me, I will always answer them honestly, okay? And I expect the same from you.'

A Blue Devil enters the room and the scream comes out of me as if it were waiting to escape. I twist and turn, yanking at the steel cuffs chaining me to the bed.

Corazzo turns to the woman in the doorway. 'Get the fuck out of here!' he orders. She rushes from the room. 'Jesus, Amy. It's okay. See? I will protect you; I will keep them away.'

The fishhook in my gut pierces my insides and my breathing grows laboured. A beeping starts up above me, getting faster and faster, and a man in a white coat rushes in.

'It's okay,' Corazzo says. 'She's fine. She just had a scare. Leave her be.'

I turn and twist, and the pain tears through me.

Corazzo keeps talking. I squeeze my eyes closed, and when I open them again I see he's standing in front of me, shielding me from the man in the white coat.

'Get out of here!' Corazzo yells.

'We have a duty of care,' the white-coated man insists.

'Please let me go,' I beg Corazzo. 'Please let me go. Please let me go. I will be good, I promise. I will.'

'Soon, Amy. I will get you out of here as soon as I can.'

'Where am I?'

'You're in the psychiatric ward of the Sacred Heart Hospital in Carlton.' He turns back to the doctor in the doorway. 'She's fine. She doesn't need sedating. It's best if she's clear-headed.'

The doctor gives a small grimace of concern then retreats, just as Mike walks in.

'I've got Maccas,' he says.

Corazzo turns to me. 'He's got you some food. Can he bring it over?'

'Food?'

'Better than hospital food.' He smiles and sits back on his seat.

Mike sets a paper bag down on the table beside the bed. When I smell the food my stomach flips.

'If you promise not to scream and not to try to hurt anyone, I'll loosen your hands. Deal?'

I nod.

'Mike, open one of the cuffs.'

Mike moves closer. My breath comes on fast as he leans forwards and reaches across me. There's a click, and then my wrist is loose. I hold it against my chest.

Mike backs away to his seat by the foot of the bed.

'See, Mike?' Corazzo says, more to me than to his colleague. 'She's not going to hurt anyone. I told you she was a good girl.

'Amy is such a lovely name; I have a cousin Amy who lives up in Toowoomba,' Mike says, shaping his mouth into a smile. These people smile when they talk, they don't stare at me too long; they are different to everyone I met at the Clearing. 'Did you have any other names, Amy?'

I shake my head.

'Let's eat,' Corazzo says. He leans over and tears open the paper bag. He pulls out two red boxes and two cartons. I reach for a box, opening it in my lap with my free hand. It's more food than I've ever seen. I look up at Corazzo, who grins and nods at me.

I take the top layer, fold it and shove it into my mouth. It's bread – or like bread, but softer. I chew it and swallow. Next there is meat. We almost never have meat in the Clearing and never this much. I shove that into my mouth too. I feel their eyes on me as I chew quickly then scoop up some lettuce.

'Jesus Christ, she's hungry, that's for sure,' says Mike. 'I'm betting she's not this thin by choice.'

I wince with pain as I reach for the second box and demolish its contents. The food is a fist, squeezing my stomach.

'Jesus,' Mike says again. 'I've never seen anything like it.'

'Are you sure she can eat all that?' Corazzo asks. 'What did the doctor say?'

'Forgot to ask. Too late now.'

I lick my fingers, wishing there was another box of food.

'Okay,' Corazzo says, 'time is of the essence. A few more questions and then we'll get you more food, okay?'

I look regretfully at the empty box in my lap. 'Okay.'

'Normally, if someone did what you did, Amy – if they hurt someone with a knife – they would be in big trouble, but I don't believe it was your fault.'

I look up now, studying his face while he speaks.

'Some people want to blame you, and they won't stop blaming you until they have someone else to blame. Do you understand? So I need to know about Adam. Tell me about your dad.'

I jerk my cuffed wrist so the chain rattles. 'It hurts,' I say.

The two men look at each other. Corazzo nods. Mike rises, fits a key into the steel cuff and turns it. It falls from my hand.

'Better?'

'Yes.'

'Good. Now, you were going to tell me about Adam.'

'Will he hurt me if I tell you what he did to Asha?'

At that, both men's eyebrows sail up their foreheads. Corazzo's back straightens. His eyes whip to the recorder then back to me.

They are both sitting forwards in their chairs now, alert. 'Who hurt you, Amy? Was it your father? Did Adam hurt you?'

'I don't know . . . I don't know anymore.'

'You don't know what?'

'If he really is my father.' I know that this is what Adrienne would want me to say.

Mike's eyes flick to Corazzo, who is holding his fist hard against his mouth, thinking, watching me. 'What makes you think he's not your father, Amy?'

'Maybe he stole me – like he stole the others.'

'The others?'

I look down. It's important that they trust everything I tell them. I've got to protect the Queen.

'What do you mean by others?' Mike persists.

I stay silent.

'Amy, what do you mean by others? Did Adam steal others? Is that what you mean?'

I let the tears come, but I don't speak.

'Mike,' Corazzo says, 'outside – now.'

The two men leave the room. *Protect the Queen, keep going,* I mouth to myself. I try to rise but my body is stiff and painful.

Corazzo strides back into the room. 'Whoa,' he says. 'Lie back down, Amy.'

He has something in his hand: a piece of grey paper. He holds it close to my face; I can make out words and, among them, pictures.

'Amy,' Corazzo says, his voice rising with urgency, 'Amy, look at the picture.' I follow his finger to a photo the size of a matchbox. I stare at it, bewildered.

'Amy?'

'That's Asha,' I say.

'Jesus fucking Christ, Mike,' Corazzo says, glancing back at his colleague.

Mike comes closer, leaning in. 'You know this girl, Amy?' he asks. 'You've seen her?'

I squint. It looks exactly like Asha, except she is smiling, her cheeks are fuller, her hair is parted at the side with a clip. It's her. She looks like she did the day we took her. 'That's my sister. Asha.'

Corazzo's mouth hangs open, his eyes are wide. I can see the sharp grains of hair pricking through the skin of his jaw. For a second it looks like he is going to cry. Then his mouth curves into a smile. What is there to smile about? Nothing is right, nothing is normal about these two men, yet somehow I'm not so scared anymore. Somehow I feel like it is all going to work out.

FREYA

Twenty-five hours missing

I UNMUTE THE news but they have moved on to another story. Where did they find the tooth? I wonder. He had one that was loose; had he pulled it out? That must be what happened.

'What is it?' Corazzo asks.

'They've found a tooth,' I tell him. 'It was on the news.'

'Where was it?'

'I don't know.'

I search the internet on my phone and find only one line in an article updated only a few minutes earlier: *A tooth believed to be that of the missing boy was found this morning near his home.* There are no stories about my connection to Blackmarsh yet. Do they know about my family?

There had been a moment of hesitation when the cops asked about my family. Did they mean Mum and Jonas, or the couple that adopted me, Christina and Dave? I'd been placed with them when I was fifteen and I left them when I was eighteen. After we came out of the Clearing I was always suspicious of strangers; even people who seemed kind I couldn't trust, especially the couple that adopted me. I hated Christina and Dave as a teenager. I hated their rules and customs. I hated their Catholic version of God. *Is there someone in your family that might have picked him up?* Not senile Mum and not absent Jonas. Not golf-playing Bee Gee-loving Christina, and not Dave, who had his third heart attack five years ago and died shortly after.

McVeigh and I had spoken about Henrik. Henrik, who Adrienne had baptised as Adam. Adam was always there when we needed medical attention. Adam could easily reset a dislocated finger or drain pus from an infection.

When Alex's fingers were snapped by a slammed door, even I was surprised by the physical damage one human could inflict on another and how some people were able to almost fully repair such damage. Alex's fingers were red-black with blood. In the following days his fingers swelled like overstuffed sausages. Adam drained them, tapping the pus like tree sap. First he lay the boy down in the Shed and put him into a deep sleep, then he opened the skin, sliding the scalpel as quick and smooth as a zip. He plucked the shards of shattered knucklebone out of his fingers then stitched them back up and put them in splints. That wasn't the only home surgery I witnessed. Someone needed to fix Jermaine Boethe's hand after I destroyed it with the back of the axe head. Then there was the home surgery of Asha. Adam was always trying to fix what I had done. What Blackmarsh had demanded of me. I was wholly committed to Blackmarsh but still there are people out there who don't understand the sacrifices I made.

Neo-Blackmarshers. There is nothing I can do about them. I've read the forums on which people talk about my 'betrayal' and the terrible punishment they would like to inflict on me. I've read posts in which they speculate on my whereabouts but thankfully only a few locals know my history, Paul the grocer, one of the other yoga instructors. They're not in a hurry to hand me over to the psychopaths loitering in those forums: the new members, or wannabe members, who have no idea what happened when I was still Amy or the truth about why I walked away that night. They couldn't begin to imagine what Adam was really like.

'I've got to head home,' Corazzo says. 'Pills to take.'

'Oh, that's fine.'

'I'll come back out later. Give me a call if there's any news, okay?'

'The detective is driving out now,' I say. 'I'm worried, Corazzo. I'm scared that if they clear Wayne they're going to start blaming me.'

He sighs. 'You've got every reason to be suspicious of them. The Blackmarsh investigation was corrupt from the beginning. So if Henrik is involved, it means they could still have sway with the police. All you can do is keep them onside and don't give them any reason to come after you.'

Mum had sway with the police, not Henrik.

•

Corazzo has been gone for an hour or so when McVeigh turns up. She eyes Rocky, who sits at attention near the door.

'Can I grab a seat?'

'Um, sure. Is this about the tooth?'

'I just want to ask you a few more questions,' McVeigh says, turning her dark gaze on me. 'I won't keep you long.'

'What happened with the tooth?'

'It's the media. We have found a tooth, but we have no idea if it's Billy's,' she says.

But I know. I am certain it is his.

'Where was it found?'

'Not far from here – in the bush near the river. Nine News got the photo at the same time as us. We've taken a statement from the searcher who found it.'

Someone has hurt him. Someone has pulled his tooth out. I imagine Billy's tiny body, pale and bloated, out there in the bush. I drop my face into my palms.

McVeigh proffers a tissue. I take it and wipe my cheeks.

'I want you to hear this from me before you see it somewhere else,' she says, her voice even, sympathy in her eyes. 'The tooth was found near a considerable amount of blood.'

My heart stops. 'What?' I open another news story on my phone, look at the tooth. There's no blood in the image. I notice a tiny chip in the corner of the tooth. My mind races. *This is the tooth he lost this week.* This is the tooth that should be in the top drawer of my dresser.

'There was something else. A pair of red pliers.' I look up from my phone. She's watching my face. 'We're running it for prints now.'

Red pliers. I get up and go to the kitchen. I open the cupboard beneath the sink and surreptitiously open the toolbox.

'What is it?' McVeigh says.

My pliers are missing. The tooth and the pliers, both taken from my home and planted outside. I keep my face neutral as I go back to my seat.

'Oh, nothing. I'm just getting a bit of a headache; I thought I had Panadol.'

They'll find my prints on the pliers. I used them recently to open Billy's paints. This confirms it. Someone is setting me up.

'So about the man you caught delivering flowers here last night . . .'

'Have you found out who hired him?'

'The username suggests it was someone called Adam, but we couldn't trace it back to Henrik Masters.'

'Who was it then?' I ask, watching her face.

'Were you alone here last night? There was no one else with you?'

I frown. Where is she going with this? 'No, no one else was here.'

'And you've never used Taskie in your life? Never been on the website?'

'No, I'd never even heard of it before last night.'

McVeigh leans back in her chair, her eyes moving around the room before landing back on me. 'I'm wondering if you have a password on your wireless router here at home?'

'You mean my internet modem?'

'That's right.'

'What is this about?'

'What would you say if I told you that we traced the Taskies account and each login, and that the most recent login came from your IP address? Whoever hired him was logged in at the time the flowers were delivered. They were using your wi-fi. So, who else could have access?'

My mind is hazy with all the possibilities. I think about Wayne, Derek, the couple by the river. How far would my wi-fi reach? Is it possible someone hacked my computer?

'Your neighbour?'

Computer illiterate Derek? Unlikely. 'No, not Derek.'

'We'll follow up with him just in case, but that doesn't leave many options.'

'Someone is setting me up,' I say. 'I don't know who, but someone is doing this to me deliberately.'

'The only lead we have from the flowers is your IP address.'

'Am I . . . am I under arrest?'

'No,' she says, letting her breath out.

'If it is alright, I want to get out with the search party. This isn't helping to find my son,' I say, my voice tentative.

'I don't think that's such a good idea, Freya. The media are all over this now. They know about your childhood. They're all waiting out there.'

'So I just have to sit here and wait?'

'For now,' McVeigh says.

I take my phone from my pocket and search the news stories to see if she is telling the truth.

'Do you want me to get some food sent out?' she says. She's not going to leave me I realise.

'I'm fine.' I open a news site and find three of the top five most read stories are about me and Billy. I read the headlines.

BILLY'S MOTHER'S DEMONIC CULT: FORMER LEADER RELEASED

HOT CAR HORROR: BILLY'S BROTHER ALMOST DIED IN SHOCKING CHILD ABUSE CASE FOURTEEN YEARS AGO

THE SEARCH CONTINUES: BILLY'S LAST DAYS RECOUNTED BY FRIENDS AND TEACHERS

I open the last story. I don't think I can stomach any of the others. I read through it, noting the tone.

Days before his disappearance, Billy showed up to school with a missing tooth and a black eye to go with a broken arm he suffered in suspicious circumstances last year.

The tooth that was recently found near Freya Heywood's property appears to be Billy's and a pair of pliers believed to be Freya Heywood's were found nearby.

Billy had reported to teachers he had seen a man near the school. Officers have not ruled out the involvement of Freya Heywood's ex-partner, convict Wayne Phillips, who was spotted in town just days before Billy's disappearance.

Police are looking closely at Heywood and Phillips as people of interest, although an arrest is yet to be made.

I stop reading and scan down to the comments. I know I shouldn't, but I'm a masochist. I can't resist. The first comment has over four hundred likes.

She's as guilty as sin. She couldn't escape her childhood and the only fix, I'm afraid to say, is a bullet.

The next comment has a number of replies.

She tried to kill her first child. Then she was abusing her second child and now he's disappeared. Who thought it would be a good idea to let this woman raise another child?

I look up, staring across my lawn towards the river. I see a searcher down at the back of the property. Except he's alone. He shouldn't be alone. He shouldn't be on my property. I step closer to the window, narrow my eyes. He's got long tangles of hair and he glances up towards the house. *It's him.* It's the man that was by the river with his girlfriend days ago. It's the man that was sleeping in the van, the same van that disappeared when Billy disappeared. *Are you in the search party or are you just snooping?* I read that criminals like to stay close to an investigation, kidnappers often join search parties but he doesn't look like he's searching. He has always been close enough to use my wi-fi so he could have hired the Taskie. The more sense it makes, the angrier I become. *You know where my son is.*

I could scream, but I simply turn to McVeigh with a neutral expression. 'I might have a shower, if that's okay?'

She looks up from her phone. 'Sure. Can we put your dog outside though? I'm not much of a dog person.'

'I'll keep him with me,' I say.

Twenty-nine hours missing

I go into my bedroom, closing the door behind me. I point at the bed. 'Up.'

Rocky jumps up obediently and lies down at the foot of the bed.

Corazzo had said, *We'll find him.* Derek had said so too. The search volunteers mouth it like a mantra and yet I know they won't find him out in the bush. He will be found if someone finds the person who took him. Everyone else has hope, but I know better. I know that soon, in days or weeks, when the entire park has been searched and the river has been trawled, they will give up and Billy will be remembered only on anniversaries of his disappearance, just like Asha. I'll be behind bars for his likely murder; the evidence is all pointing towards me. I can't trust the police to listen – I have to take things into my own hands.

Going into the ensuite, I open the shower door, twist the knob then close the door without stepping in. I slip back into my bedroom, walking on the balls of my feet. The bedroom window rises gently, noiselessly. I step through it, out into the mid-afternoon heat.

Adrienne's voice is in my head: *Think, Amy, you stupid little bitch. Think. You shouldn't be there in your house. Never trust the police.* Her voice is telling me what to do now, just as it did all those years ago. But Mum has changed. That woman with the fierce eyes and sharp mind is gone; now she is a mere shell. Finally the world can see her for the fraud she is.

I run from the house towards the cover of trees, and then continue on to the river, hurdling the gate. I can see the volunteers' tent in Derek's yard from here. The media up near the road. I keep running, getting closer to the river.

Billy could be with Henrik Masters and this man is probably involved. *Or Billy could be rotting beneath a foot of earth.* It's a punch to the gut, this other possibility. I think about the times I hurt Aspen, striking out with my palm, pinching his wrist, flicking his nose. Tricks I learnt at the Clearing to punish children. Wayne called me a bad mother, he told me I was cruel, and he was right. I had no idea what I was doing.

I hear Rocky barking back at the house, but I don't stop. As I emerge from the trees by the river I almost slam into the man.

It's him – and he's alone.

'Who are you?' I demand, bringing my face close to his. 'Who the fuck are you?'

Silence. His lips curl a little at the edges. His eyes meet mine. 'You miss your son?' His voice is so quiet I wonder if I hear him at all.

'What did you say?' I grab his hair in both hands, pulling him close. He's younger than I thought. He couldn't be older than twenty. He doesn't fight back. 'What the fuck did you just say?'

'You ever wonder what happened to him?'

'Where is he? Tell me!'

He smiles then, opening his mouth wide like he's going to laugh. 'You really don't know, do you? You have no idea. You never gave a shit about him.'

I swing my fist so hard that when it connects with his jaw my hand explodes with pain. The man stumbles back, cupping his chin. He rights himself. Blood on his lip, covering his teeth as he smiles again.

'You're a fucking bitch,' he says, the grin spreading, but his eyes are wild. 'You've finished killing children now, have you?'

I rush at him, throwing my fists, knees, elbows. The man doesn't fight back; he covers his head, turns, lifts his knee to protect himself. It's all fists and flesh, thrown with pure anger. I drag him by his hair and I hold his face beneath the water, pressing as hard as I can. I pull him up, look down at his head turned back to me. In that moment I see the vulnerability in his eyes. I recognise something familiar. He's just a boy really. I release my grip and he surfaces, gasping for air. I hear voices behind me now.

'Freya!' It's McVeigh. A second later, her body crashes into mine and together we go over into the river.

Someone else is there, pulling the man up from the river bank. Watery blood drips from his face.

McVeigh is deceptively strong, so deft and quick that I don't even realise my hands are cuffed until she takes me by the elbow, guiding me from the water. The cameras are clicking.

My nose is bleeding, but there is no pain. I look up and see them all waiting, the crowd gathering. Volunteers, media, police. *Did you all see my mask slip? Did you snap a picture of me holding his head under? Enjoy the show?*

'Get them out of here,' I say. 'Clear off, the lot of you. Get the fuck off my land.'

I look up and see the woman who was with the man that day I'd caught them by the river. She brings one hand to her mouth as our eyes meet. Her other hand rests on her navel. There's a bump, small but unmistakable. She's pregnant.

Casting one last glance at the man being pulled away by a cop, I feel that jolt of recognition again. *Where have I seen you before?*

AMY

ADRIENNE SAYS THAT everyone in the world is fake, that they're all pretending. That means these two men beside the bed. That means Corazzo.

They're both reeling. I can see it in their eyes. This is the moment they were waiting for. They know about Asha. They know we took her away.

'We need to move on it tonight, Mike. We need to get her and the other children out.'

'But—'

'Use the phone,' Corazzo says, pointing to the hallway. 'Speak to Jackson, make sure this doesn't get to anyone outside of the task force. No one. Not even the guys on the McFetridge case. We can't take any risks. Then get back out to that house and search for the journal. It could be useful.'

The room is thrumming, it's all happening so quickly. Just then the lights dim a little, just a flicker. Corazzo looks up. I feel the tears coming again, the fear cooling me from the inside out.

I don't want to let Adrienne down. I'm so scared, so scared I have done something wrong.

The hard lines and edges of Corazzo's face soften and he leans forwards. 'Hey now,' he says. 'Don't cry, Amy. Don't cry. You don't know it, you might not realise for some time, but you've just saved lives. You're a hero.'

Mike steps back into the room.

I look at him, then back to Corazzo. 'He killed her,' I say. 'Adam killed her.'

And just like that the smiles disappear.

FREYA

Twenty-nine hours missing

'GET HIM, NOT me,' I say, as McVeigh shoves me along the path towards the house. The mask of Freya Heywood is gone. 'He's got my kid. He told me. It's him.' She pushes me through the gate and across the lawn.

'Just get inside. He's not going anywhere.'

For a second, I wonder who is in my shower before remembering that I left it running. Rocky is barking, staring out the window at me.

Inside, McVeigh sits me down on a towel on my couch. What would have happened if she didn't stop me? I might have drowned him. She holds a warm damp cloth to my nose. I can feel the blood running. Another officer is standing nearby, talking into his radio.

'What on earth were you thinking?' McVeigh demands.

'Can you take these handcuffs off?' I ask.

'No. You've put me in a really awkward position, Freya. We all want to find Billy. We're all on the same team. Then you fly off the handle like that. That man has every right to press charges.'

'He took Billy! He confessed.'

She looks at me sceptically. 'What did he say?'

'He asked me if I wondered where my son went. He just did it – I know he did it. You need to start questioning him!' I stand up, move to the door and look out across the yard, trying to catch a glimpse of him. The lawn shimmers, the heat presses its nose to the glass.

'I will question him, don't you worry about that. In the meantime, they've called an ambulance for him.'

I turn back to face her. 'Imagine if someone took your kid and you knew who it was and—'

'I get it.' She raises her eyebrows, gives me a knowing look. 'Take a seat, Freya. I'm not going to ask you again.'

I sit back down with my hands behind me in the cuffs. 'What are we waiting for?'

'We're waiting for a car to take you to the station.'

The cop with the radio steps outside onto the deck to watch what's going on by the river.

I let my breath out. 'Can I at least make myself a cup of tea?' It will mean removing the cuffs.

She's standing with her hands on her hips, staring out the kitchen window up the driveway, as if willing the car to appear. She turns back to me. 'Where's the tea then?'

'In the cupboard above the sink.'

She's a little taciturn. Follows instructions. McVeigh would have made a good little Blackmarsher, I think. She's the right age to be one of my siblings but she never would have appealed to Adrienne with her coffee brown hair and dark features. I know others have since changed their appearance after Blackmarsh, dying their hair dark, letting it grow wild as a final act of defiance to Adrienne.

When I searched for my brothers and sisters online I found suicides, lives spent institutionalised, some were in and out of rehab and perpetually medicated. One of the children went on to have a relatively successful career as a lawyer before one night she ran a hose from her car exhaust to the driver's window. The past,

I realised, was a parasite. It could lie dormant inside for years and eventually flare up and kill you. They all must have resented me and Jonas – especially me. *Well adjusted, normal.*

Andrew was placed in foster care and grew up as 'Liam Stein'. At the Clearing he had the first signs of facial hair, a kind of blond down that shone in the sun, but in the newspaper photo he was hairless, heavily tattooed and wore silver reading glasses. He gazed into the camera lens with a melancholy expression. The article was about the children he hurt. It mentioned his time in the cult as a sort of excuse. *Stein was raised in the Blackmarsh cult, where he himself was abused as a child.* Andrew had sharpened his toothbrush on the concrete of his cell as he waited for the trial and in the night he pulped his wrists. I know what he was thinking. He was thinking that everything is inevitable. He was thinking you never leave Blackmarsh.

•

'Chamomile, turmeric, sleep tea or rooibos?' McVeigh is searching through my pantry for the teabags.

'Chamomile,' I say. 'That would be fine. Can you take the cuffs off? I need to change out of these wet clothes.'

She turns and gives me a long, hard look. 'You need to stay away from that man for your own good. I'll release you, but I don't want you leaving my sight.'

She flicks the kettle on and walks over to unlock the cuffs. She lets me take a shower, watching me walk in and then standing outside the bathroom door. Afterwards I pull on clean clothes and brush my teeth. Rocky stays in my room as I walk back into the lounge. McVeigh pours me a cup of chamomile tea and places it on the table.

'So what happens now?' I ask.

She's about to answer when her phone rings on her belt. She raises a finger to tell me to wait, then steps out onto the back deck to take the call. I stalk her with my eyes. She glances back at me, her phone pressed to her ear, brow furrowed. Something is wrong.

She places her phone back on her belt and steps inside. 'Take a seat, Freya.'

'Why?'

'Trust me, you'll want to be sitting for this.'

I shake my head, my body gripped by an invisible fist. 'No,' I say, a whimper in my voice. 'No, no, no. Don't tell me, don't say it.'

'It's not Billy, Freya. It's Masters.'

Now I do sit. 'What? What's happened?'

'Masters is under surveillance. He is not allowed to leave his place of residence. However, between 1:00 and 2:00 pm this afternoon, after his doctor checked in on him, he left his property in breach of the terms of his parole.'

I catch my breath. It's not so bad. Well, it's bad, but I'd been preparing myself for much worse news.

'Sometimes these things happen when people have recently got out of prison. In this case he managed to shed his electronic monitoring device.'

I lean back in the chair. Okay, this *is* bad.

'There's more. That man you beat half to death is hardly a man at all. He's a seventeen-year-old runaway.'

My stomach hits the floor. 'No,' I say. *You ever wonder what happened to him?*

'He was removed from an unsafe family environment when he was a child and lived with his father subsequently. His mother was prohibited from having any contact with him.'

'It can't be him. It's not him. You're lying.' But I know she's not. I saw something in his eyes.

'He's your son, Freya.'

Aspen.

AMY

'WE'RE GOING TO need you to sign a couple of pieces of paper, all very standard.'

Corazzo stands near the bed with his arms crossed. He is always close now, always nearby. When he is not here, I feel the fear again.

A new man with too-small spectacles and tiny hands folded in his lap sits nearby, speaking quickly. When our eyes meet he instantly looks away. I'm finding that happens more and more. Most people don't maintain eye contact with me, only Corazzo does. It's like I'm a dangerous animal. They all look away, staring at their hands, or the ceiling, or at something just over my shoulder. This man looks at Corazzo when he is talking to me.

He rises to pass me the clipboard but Corazzo tenses, stepping between us. He takes it from the man and hands it to me.

'Sign?' I say. 'What does he mean?'

'Write your name,' Corazzo says, leaning over to jab his finger at the page. 'On that line.'

'My name?'

'It just means you agree with what is written in the statement here.'

I quickly read through both the pages, recognising my own words. All the things I told Corazzo and the others. I write my name. *Amy.* I hand the clipboard to Corazzo, who passes it back to the man. He leaves without another word.

'I didn't mean it,' I say, looking up at Corazzo. I remember everything Adrienne told me about the outside world. *Everyone pretends. Everyone wears a mask.*

'Mean what, Amy?'

'I didn't mean to cut that man with the knife. I was scared.'

'He's a big boy. He's patched up now. No harm.'

'Will you protect me?' I say.

'Of course. We all will.'

'My dad is going to be so angry.'

He sucks his lips. 'Amy, you look at me. You just keep telling everyone what you have told me, and I will make sure you are safe. We've got your Adam, he's been arrested.'

'I don't want to talk about it again.'

'Well, you will need to do it one more time, okay? But we'll make it really easy for you. You'll be in a big courtroom with a lot of people to look out for you. It's important that you tell them what he did. Otherwise your mum will get the blame. And others.' He crouches so he's at my level and looks me straight in the eye. 'Don't you worry, Amy. We're going to practise – you, me and Mrs Bourke. We'll practise what you need to say over and over until it is easy. That way, when you have to do it in front of everyone in court, you won't need to think at all.'

Mrs Bourke comes and sits with me most days. When we were first introduced, she smiled at me. It was a smile so warm and broad that her eyes almost closed. I tried the smile on myself. It felt good.

Corazzo is never far away. Sometimes he goes out to help at the Clearing, but then he comes back to see me to tell me what has happened. He reports back about my brothers and sisters.

Mrs Bourke asks me questions and I do my best to answer. I know it is easier if I answer the questions the way she wants me to, if I tell her that I'm feeling better and that I can see that Adrienne is not really my mother. I know that if I act like everybody else, if I greet them with a smile, if I sit still and don't try to escape, they won't keep such a close eye on me. So that's what I do. I try to act like them. I act the way people do out in the world, just how Adrienne would want.

'You can't protect me,' I say to Corazzo now. 'You think you can but you can't.'

FREYA

Thirty hours missing

'CAN I . . . can I see him?'

'That's not the best idea.'

Aspen was here. It was Aspen camping out. What did he want? To meet me? To watch me and know me? To punish me?

I feel something a lot like sadness deep inside. I let a few tears slip from my eyes. McVeigh watches me, her head slightly tilted. I dab at the tears with my sleeve.

'I can't just sit here – I need to be doing something to help find Billy.'

'I'll have to arrest you if you try to leave,' the detective counters.

'Can you at least give me some space?' I plead. 'Just an hour or so to clear my head?'

The sun is descending behind the tree line. 'I can't leave you alone.'

'Am I a suspect?'

'A suspect in what exactly?'

'Do you think I've done something to Billy? Do you think I'm involved?'

McVeigh touches her ear and licks her lips – a tell, she is about to lie or she's simply nervous about something else. 'Can I be honest?'

'Please.'

'The media are all over your history. They know that you were abusive in the past.'

'With Aspen? That was Wayne lying. I was—'

'Not Aspen but Billy.'

'Abusive to Billy?' I think about the black eye, the broken arm, the bruises on Billy's wrist and his missing teeth. Then again I feel that vacuous pain inside, I miss him so much.

'The police believe you may have a case to answer.'

I can hear Rocky scratching at the bedroom door. I look at McVeigh, who nods, then rise and cross the lounge to let him out.

Maybe Aspen only wanted to meet me. If I hadn't been so curt and dismissive when I first encountered him near the river maybe we could have talked.

'Is it okay if I use my phone?'

McVeigh sucks her lips. 'Sure.'

I pick up my phone to text Wayne.

I found Aspen. He will be at the police station soon. Long story.

The sun is setting. I know it's only a matter of time until they arrest and charge me. Who can help me? Corazzo. I text him.

I've been set up. The police have got my prints on pliers that they think have been used to pull out one of Billy's teeth. They think I've got a history of abuse. I don't know what is coming next.

Corazzo's reply is almost instant. *They've got someone in the police, Freya. Be careful.*

My heart begins to thump. McVeigh is watching me. I don't let the mask slip to show her my suspicion; I shape my face to casual indifference. I bow my head and flick my thumb up the page as if scrolling through Instagram, but in the meantime, I slide my eyes sideways. Through the kitchen window, I see the Disco, parked only ten or fifteen metres away.

They won't let me leave my house, I type.

A reporter is holding one finger to her ear and talking into a microphone at the top of the driveway; she must be doing a live cross. I stand up, walk over to the kitchen window and drop the blinds.

Corazzo messages back. *NOT NORMAL. Who is the cop?*

McVeigh.

Get out. Run. Go somewhere no one will find you. Then let me know and I'll come to meet you.

'Are you texting someone?' McVeigh asks.

I glance up. 'Oh, just my brother.'

'He's in Bali, isn't he?'

'How do you know that?'

'It's my job to know.'

'Of course,' I say. I take my teacup and go back to the kitchen. 'Are you sure you don't want some tea yourself?' I ask.

'I'm more of a coffee drinker. Have you got anything else?'

'I've got kombucha.'

'Alright, I'll try a kombucha.'

There's only a third of the bottle left. I pour it all into a glass and take it back to the table.

She sips. 'That's . . . sweet.' She takes another sip. She blinks rapidly, licks her lips.

I lean against the bench watching her, thinking about Corazzo's message. *Get out now.* She drains the glass then looks at me. Her eyes seem to be having trouble focusing. Suddenly, she pushes herself to her feet.

'What is it?' I ask.

She holds herself up over the table, blinking hard.

'Jennifer?'

'What did you do?'

'What do you mean? I haven't done anything.'

She blinks again, her eyelids drooping. 'You drugged me,' she slurs.

'That's impossible,' I say. 'You saw me pour it.' And then it dawns on me. I had drunk a glass of kombucha from this bottle just before I fell into a deep sleep the day Billy was taken. It had tasted sweeter than usual. Whoever took him knew my routine, knew I drank a glass with breakfast every day. Knew I gave Billy a glass too. It was all planned. 'No,' I tell her, 'it wasn't me, I swear.'

She takes her radio from her belt. 'I'm calling this in.'

'No,' I say, frantic. 'You can't. I didn't do anything – I'm being set up!' I have to stop her from making the call. 'Rocky, defend!'

Rocky leaps forwards, his entire body tense and bristling.

'If you move, he will attack you.'

The hand holding the radio begins to tremble. I see her throat rise as she swallows.

'If I give the command,' I continue, 'he will latch on to you and he won't let go.'

She's watching my face, struggling to keep her eyes open, her breathing slow.

I've been played by someone who knows my habits, can predict my every move. Someone who can ensure that all the evidence points to my guilt. I reach for the keys to the Disco, then hit the master switch for the roller shutters.

'Freya!' McVeigh says, her voice urgent but faint. 'What the hell is this?'

Rocky takes a step towards her, growling.

The shutter over the door is getting lower and lower. I bend and step backwards through it.

'Rocky, here now.'

He bolts towards me, just squeezing through the gap in the door before it is fully closed. McVeigh is entombed within my home. I run to the electrical mains at the side of the house and kill the power.

The cameras at the top of the driveway are trained on me, avidly watching my every move. They machine gun their shutter clicks.

I climb into the Disco, leaving Rocky outside – with any luck Derek will collect him – I gun the motor, and the Disco shoots up the driveway. The reporters scatter as I fly towards them.

My mind is racing as I try to put the pieces together. Henrik has escaped, but he can't have taken Billy alone. If this has something to do with Blackmarsh, there's only one place to go. I set out towards Eucalyptus Acres.

UnCULTured Podcast – Episode 37
**'Breaking Blackmarsh: The disappearance of
Sara McFetridge'**

*On a sunny summer afternoon in February 1997, the small
figure of Sara McFetridge was seen rounding the bend less than
a football field's length from her home. Sara had a skip in her
step; it was a Tuesday, which meant she and her grandfather,
Tim Yule, would be eating fish and chips for dinner. Less than
a minute later, Sara was snatched from the side of the road
and never seen again.*

*Today, we are in Victoria, Australia to take a closer look
at what really happened.*

*It wasn't until eight days after the disappearance, when a
peculiar case landed on the desk of Chief Inspector Dominic
Corazzo, that a break in the investigation came: seven-year-
old Sara had been abducted and murdered by the secretive
Blackmarsh cult.*

*Sara's body was never recovered, despite the tireless efforts
of search parties scouring the North Tullawarra National Park.
They searched the seam of native bush that runs all the way
up to Wallaby Station, twenty kilometres north of the Clearing
where the cult was based.*

*Sara, described as inquisitive and clever by those who knew
her, had made several attempts to escape, facing increasingly
cruel punishments.*

*'When Masters decided to kill Sara, it was not in anger
but in a move calculated to instil a sense of consequence
in the other children,' explains Andrea Bourke, one of the
psychologists who worked closely with the children rescued*

in the subsequent raid of the cult's headquarters. 'It was a sophisticated brainwashing regime; he knew exactly what he was doing down to the very last detail. These people were extremely intelligent. I mean, Adrienne Smith-Atkins served only two months in a cushy jail cell. They abused these children for fifteen years and she gets two months.'

Even though police had a reliable statement from one of the children who had witnessed the torture and death of Sara McFetridge, they feared it wasn't enough.

'It's difficult to get a prosecution after a certain amount of time has passed, and it's almost impossible when no body and very little physical evidence is recovered.'

That's retired detective Dominic Corazzo.

It was Corazzo who first encountered Amy Smith-Atkins, a teenager who fled the cult after Sara's death, and his early work on the case gave prosecutors a real chance of securing a conviction. Amy was the only one of almost a dozen abused children deemed fit to stand trial. This is me speaking with him.

'Why was Amy the one to testify?'

'We made a decision that Amy had to be the one. There was something different about her. She could keep it together and was the only one we felt we could ethically put in front of the defence lawyers.'

'Did any of the other children contradict Amy's testimony in any way?'

'Well, there are always going to be inconsistencies when you're relying on the memory of ten extraordinarily damaged children.'

'I read the book about the Blackmarsh group, Dark Paradise, *which contains extracts from Amy's journal. Pretty confronting stuff in there.'*

'*Oh yeah. I saw it first-hand. Burns, cuts, broken bones –*
you name it.'

'*And Adrienne Smith-Atkins . . . was she more involved*
than people think?'

'*No, I don't think she was. She was away travelling much*
of the time and was largely oblivious to what was going on
in her absence. We got our guy.'

It should also be noted here that, as a result of the
Blackmarsh investigation, a separate task force was set up
to investigate police corruption in Victoria. Although no
charges were laid, many links between the Blackmarsh cult
and members of the police were discovered.

'*Were there Blackmarshers within the police force?*'

'*The balance of probability suggests there were.*'

FREYA

Thirty-one hours missing

I ROAR OUT onto the road. For a moment I imagine Adam standing there, his beard scraggly, black hair curling about his ears. *What does he look like now?* I wonder. I blink the vision away as I cross the dip over the drain. A dozen or more cars are parked along the narrow verge.

I switch my phone off and the radio on, scrolling through static until I find a talkback station. As I near the town, a police car flies past me heading in the opposite direction, back towards my house, its lights flashing and siren blaring. I hold my breath, watching in the rear-view mirror, expecting to see red brake lights, but it continues on, disappearing around the bend. They didn't recognise my car.

My gaze still on the road behind me, I notice headlights turn on in the twilight; there's a car following me. I frown. I drive on, my eyes flicking between the road in front and the rear-view mirror. It can't be a reporter; they weren't expecting me to leave the house and they were too slow, too stunned to follow. It can't be the cops either. The car tailing me is staying back, not crowding me; if it was the police they would be in pursuit mode, ordering me to pull me over.

Posts tick by at the roadside, the white centre line flickers, sliding ahead like a lit fuse. I know I'm driving too fast.

Adam, I think. *Always Adam.*

Ghost gums line the road, anaemic limbs reaching out above me. It reminds me of the road down to the Clearing. It isn't so far from here but of course no one would be there. I'm sure some people visit. Those fanatics online. They brag about the memorabilia they have collected – a hairbrush, notepad, pillows – all purported to have come from the Clearing. Some still search out in the bush for Asha's remains, hoping to stumble upon them, as though they're better equipped than hundreds of police and search teams.

I once took a perverse sort of pleasure in reading those Blackmarsh forums deep into the night. It was like reading the diary of an ex-lover. I'd scroll through the conspiracy theories, marvelling at both how close they were to the truth about what happened and how far off, how inane, how fantastical. Occasionally a thread would descend into the cobwebbed corners of the darkest fantasies. Orgies of hate. Sex. Rape. Murder. Fantasies projecting onto each other. Want to know how to find a psychopath? Easy. Download a Tor browser and search almost any forum, you're likely to find at least one. The challenge is separating those who wish for violence from those few insane enough to actually perpetrate it.

I round a gentle bend, the needle drifting towards one-twenty. The lights of the trailing car recede into the distance. I exhale and ease my foot off the accelerator.

Adrienne only wanted blonde, blue-eyed, pale children because she wanted to create a family in her own image. It was the ultimate act of narcissism, not some Aryan dream. The prophecy was false, there was no plan to save the human race; it was all just plain narcissism. Adrienne convinced all of us at the Clearing that if she died the world would end and the only way to save it was to find her twelve perfect children. In moments of weakness I wonder if she really is my mum. Maybe, like the others, I was stolen away. But the truth is her blood flows in my veins. I know I am different. I was there first, before she set about collecting the rest of the twelve.

The police were never able to pin anything substantial on Adrienne; she escaped with only a couple of minor charges. She could still travel the world freely. It must have killed the police. Perhaps her dementia is just another deceit. Perhaps that's what I inherited from her: the power to wear the skin of another. But it can't be; some things you can't fake: the vagueness in her milky eyes, the lapses into confusion, the rambling . . . Not even I'm that good at being someone else. I know her memory really is failing and soon I will be free of her.

I pull off the highway and take a back road up through the hills. I turn down a dusty track, cutting through farmland, then turn again and begin to descend.

Death makes life real, Adrienne told me once. There were other deaths out there. Deaths that would never be reported. They were not memorable enough. Adult deaths. Deaths from infection, accidental drowning, deep sleep therapy. Oversupply of insulin. Then the bodies disappeared, and we never spoke about them again.

The radio drops out in a bray of static, and for a moment, while I search for another station, I hear only the smooth heavy purr of the disco. The radio locks on to a frequency. A slow melody comes from the speakers.

I pass through the town where I stopped for fuel the last time I came to visit Mum. It's all dark now.

Soon the music is interrupted by a breaking news bulletin. I turn up the volume and listen closely.

. . . In a new development, a blood-stained pyjama top believed to belong to Billy Heywood has been recovered from a fire bunker near his home, along with evidence of what police believe was a significant volume of blood inside the house. Police have also confirmed the pliers found near the child's tooth did belong to Freya Heywood and her fingerprints were recovered from the tool. Heywood fled her home and police supervision earlier this evening. Police are asking members of the public to remain vigilant and to call triple zero if Ms Heywood is sighted.

•

I exhale. It's happening. I turn into the track leading to Eucalyptus Acres. The stars are out, filling the sky.

I pull in beside Mum's unit and switch off the ignition, listening to the engine tick. The breeze outside is shifting the leaves. I lower my window and feel the cool change has come, sweeping through the country. Rain will come next. The lights are off in all the units, including Adrienne's, which happens to be the furthest from the road, right at the edge of the national park. Any staff on the premises would be over in the office, out of sight behind the trees.

Like me, Adrienne always had to be close to the river, close to the bush, breathing in the eucalyptus-rich air. I walk to the back step and wait a moment, straining to hear if there's any sound inside. I can almost hear the trickle of water from here.

I see something familiar in the darkness. Near the bin, stacks of yellow wattle – the same as the flowers I received. So she has been receiving them too. Or was she sending them? No, impossible. The sender was close enough to be using my IP address. I gaze at her door, a quiet moment of meditation in the dark, before gripping the handle and turning it slowly.

I hit the lights. The room is lightning-strike white. I see her, Adrienne, sitting on the couch, her back to me. She doesn't turn to see who's entered. Is she sleeping?

'Mum,' I say.

No movement. The air is still. Too still.

Something's not right. I have the feeling of being watched, as though she has eyes peering out through the thin grey hair at the back of her head. I step closer. *Blind bravery comes from ignorance of the real threat.* I move around the couch to face her. I've never seen her so vulnerable: no make-up, her hair faded and wispy. This confirms it. She would never let herself get to this stage, not in her right mind. Eyes closed, chest completely still.

'Mum,' I say, desperation rising in my voice. I reach out and touch her shoulder, shake her gently. 'Mum?'

Her blue eyes snap open like the eyes of a porcelain doll. She is staring straight at me.

'Amy,' she says. 'You shouldn't be here.'

I search her face for any sign of deceit, any sharpness or cognisance. 'Mum, someone took Billy. Someone stole him away.'

'*He* took the boy.'

'Who?'

She closes her eyes.

'Mum, who took him? Who took Billy?'

'Billy?' she says, shaking her head as if waking from a trance. Suddenly she looks uncertain, her eyes peering around the room before settling on my face. 'Amy,' she says. 'What are you doing here? It's late.'

I lean closer, holding her shoulders. 'You said *he* took Billy. Who do you mean?'

She moves her hands in the air, making small birdlike movements. 'Who took who?'

That lucid moment has gone.

'Who took my son?' I demand. 'Billy – you remember Billy?'

'Oh yes. How is Billy?'

I shake her. 'Think, Mum. Who took him?'

'Ouch. Stop it.'

My fingers are gripping too tightly. She winces. *You old witch. This is your fault. You did this to us.*

'I didn't do anything,' she says plaintively.

That strange tingling washes over my skin: the feeling that she can see inside my head.

I draw a breath, step back. 'Mum, I need your help.'

'Leave me alone now. Just like you left me here before. After everything I did for you children, you abandon me.' *You taught me how to act, how to conceal Amy and show the world Freya.*

'I didn't abandon you, Mum. I didn't mean to.'

She won't look at me. 'Leave me to sleep now.' She puts a palm to her chest as if her lungs require the weight of her hand to compress.

'Mum,' I say. 'Are you okay?'

'I'm fine. I just need to get to bed.'

Again I notice the artwork on the walls, the Olsen, the Whitely, the *Heywood*. Hundreds of thousands of dollars' worth of art adorning an otherwise bland, unremarkable unit. It strikes me as a waste, how can someone who can barely recognise herself in the mirror recognise the great art around her? I look up at one of the paintings. It's mine. It's a painting of the Clearing with the black square at the centre and all those flowers blooming at the edges. *The flowers.*

'Look at me, Mum.'

She keeps her face averted.

'Mum where did those flowers come from? Did someone send them?'

'Flowers?' Finally she raises her eyes to meet mine. 'What flowers?'

I stride across the room, out the door and pick up one of the bouquets. Returning to her side, I hold it out. 'These flowers. Where did they come from?'

She squints at them, puzzled, then her face clears. 'Oh, those flowers. I don't know. They just turn up. Someone puts them out there.'

'Is it Adam? *Think*, Mum. Did he take Billy?'

She smiles then, her eyes settling on mine. '*You* are the killer, Amy. Not Adam.'

It hits me hard, right in the stomach. Is this the real Adrienne speaking? Has she been acting all along? I hate that this woman has held something over me for so long.

'Where are the photos?' I say. 'Where are they?'

She gives a tiny, almost imperceptible smile.

'You're a fraud. That's all you've ever been,' I say.

Is there hurt in her eyes?

'I can't help you, Amy. You turned your back on me.'

My phone buzzes in my pocket. I look down, the message is from Corazzo.

Just saw the news. They're after you. They'll be watching main roads and checking in with your family. Turn off GPS on phone or get rid of it.

Family. I know what he is saying. The first place someone flees to. The police could be on their way here right now. I rush out to the Disco, pulling the door closed behind me.

I floor it, the engine growling, the headlights blasting through the darkness. I swing out onto the road, heading away from the city. I'll take the long way. Corazzo lives west of the city. It's a couple of hours from here but he's the only ally I've got left.

Thirty-four hours missing

A dead wallaby lies near the centre line. I swerve to avoid it. I wind down my window and hurl my phone as far as I can into the dry shrub without slowing – Corazzo is right, it's the easiest way of getting caught. It won't be easy to find my way to the western side of the city from here without navigation, and I only have half a tank of fuel. I'll just have to figure it out as I go.

I'll need a lawyer, but then again there's not much any lawyer can do from this position. It's like calling in a chess master when you're three moves away from checkmate. Whoever has set me up has me comprehensively screwed. My last lawyer kept me out of prison, but I lost my son. Not exactly a fair trade-off. What's the best I could hope for this time? A decade in prison? I glance down at the speedo, making sure I'm not over the limit. My number plate, make and model have no doubt been broadcast to the police and probably the public. I need to avoid being seen, which is easier now, on a Sunday night at 10 pm, than it will be tomorrow morning.

I keep the radio tuned to one of the news stations as I drive away from the city, up deep into the bones of the country. I pass through towns where shops are boarded up. Towns that aren't towns but names on maps, now populated only by farmers.

I could drive all the way to Jonas's place and camp out there until he gets back, but I doubt I could find my way there. I don't have enough petrol, and police will likely check there too. Corazzo is my only option and time is ticking away to find my son. It still hurts, that phantom pain of missing Billy. Even when I forget, for half a second, I still feel sick and scared, then I remember.

There comes a point when *missing* becomes *missing, presumed dead*. Whether it's years or months or days, the moment always comes: the moment when all the evidence suggests a murder has occurred; when volumes of blood are found and possible weapons; when the search for a missing person becomes a homicide investigation. I know this because I have keenly watched every news story about every disappearance over the past two decades. I know how perpetrators trip up and are caught. I know that nine times out of ten when someone disappears and is presumed murdered, a family member is responsible. Whoever took Billy also knows this. They've done their research and set the trap perfectly. I could almost laugh – and then I do.

•

I keep driving through the night. Eventually I have circled around the city and start heading south towards the western suburbs. I know I can't park near Corazzo's house in the Disco, but there are plenty of industrial estates nearby.

I cruise along back streets, looking for somewhere inconspicuous to leave the car. Finally, on the other side of the train line, I find what I'm looking for: a semi-derelict warehouse abutting a vacant lot. I park up close in the shadow of the warehouse, and hurry down the street in the direction of the train station. I walk through the underpass, and stride down the main street. A man passes me, walking the other way. There's a moment of eye contact, then I look away. After I have passed I hear his footsteps stop. I walk faster. When I turn back a few seconds later I see him standing still, staring down at the phone in his hand. He could be ordering an Uber, I reason, or messaging his mum, or checking Google Maps to make sure he's walking the right way to his girlfriend's house . . . or he could be looking at a news site for a photo of me. I'm not prepared to stick around to see which it is. I pick up my pace and turn down the first side street.

I'm not far from Corazzo's now. Twenty minutes of striding through the cool of the night, keeping my head down, turning away when I see headlights. Avoiding anything that resembles a CCTV camera.

At last I arrive at Corazzo's. It's a small squat weatherboard house. Red door, wild garden. Sweating in my jeans and dusty blouse, I raise my hand and knock three times, hard enough to wake the occupant but not so hard that a neighbouring insomniac might look out to the street.

I listen to the night, hear the distant sound of trucks on the motorway, the creak of a swing set. No sound comes from inside. *He's not home.* Even as I think it the door swings open and a hand snatches my shoulder, jerking me inside.

He holds me there, near the door. His face half in shadow, half illuminated by the streetlight coming through the window.

'Freya, what the hell are you thinking coming here?' He looks over my shoulder, peering out at the street, then closes the door. He turns back to me, eyes full of accusation.

'I–I've got nowhere else to go,' I say.

He points towards the door to the kitchen and follows me as I walk through. The place looks as if it's still haunted by Corazzo's ex-wife. Floral table cloth. Framed cross-stitch on the walls along with a photo of Corazzo as a new recruit to the police, standing stiff and proud, with much darker hair, a thinner moustache and fuller face. He drags two stools over to the island bench and turns the kettle on.

The clock on the stove says it's 2:14 in the morning.

'You made me look like a fool, Freya,' he says, pulling a pair of cups from a cupboard. 'The Blackmarsh case was the pinnacle of my career.'

'What are you talking about?'

'We'll discuss it in the morning.'

He places a teabag in each of the cups and fills them up with water.

'For now, I want you to tell me everything you know about Billy's disappearance. Run me through the past twenty-four hours, no bullshit, just facts.'

I glance up from my cup and see him rubbing the stubble on his chin. He's stressed about Blackmarsh, I realise. I've brought the past into his home.

I recite the events of the days, exactly as they unfolded. When I get to the part where I saw Adrienne, he raises his hand for me to stop.

'You visited her?'

'Yes.'

'And it wasn't the first time?'

'No.'

He closes his eyes as if in pain. 'Okay, tell me honestly: how often do you see her?'

'Once a week,' I say.

He looks surprised at that – and hurt.

'I see. And you still believe she's a reincarnation of Jesus Christ? You still believe in all the Blackmarsh stuff?'

I take a sip of my tea to think. I need him on my side, I need to deliver this with conviction. 'Of course not,' I say. 'She's a delusional old woman. I don't believe any of that stuff. I go because if she realised how much I despised her she would ruin my life.'

'You swear this is the truth?' he asks, his eyes intent on me. 'You promise?'

'It's the truth.'

'Alright,' he says, draining his cup and standing up. 'Where's your car?'

'I parked it near an old warehouse on the other side of the station.'

'Good. Let's make a plan in the morning. You're still not off the hook.' As he walks away towards his bedroom he says over his shoulder, 'The bed is made up in the spare room.'

I shed my clothes and climb into the bed, more for something to do than out of any expectation of sleep. But the moment I close my eyes it's as if I've pulled the power cord of my brain, and the black tide of sleep rushes in and overwhelms me.

Forty-four hours missing

Morning arrives abruptly, light seeping in through a gap in the curtains. I don't know where I am at first, and then with a pang I remember. I'm at Corazzo's house. Billy is still missing.

I can smell bacon, eggs, grease, and I sit up, my body feeling weary despite the sleep. I throw on my clothes and move to the door, pulling it open gently.

I find Corazzo sitting in a chair in the living room watching the road. He has a shotgun laid across his lap.

'Morning,' I say.

He turns to me. 'She wakes.'

'What time is it?'

'Almost time for breakfast.'

He stands and leans the gun by the doorframe. A moment later he returns holding a plate heaped with eggs, crispy bacon, grilled tomatoes and mushrooms. A thick wedge of toast sits beneath it all. The plate is warm, as if it's been sitting in the oven, waiting for me.

'Oh, you shouldn't have,' I say.

'No worries. You need your strength today. You need to eat.'

I think about what he said last night. About his reputation, the case that made his career. I decide not to broach the subject yet.

'TV?' he says, but he's already aiming the remote before I answer.

The house is cool and air-conditioned. He flicks through the channels, landing for a moment on a morning show before he quickly moves on.

'Go back,' I say, lowering my fork. 'What was that?'

He changes the channel. I see a series of photographs of Wayne and Aspen. They're leaving a hospital. A banner screams *Nine Exclusive*. Then the camera zooms in on his face. He has a black eye, a scratch beside his nose. He's shaved and looks so much younger now than he had by the river the day before.

Why did you track your Mum down, Aspen? What did she say to you?

He doesn't look at the camera when he responds.

I just wanted to meet her. I don't know. I wanted to ask her why she hurt me, but she wasn't what I expected.

It cuts back to the studio. A woman, blow-waved, lips shining with gloss, is wearing her best *how awful* expression. Beside her sits a man in a blue shirt who might have just stepped out of a teeth-whitening commercial, and next to him I recognise a goateed shock jock: Des Holder, the most self-righteous man on radio.

The woman tut-tuts.

It's appalling, isn't it? The entire story. Des Holder joins us now. Des, what do these latest photos mean for Freya Heywood?

Latest photos? Pinpricks of sweat break out all over me. *She hasn't*, I think, *she can't have.* Images appear on the screen. My heart plummets as I recognise the scene, the grainy images. The photos are from the Clearing. The photos are of me: one in which I'm holding Asha's head under water, another where I'm helping to dig a hole next to a pixelated body. There's a manic grin on my face. It's Adrienne. These photos belong to her.

Des Holder is shaking his head sorrowfully.

Well, anyone can see that this girl at the age of fifteen helped to torture and murder Sara McFetridge. It shows us that the police involved in this case wore blinkers when it came to all the perpetrators of the crimes that were committed at Blackmarsh. Henrik Masters might have been the mastermind – but he didn't act alone.

Corazzo clears his throat. On screen the other speaker chips in.

Des is exactly right, but there is no precedent for this in Australia. A historical crime committed by a minor who was essentially raised in a cult. I can't see how she can be viewed as culpable.

Des Holder interrupts.

Well, look at what she has done since. She tried to kill her first son and now, after she tortured her second child, he has disappeared. At what stage do we as a society ask ourselves, why do we let people like Freya Heywood, with Freya Heywood's track record, raise this country's most vulnerable? It's absurd. And some Neanderthals still believe she might be innocent. Despite the tooth, the pliers, the blood beside Billy's bed?

Blood beside his bed, this is news to me.

And now a blood-stained pyjama top has been recovered from her fire bunker. We need to find this woman and get her behind bars as quickly as possible.

I turn to Corazzo.

'I'm sorry,' I say.

'You said you never saw a body; you said it was Adam alone.' He turns away, squeezes his eyes closed as if in pain. 'Looks like that was a lie. What else did you lie about?'

'You don't understand.'

'You can say that again.'

Once more, we urge anyone who has any information regarding the whereabouts of Billy Heywood or Freya Heywood to contact Victoria Police.

The only way the media got those photos was from Adrienne – or, if not her, someone close to her. The truth is back at Eucalyptus Acres. I've got to go back.

Corazzo is watching me through narrowed eyes. 'What are you thinking?'

I'm thinking the entire Australian public has turned against me. I'm thinking if this has made international news even my brother would know about it. I'm thinking I'm going to get the truth out of my mother even if I have to squeeze it from her throat. 'I've got to go to Adrienne's,' I say.

He's silent for a moment. Then: 'Not now,' he says. 'Wait till tonight. And take my car.'

He's right but I don't think I can wait much longer. Every second away from Billy, wondering what he is going through, wondering if he is alive, is agony. Almost forty-eight hours have ticked by and my son is still missing.

Fifty-five hours missing

We plan the route, the timing, everything. Corazzo takes the car out to fill it with petrol for me before I leave. While I wait, I study the printed map of my route. The idea is to avoid toll roads and any high traffic areas.

I have spent the whole day watching the news for updates, checking stories online with anxiety flipping my gut. But there have been no further developments. Every time I see those old photos of me – dunking Asha, burying her – I am overcome with anger. The situation is now irreversible. I'll never escape, I'll never have a normal life. Someone will pay for this.

The car, a thirteen-year-old Holden Commodore, handles well. It's probably the exact model Corazzo had when he was a cop. Probably the exact car, now that I think about it. I cruise along the straights, staying under the speed limit, wearing Corazzo's wraparound glasses with the driver's seat back. I guess I look a little suspicious, but that's okay so long as I don't look like Freya Heywood.

I've been in the same clothes for twenty-four hours but there's no chance of me going near my house to get changed. It will be crawling with cops. The caravan of reporters has likely moved on to the next story but the searchers would still be scouring the bush, combing the undergrowth with eyes down, insect repellent and drink bottles at hand.

The car warns me with a beep whenever I drift over a hundred. I smile at that; Corazzo will never stop being a cop. When we hit a gravel back road, the Commodore digs in, leaning into corners as the wheels slide a little. The gravel rattles against the bottom of the car.

As the farmland gives way to trees and the roads wind through the thick bush, a news bulletin runs. A factory fire is burning in the west. A package of heroin with a street value of four million dollars was found in the possession of someone passing through customs at Tullamarine Airport. And one last item.

> *Henrik Masters, who served a nineteen year prison sentence for his role in the kidnap and murder of Sara McFetridge, was found dead this evening near the location of the abduction. Masters had left his flat in breach of parole conditions yesterday afternoon, Police are not deeming the death suspicious at this stage.*

My heart beats his name.
Ad-am. Ad-am. Ad-am.
Adam is dead.

Fifty-eight hours missing

I'm still reeling when I see the sign for Eucalyptus Acres. My heart is thumping. My hands are damp on the wheel. I drive a little further along and pull off the road, sitting there as the sweat cools on my spine. Adam, Henrik, who spent twenty-one years in jail, is dead. I think about what he did for Adrienne, what he gave to the cult. *Suicide?* Unlikely. My mind is whirring. I think about Adrienne's travel records. They could never pin anything on her because, according to her paperwork, she was always out of the country. She was overseas when Asha was kidnapped. Except she wasn't. Adrienne's influence extended beyond the Clearing – police, academia, and even immigration.

I think about what Adrienne made me do at the Clearing. Everything she did to protect herself. *Maybe she hasn't changed at all.*

The car is on the shoulder of the road, out of sight of the entrance, when I open the car door. The air is unsettled, clouds obscure the stars. Dry grass crackles beneath my runners. The truth is here – I'm sure of it. Only Mum can help me find Billy before the net closes.

I lock Corazzo's car and walk, hugging the tree line, down towards the entrance. I can approach the unit through the bush without having to enter the village at all. When I draw near, I see a light burning. *She's awake.* I creep closer, close enough to see through her window.

She's sitting on the couch again, her head tilted back. I watch her. Even if she were to wake it's unlikely she would see me here.

Adrienne took the photos that appeared on television; they were her insurance plan for if I turned my back on her. All these years she has kept those photos safe, but perhaps in her old age she's become careless. Perhaps someone else found them. Or, of course, there's the other possibility: that she has been pulling the strings all along. That she is much more lucid than she would have me believe.

I've made it this far – now I need to get inside to find what I am searching for. Some evidence that Adrienne is involved, or someone else close to her is. Something that might lead me to Billy.

I step closer to the window. Her eyes snap open. Can she see me? Her mouth is moving. But no, she has turned her head. She is speaking to someone inside with her. Who?

At that moment he walks into view. The familiar shape, the lumbering gait, thick brow, scraggly hair. He hasn't changed much since he was sixteen. He still loves his mother. He walks to the external door, opens it and steps into the night. *Jonas.*

PART SIX
PROTECT THE QUEEN

AMY

'YES, MOTHER?' I say, entering the room at the back of the Great Hall.

Adrienne is sitting at the teacher's desk with my journal open in front of her. 'Bring a seat over.'

It's late. The last of the day's light streams through the high windows and Adrienne's brow is creased, her lips bunched, her eyes crinkled. She usually wears an open and loving smile, but not now. Sweat prickles my skin.

I pull a chair from the stack in the corner and set it near her. My heart is racing. Adrienne wanted me to write this journal, she wanted me to write it as though it were a secret, as though I was keeping it even from her.

Tension has been high, and the children have been spending more and more time in the Hole. We've gone days without food. Anton says the Blue Devils are close, that they are conspiring to get Adrienne, and someone within Blackmarsh has been sharing our secrets with them.

Adrienne plants her elbows on the desk, links her fingers, and rests her chin on her knuckles.

'It's good,' she says of the latest draft of the journal.

Jonathan had helped me to rewrite it, to make sure it was 'convincing'. Adam is mentioned much more frequently now. No matter who among the adults had hurt us, who hurt me, I only referred to Adam. That's what Adrienne wanted. *The world outside will need someone to blame. They need a villain.* And Adam was the most loyal, the one that outsiders knew as Adrienne's right hand man, the one who had severed all ties to the outside world, the one who could be sacrificed.

'I think it's almost ready,' she said now. 'I need you to write it all once more, but we will have to make one or two more changes.'

When it is ready I am going out into the world. Part of me doesn't want it to be ready, part of me never wants to leave, but it needs to happen before the Blue Devils swoop down. Adrienne has a plan, she always has a plan. 'Yes, Mother.'

'Your brother Anton is eighteen, he is an adult in the eyes of the world outside. So we need to protect him. When you go out into the world, always stick to what I've told you. They're going to ask you questions, they are going to try to trick you, but if you repeat the story often enough it will become true and we can all stay together on the outside. Do you understand? You must never talk about how Anton hurt the children.'

'Yes, Mother.'

'Everyone has their role to play.' She pins me with her blue gaze. 'This journal will tell them everything they need to know, and you will barely have to speak at all.'

'What would you like me to change?' I ask, eyeing the journal on the desk.

'It's good that you've removed your brother and me from the realignments. But now I want you to write it so that Adam is the one who kills Asha.'

'Adam?' I say. I'm thinking of how Adam adores Adrienne, how he tried his best to fix Jermaine Boethe's fingers and tried for so long to bring Asha back to life. Breathing oxygen into her lungs, pumping her heart, cutting her open, shocking her. Adam, who is softly spoken, quiet as a mouse. Adam, who had given up everything to be here.

'Yes,' Adrienne says. She wears an open, kind expression once more, has that beatific look in her eye. 'It has to be Adam.'

FREYA

Fifty-eight hours missing

JONAS. ANTON. MY brother. *You're supposed to be overseas.* I feel winded. He never stopped believing. Even when he moved up to that farm in the country, even when he stopped visiting her so often. He was still always doing her bidding and now it's clear to me that he knows what happened to Billy. He has been lying to me. He wanted me to believe he was away overseas but he was here all along. No doubt his travel records will confirm his story, proving that he was not in the country, just as Adrienne had appeared to be overseas when she was really at the Clearing all along.

A woman with dementia and a man on another continent – no wonder the police never considered them as suspects. No wonder they focused on me, Henrik and Wayne. Oh God, Wayne. I was distracted by him, I put him in the sights of the police. He was here looking for Aspen and I made him a suspect of Billy's disappearance.

I'm stepping back slowly, away from the house. Jonas is out here somewhere. I can't let him see me. I rush up through the trees towards the road.

Henrik was found dead. Could Jonas be involved with that too?

I'm running now. Leaves and twigs catch in my hair. I need my phone; the lack of it is a painful, physical sensation, as if I'm missing a limb. I will have to drive somewhere or wave someone down. I could call the police, or Corazzo and tell them everything.

I reach the road and see the car still parked up at the shoulder. I'm almost there. I sprint the last stretch, chest heaving from the exertion, and slam the key in the lock. I yank the door open and get in. My hands are shaking so much I can barely get the key into the ignition, but at last I manage it. I turn the key.

Nothing.

I turn it again.

Still nothing. No lights, no sound, no roar of the engine.

There's a tap on the window. I turn.

I see his eyes first. Sunken, dark. Then his long thick hair, his crooked smile. He motions with his finger for me to lower the window. I'm trapped. There is nothing I can do now. He motions with his finger again. I steady my breath, then wind the window down.

I paste on a smile, look up into his eyes. 'Jonas, you're . . . you're back.'

'Sister,' he says. 'We weren't expecting you. You're leaving already?'

'It's late,' I say. I understand how ridiculous this pantomime is, but what else can I say? 'My car won't start though.' *Because you did something to it.*

He tilts his head to one side. '*Your* car? It looks a lot like a cop car to me.'

I swallow. 'I borrowed it from a friend.'

'A friend,' he says impassively. He opens my door. 'You'd better come say hi to Mum, since you're here – she's still awake.'

I watch his face in the darkness, my heart slamming against my ribcage. I need my phone, or a weapon. I need something. I know what he is capable of.

'I thought you were away,' I say casually.

'I just got back. Heard the news and booked the next flight out. Don't worry, Billy will turn up.'

'What's happening up at your farm? Is someone looking after it?'

'I've got people helping.'

He walks behind me, down the road leading into the retirement village, giant eucalypts lining our path. There are no lights other than the security lights around the reception area. Just me and Jonas. When Adrienne dies will the spell be broken? The idea was to collect the twelve for her, surely he knows that Blackmarsh is running out of time. She won't live forever.

'This way,' he says, pointing down a path that skirts the perimeter of the village. I'm unlikely to be seen by anyone from the other units here, I realise.

'How was your holiday?' I ask, my voice tight.

'It was nice.'

He's almost translucent in the moonlight, no colour, no tan. He looks like he's been inside for the past month.

'But that's not important at the moment. We need to find that boy of yours, don't we?'

He is walking beside me now, a great presence, hands like slabs and that thick neck. He moves in front to open the side gate of Adrienne's unit. I walk through and climb up the back steps. It's darker in the moon shadow of the house. Through the window I see Adrienne sitting on the couch, a corona of white hair floating about her skull.

'She's never lost control, Amy. Not once. You've been in her web your entire life and you didn't know it. The more you struggled to free yourself, the more you turned your back on her, the tighter the binds became.'

'Did you take him?'

Jonas sighs, then slides the door open. 'Come on, get inside.'

'Hello?' Adrienne says, turning towards the door.

'Mum, it's Amy.' Jonas's voice is light and buoyant, as if he's speaking to a child.

'Amy?' she says. 'Oh my.' She looks up into my face. 'You're back.'

'Grab a seat,' he says to me, gesturing towards the small table. I sit down. Jonas puts the kettle on.

'I'm actually okay for tea,' I say, my eyes casting about for a weapon. Something solid. Something that could break a bone.

'Water? Juice?'

'No, thanks. I'm fine.'

'Fair enough,' he says. 'We need to be focusing on Billy. I think the Clearing is the first place to look. You know what the fanatics are like, Amy. They're not the real Blackmarshers; they don't know what you sacrificed.'

'No they don't,' Adrienne agrees. 'You sacrificed a lot for me, didn't you?'

I ignore her. It's clear to me that Jonas's the threat. I wonder what kind of game he's playing.

'What do you say, sister? Should we head out to the Clearing and take a look?'

'Sure,' I say.

'After our tea.'

I see him setting two cups down. He takes the kettle off the burner. I know it would be suicide to drink anything he prepares for me. *What are you planning, Jonas?*

He carries the cups through and sits across from me at the table. He sips his tea and gestures for me to do the same. I know now that he drugged me with the kombucha. I'm not stupid enough to fall for it again. I take the cup and raise it to my mouth. He's watching me closely. I let the liquid touch my lip. It's hot. Perfect.

In one swift motion I stand and hurl the scalding liquid into his face.

Then I run. If he's here, if they have him, I will find him. I sprint up the hall. 'Billy!' I scream. 'Billy!'

I fling open the first door to reveal a bedroom, Adrienne's. There's no sign of Billy.

'You bitch!' Jonas screams behind me. 'You don't know what you are doing. You have no idea!'

I rush to the next room and throw the door open.

'Billy?' I call. I find the light switch. The room is empty but for a few boxes.

Where is he?

Footsteps, then something hits me hard in the throat. It tightens and tightens. I throw all my weight backwards. We hit the wall. My eyes bulge.

'He is part of her plan, Amy,' he says, his voice breathy in my ear. 'Billy belongs to a higher cause now.'

He is choking the air from me. I think back to my self-defence training. Twisting and turning, I fight to break the chokehold, but he is too big, too strong. I get my jaw into the kink of his elbow and pull at his hand, releasing his hold just enough to allow me to take a quick breath.

I feel something press against my face. A hand gripping me. Cotton rubbing against my nose and mouth. I know the smell. *Don't breathe.* I hold my breath, but make my chest rise and fall.

I make the movement slow, let my eyelids droop. I slump in his arms. He keeps the cloth there for a minute at least. I imagine myself underwater, floating in the river, blocking out the world. I know I can make it to ninety seconds before coming up for air. We must almost be there now as my brain is starting to ache and my limbs are tingling. I close my eyes and make my body go completely limp, completely still. It's the trick Asha tried to pull when she was dunked in the Cooler. This time it works.

He takes the cloth away, loosens his grip on my throat. I fall heavily against him as if unconscious.

He hauls me up over his shoulder effortlessly. Then he speaks.

'Go sit down, Mum. I'll take care of this mess.'

'What happened?' Adrienne says. 'Put her down! Where are you taking her?'

'We're going for a little drive, Mum. I won't be long. It's for the best.'

Fifty-nine hours missing

There's a fierce throbbing in my head and my throat is still sore but I'm awake. That's the one advantage I have: he thinks I am unconscious. He carries me outside. A car boot opens, and I tumble into it. He folds my legs before thumping the boot closed. The air is thick in here, and there is almost no room to move. I'm trapped now, I realise. He could leave me in here until I starve to death, or he could drive the car into a lake. I might not be found for years – if at all. I dimly hear the sound of a car door opening and closing, and then the purr of the engine. *Think, Freya.* He's too big, too strong for me to have a chance in a fair fight. I've got to catch him off guard. I feel around the boot, finding the flap of carpet covering the tyre-changing kit.

It's close and dark in the small space, and it feels a little like I'm trying to breathe underwater. *Stay calm, Freya.* The car bounces along the gravel track, and then we are turning, accelerating away on smooth bitumen. I can hear a faint murmuring now. Is Jonas talking to himself? Maybe he really has lost it.

'. . . so we're just going to have to cross our fingers and hope she's not found any time soon. I've got the note with me; I'll put it in her pocket. What's that?'

There's a pause. He's on the phone, I realise, but who is he talking to? Is it a Blackmarsher?

'The moment it's ruled a suicide we're in the clear,' he continues. 'They'll assume she's got rid of the body. All the other pieces are in place: the phone records, the pyjama top, the tooth.'

I can feel rage boiling inside. He's planned it all. My own brother is planning to murder me and make it look like suicide.

'There won't be any marks on the body and you can help clean the boot when you get here. I'll make sure she's somewhere she could have climbed to herself.'

They're going to hang me from a tree. Billy will believe that I gave up, I left him behind. I think about Jonas's farm up north. Is that where my son is now?

'It's perfect – they'll think she killed Billy herself and then concocted this whole kidnapping story. Then, racked with guilt, knowing the police are closing in, she drives out to where it all started. And you're certain the rain will wash away our tracks down there?'

The call ends. So this is it. Jonas has Billy. They have my son. He's in the clutches of Blackmarsh and will never escape. *You never escape a cult.* I was naive enough to think I could walk away but Adrienne always had me, a fly in a web. Now that the photos are out in the world, Adrienne and Blackmarsh have nothing over me so they're disposing of me altogether. I feel no fear for myself, nothing but an implosion of sadness for my son. My brain whirls through the possibilities, the corridors and alleyways and they all lead to one inevitable truth: Billy will live the life I lived. Brainwashed into believing that Adrienne is divine and Blackmarshers will be the guardians of the planet when the new age dawns. But eventually

Adrienne will die, and then what? Jonas will proclaim himself the reincarnation? Someone else will rise to the top?

The car stops. A door opens. The creak of hinges as a gate swings. And then the car begins to move again. I'm thrown forwards as the wheels hit ruts in the track. Long grass swishes against the underside of the car and branches and leaves screech against the duco. My body senses it before my mind; the scar on my hip throbs, and I feel a phantom pain in the toe Jonas hacked off with pruning shears to punish me for taking extra food. I know it without any doubt; we are in the Clearing.

When the car stops I reach into the hollow of the spare tyre and grasp the solid shape of a wrench. I breathe slowly and deeply, steadying my heart.

The engine dies. A door thunks open and closed. I let my head fall back, my neck bent like a flower stalk. The wrench is concealed beneath me. I hear footsteps rounding the side of the car. There is a light patter of rain. *Finally, rain.* The boot opens. Brightness presses briefly against my eyelids, then it's gone.

'Wake up, Amy. You're home.' Jonas touches my shoulder, turning me towards him.

I open my eyes, roll and swing my arm. The wrench connects with something too soft to be a skull. An arm?

I quickly haul myself from the boot. Jonas has been momentarily knocked off balance, but he quickly steadies himself again.

'Amy,' he says. 'You hit me.' There's laughter in his voice.

'Why, Jonas?' I say. 'Why did you take him? Why now?'

I can hear his breath becoming short. The sky is moonless; I can only just make out his dark shape. My fist trembles with adrenaline as I grip the wrench.

'We gave you every chance to return,' he replies. 'Every chance to prove yourself loyal. We chose you to be the one to save us when they conspired against us.' He steps closer. 'You were supposed to lead us. Instead you turned your back while I've been busy rebuilding what they took from us. You called her deluded, a fraud. We must complete the twelve before it's too late.'

'She *is* deluded, Jonas. She's demented. There is no end of the world, she's not going to save us. The twelve was always just a way for her to surround herself with children.'

He steps closer still. Before he can say another word I swing the wrench. He dodges it. This is a man not merely acquainted with violence; this is a man who grew up in violence, who *became* violence.

I rush forwards, swinging again. The wrench connects this time, smashing into his forearm with a thud. He roars in pain, grabbing at his arm, then lowers his head and rushes at me like a bull. His left arm hangs limp but his shoulder hits me below the ribs. We tumble together to the hard earth.

'This only ends one way,' he says, his mouth close to my ear.

I raise my knee and feel the breath leave him. I swing the wrench at the back of his head. I swing it again, feel the reverberation in my palm. I try to wriggle out from beneath his weight, but he pins me down with his forearm across my throat. With his good hand he grabs my wrist and holds it at my side, the wrench still in my grip.

I try to breathe, but no air comes, just gurgling. I squeeze my jaw beneath his forearm, open my mouth and bite. I taste blood.

He releases my wrist and brings his hand up to my throat, choking me. I swing at him as hard as I can. The wrench strikes again and again. There is little force behind the blows now, but I can feel his limbs softening, his fingers loosening around my throat. He's dazed.

Twisting, I squirm from beneath him and rise to my knees. My breath is loud and rough in the still night. I could run, take the car and escape. *You never escape a cult.* They will always come for me. I turn back to him.

He moves as if to stand but before he can I bring the wrench down on his skull. This time the blow is wet, meaty. He falls face first, hitting the earth as heavy as a stone.

Each breath I take rocks my entire body. I let the wrench slip from my hand. The rain is coming down steadily now. I stare at the slumped form hesitantly, half of me fearing he might suddenly fly up and grab me. But even in the dark I can see the blood. I know he won't be waking any time soon.

I heave him over and find his eyes are closed. His chest rises and falls, but blood is darkening the pale grass beneath his head.

He had a light, I recall. I search his pockets for a torch but find nothing except a piece of paper. *The note.* He must have dropped the light near the car. Dropping to my hands and knees, I search around the boot until my hand touches something small and rectangular. My pulse pounds at my temples. It's a phone.

Clutching it in my hand, breathing heavily, I turn the phone's torch on and take a moment to look about the Clearing. It's the same and yet so different. The place is overgrown, wild. The Great Tree is still there, the leaves shimmering in the breeze. I can see the outline of the Great Hall in the distance, all boarded up now and collapsing in parts. Reclaimed by the wild.

The rain becomes heavier. It dampens me, cools me, clears my head.

I use Jonas's phone to dial triple zero.

Billy must be up on Jonas's farm, I surmise. It's hours away from here, so I need to get moving. I feel the cord between us pulling taut. I need to see him, to know he is okay.

'What's your emergency?'

'Police,' I say. 'Someone tried to kill me. I'm at the Clearing. The end of Blackmarsh Road.'

I wait with her on the phone until she tells me that police are on their way. Then I climb into Jonas's car and find the keys in the ignition.

AMY

FOR THE FIRST time I'm allowed in the minders' quarters. I feel guilty. I fear that Adrienne might snap at any moment, and hurt me.

She leads me in by the hand and gently guides me onto a couch, then takes a seat beside me.

Through the window I can see the Burrow, the Great Hall, the Great Tree, our vegetable garden and the chicken coop beside it. I can see the whole of the Clearing spread out before me and it really is beautiful. It is our own Eden. I'm going to miss it, I just hope I can return soon.

'Amy,' Adrienne says, 'you have to go tonight. The Blue Devils are planning to swoop in the next few days to take you all away. You know the plan; you know where you must walk to in the night.'

'Yes, Mother.'

'I have something to show you before you go.'

Her blue eyes turn from me to the envelope beside her on the couch. She touches it lightly, seeming uncertain for a moment. Then she picks it up and removes three brown strips. She holds them up to the light, peering at them. Then she slips them back into the envelope.

'I want you to remember this moment for the rest of your life, Amy,' she says. 'You are going out into the world. You will wear a mask for the rest of your life to hide who you really are. No one will love or accept you like me, because they hate us, they don't want us to succeed. You will look and act like them but, in truth, you will never walk away from us. Do you understand?'

'Yes, Mother,' I say, though I'm not sure that I do understand.

'Now remember this.' From the envelope she pulls a small stack of photographs. One at a time, she holds them up in front of me, giving me enough time to study them.

I turn my face away.

'Look at them,' she says, her voice a slap.

I turn back, but I can't focus on them; I can't relive that day without remembering Asha, remembering how sick with excitement I was when she arrived, how quickly we snuffed her out.

'No one other than you and I will ever see what you did to Asha. Because if they should see this out there, they would lock you up and throw away the key. They would always know what you are.' She places the photos back in the envelope.

My heart is racing now.

'I'm leaving today, a few hours before you, and I am taking these photos with me. I will keep them safe, but if you should ever disobey me, the world will see that you murdered little Asha.' She takes my hands in hers and warmth rushes through my body. I feel like I am home, that this is the last time I will ever be home.

I would never disobey my mother. I can't imagine doing such a thing. I would never do anything to disappoint her.

'Mother, I will never disobey you,' I say. 'I promise.'

'Good girl. Protect the Queen.'

I say it back.

'Now go on, get yourself ready. Brush your hair and your teeth. Make yourself beautiful for the world out there. Be brave, my child, as you step into the darkness. But know that blind bravery comes from ignorance of the real threat. If you are true to me, you will always be safe, but waiver and you will find what the real threat is. So now go out there, fit in, wear the mask, do what you need to, but think of me every day, find my voice in your head and I will guide you, I will give you the strength to keep going. We will be back together soon.'

FREYA

Sixty hours missing

THE CAR STARTS. The rain is falling harder now, like bullets in the headlights. It rattles on the roof. Through the windscreen I see the shape of the Great Hall against the dark sky. For some reason I always thought they would have knocked it down. Burnt it like a funeral pyre to exorcise the demons contained within. Those walls have seen horrors. Even Adrienne seemed to forget the Clearing and left it behind. This place where I grew up was nothing in the end. Just a space to occupy like any other. Why then does it feel so heavy, like I'm sitting in a car at the bottom of the sea? I squint through the rain, leaning over the wheel. Listening to the *zomb-zomb* of the windscreen wipers. The door to the Great Hall is open. *Could Billy be inside?* I wonder suddenly. *Tied to a chair in the kitchen where we used to eat?* I need to leave, to get as far from Jonas and the Clearing as possible before the police arrive, but what if my son is here, scared for his life? *What if,* two little words that have me snared.

I drive the car forwards, flattening the long grass before me, and pull up in front of the Great Hall, the headlights shining in through the open door. I can see only the grey of the faded wood panels. I kill the engine and open the car door.

It's dark and damp inside the Great Hall, like walking into an eye socket. I peer into the corners then remember Jonas's phone in my pocket. With the torch there is just enough light to see a few feet into the room. There's mould and mildew. Rain streams in where a section of the roof has collapsed. The floor is rotting in places and I step tentatively, testing the boards before putting my full weight on them. I move deeper into the building. It's so much smaller than I remember. I'd thought of it as an enormous building, grand, but now I can see it's just an ordinary hall, plain and functional. I reach the room that was once our classroom. My skin is tingling.

When I shine the light into the corner I think I see something move and my heart leaps, only to find it was nothing but the shifting shadows of the desks and chairs still stacked there after all these years. The blackboard is in its usual place down one end of the room and the windows are unbroken, though battered now by the growing gusts of wind.

The rain continues to drill down. I hear it trickling through the seams of the building. Dripping down onto the wooden boards. When I try to get to the kitchen I find I can't; the floor has rotted through. By the weak light of the phone's torch I make out the shape of the bench, the sink, the old pot-belly stove.

This was my childhood. People think I was born into it, that I simply had bad luck, but they don't think about their own luck. They don't realise that everything is chance. The trajectories of their normal happy lives are solely determined by chance. They only seem to remember when they compare themselves to someone like me.

The phone starts to vibrate in my hand and I am so startled that I drop it. The room goes dark.

The phone continues to vibrate. I bend over and pick it up, stare at the number on the screen. I press accept and hold it to my ear.

'Anton?' a man's voice says; calm, quiet. Anton, not Jonas. The voice must belong to someone who knows our past. I can hear the hum of a motor; the caller is in a car.

I don't speak. The pause drags out. The man on the other end of the line sighs and ends the call.

Whose voice was it? I can't be sure, but I know that I need to leave, and soon.

I shine the light about the room, scanning one last time for any sign of Billy. I call his name gently into the darkness, as if to summon him like a ghost. But he's not here.

I step out into the rain and walk down the stairs at the front of the building, the wood soft and slippery under foot.

A second later I see the flash of headlights through the bush. I duck down behind the car, holding my breath as a four-wheel drive emerges from the track and crawls across the grass, coming to a stop nearby. A door opens, boots hit the ground. 'Anton?'

More footsteps. I raise my head just far enough to see through the windows of the car. I can make out the silhouette of a man. He's looking up at the Great Tree.

'Anton, where did you put her?'

My eyes follow the shape as he steps closer to the tree, then I turn back to his vehicle, squinting at it through the rain and the dark. I feel a physical shock, a gut punch that almost folds me in half. My eyes have come to rest on something familiar. Something I have seen every day for years ... A broken badge with the word *Disco*.

'Anton?' The voice is less certain now but I recognise it, though it doesn't make any sense.

Corazzo.

Two months earlier

'HE'S COMING OUT,' I say. 'On the twenty-ninth of February.'

Corazzo picks up his coffee cup, sips. His eyes are fixed on something outside the cafe. 'Henrik Masters?'

'Yeah.'

'I saw,' he says. 'You worried about him?'

'A little, I guess.'

He turns his gaze back to me, a smile playing at his lips.

'What? You think that's wrong?'

His dark eyes bore into mine. 'I think you've got nothing to worry about either way.' His voice is warm, reassuring. 'He's probably no longer involved with Blackmarshers. People change in prison.'

I shrug. I don't care about Blackmarsh anymore. I want nothing to do with my old family.

'I don't know. Maybe you're right. He's still got reason to hate me though.' I think about the journal, how it was manipulated.

'Is he still in contact with your mum?' he asks.

'How would I know?'

'Well, you are still visiting her if I recall correctly. Maybe . . .' He pauses, flaps his hand as though waving the idea away.

'We don't talk about that. She's not herself anymore anyway.'

'What do you mean?'

'She's lost it.'

He raises his eyebrows at this. 'You certain?'

'Yeah. She barely recognised me last time.'

'So what are you going to do now? Will you keep visiting her?'

'I don't want to but I don't want to piss Jonas off, and I kind of have to. But I'm not taking Billy out there again. I don't want Billy near her at all.'

'That's good to hear,' he says. His gaze shifts away from me, back to the street outside the cafe window. He takes another sip of his coffee.

'I still feel like such an idiot,' I say. 'I believed in the twelve and the new age for years after I left. Then even when I knew it was bullshit, I couldn't walk away. She always held a power over me.'

Corazzo has a complex expression. He watches me closely. 'You don't believe in all that anymore?'

'God no. Olivia says it's conditioning. She says I have been wearing a mask my entire life, I've always felt different, I've always felt like I'm full of violence and it's only a matter of time before it comes out. She says most people never escape a cult even when they leave it.'

'A cult,' he says to himself. 'So you'd never go back?'

'No,' I say, smiling. 'I can finally, honestly say Billy is much more important to me than Adrienne. This might sound callous, but when she dies I'll feel entirely free for the first time in my life.'

'So that's it, you're done with her?'

'I am,' I say.

There's a moment, a pause, before he smiles.

'I thought you would be happier,' I remark.

'Oh, I am happy. I'd be careful though. The fanatics might still be out there. I wouldn't go broadcasting the fact you're no longer loyal to her; you never know who might be listening.'

FREYA

Sixty-one hours missing

'ANTON?' CORAZZO SAYS again.

I risk another look. He's squatting down now by Jonas's inert body.

'Shit,' he says.

I stay dead still, concealed behind Jonas's car, trying to form a plan. If I could make it to the driver's door, I could take off. But what if he tries to stop me? Corazzo is old, I remind myself, with a heart condition; maybe I could fight him off. On the other hand, he's still so much bigger than me, still so strong. *Think, you idiot,* I scold myself.

The rain has eased to a light drizzle, but the wind is still gusting, pulling through the bush.

I feel something against my hip, a vibration. It's loud in the still night. I stare at it in horror, recognising the number that had called earlier, knowing now that it's Corazzo, and that he's looking for me. I stab at the screen, trying to stop it, but by the time I do he's there, looming above me.

I stand up, staring at him, speechless.

'Amy,' he says. My old name. I hold the phone out towards him to see him better.

He is holding something in his hand. It glints in the meagre light from the phone screen.

A blade.

Laughter bursts from him. 'You're not the only one who wears a mask, *Freya*. This is what we do for her, this is how we pass in the world.'

The police can't be too far away now, but he's drifting closer to me. I step back. 'No,' I say. Tears, *real* tears, fill my eyes. 'Not you.'

His expression softens. 'Don't make this difficult, Amy. You've already nearly killed your brother. You've done enough damage.'

'Where is Billy?'

'He's safe. Don't worry. We will take care of him.'

'When did they get you, Corazzo?' I try to keep my voice even, but I hear it crack. 'What did she offer you?'

He ducks his head a little as if to see me better. 'She never got to me. I was always with her. I was with her when you were a baby. She knew you wouldn't be able to control yourself on the outside, so I stayed close.'

His face is expressionless. I steal a glance at the blade in his hand.

He's the one who convinced me not to trust the police, that he was the only one who could protect me, the only one who was really on my side. He probably concealed evidence, pursued Adam but not Adrienne, manipulated me at the hospital. When the police were closing in on the Clearing he tipped Adrienne off. He was there at the house by the river when I fled with my journal. He was part of the plan all along.

I step back, drawing a deep breath, filling my cells with oxygen. Then I turn and run.

He moves quickly for an old man, but I'm faster. My sneakers slide in the mud as I round the Great Tree, instinctively heading for the gate. After years of neglect, the gate and the fence have been swallowed up by blackberry bush. I sprint. The night air shrinks my lungs. I can hear him close behind, but I don't risk looking back. I'd been shot that night at the house, all those years ago. Shot but not killed. Was that a mistake? Was I supposed to die that night, leaving my journal to exonerate Adrienne? Instead I survived.

I hurl myself up and over the fence. The thorns of the blackberry bush shred my palms but I don't slow down. I am wired with adrenaline.

I hear him hit the ground behind me a moment later.

The track through the bush is so overgrown I don't recognise it, but sometimes your body remembers what your brain forgets. My heart pounds and my lungs burn as I weave through the bush along the overgrown path. I can hear him close behind, hunting me.

I put on a burst of speed. Blackberries catch my hair, tearing it. The sky cracks open and I can hear the rain again before I feel it, spitting at first, dripping through the canopy. Blood pounds at my temples, in my chest, and sweat starts on my back.

I keep going, ignoring the searing pain I feel in my throat with each intake of breath. He is close now, so close. I feel his fist snatch my hair and I drive an elbow back in the darkness, hitting something solid. His grip loosens.

'There's no escape, Amy,' he calls. *Amy* – hearing that name coming from his lips hits me in the guts.

The bush is so thick here; curls of ferns, a fallen tree rotting on its side. I leap over it. I hear him coming down, the swish of ferns moving, the crack of twigs snapping. I move again, lightly picking my way through the undergrowth, shifting between trees. I need to get to the river.

'I know this bush as well as you,' he says. 'You think you're safe out here but she is with me, she is guiding me.' His voice booms over the storm. 'I led the search for Asha, knowing all the while we would never find her. Making sure we never found her. I scoured this bush with the rest of them, Amy. You can't escape.'

I keep moving, picking my way in near silence. Then I slip. I slide down a slope, grabbing at roots and shrubs. A bone-shattering crunch. My ankle. I bite my palm to keep from screaming. I try to stand but the ankle won't take my weight. I'm trapped. Desperate to keep going, I start to hop. Then I hear it. Just a whisper at first. *The river.* It's near, summoning me. I hop faster, scrambling through the dense bush, using my hands to tear away the foliage. It's so close. But he's coming.

I emerge near a bend in the river, a place from which we once leapt into the water below. But the river is too low now to risk jumping. Down below it's all rocks and shallow pools.

My ankle is throbbing; I can't run. I'm trapped here. I can hear him coming, the bush crackling around him. I look around urgently for some kind of weapon, something that will give me an advantage. Spying a log close by, an idea forms. I heave the log up and hurl it off the cliff and into the river below. The splash is loud. I hobble back into the undergrowth and crouch beside a tree.

Focus. Control your breathing, Freya. Don't mess this up.

He rushes out of the bush, the blade in his hand. He's so large, squinting down at the river, searching for my body.

He turns back towards the bush, eyes searching the dark. He senses me. He knows I'm near.

He glances back down at the river. This is the moment. I don't hesitate. Despite the crushing pain in my ankle, I run.

I hurl myself at him, shoulder into his spine. He's surprised. He stumbles, twists, falls. A moment of flight, then the cartwheeling descent.

I watch. Not with sadness, exactly, but the feeling is similar. There's a sense of loss as the only person I ever truly trusted tumbles, falls and hits the water. The rain pounds. For a moment nothing happens, then Corazzo resurfaces, floating face down.

I remember playing in the river with Adam. I remember how happy I was, how much he cared for us children. I remember the look on his face in court, the hatred in his eyes.

I glance down once more at Corazzo before turning and starting back, limping towards the Clearing. I think of everything I did for my family as a child, and what I'll do now for Billy. It's not so different.

Three weeks returned

Olivia smiles when she sees me. I can smell the chamomile tea in the pot on the low wooden coffee table. The warm autumn sun streams in through the blinds.

'Freya,' she says. 'Take a seat.'

We have a lot to work through now. The yoga mums, the school parents and teachers, everyone knows who I really am. They've all seen the photos and read the stories. They all want to hear about Blackmarsh and that night in the Clearing from me, but I've taken time away. I've got to accept who I was, where I came from and who I am now.

I pick up my cup and sip.

'So, how have you been the last couple of days?'

I think for a moment about what has happened since our last session a few days ago. Billy had another check-up yesterday at the hospital. He's been home for a week now.

'I spoke with Aspen last night,' I say. 'I've got a lot of making up to do after almost killing him for the second time.' I try to laugh but only issue a sad deflating sound. 'Wayne's happy for me to have some contact with him too.' He's almost an adult now, after all. We've agreed to let bygones be bygones; we've both changed a lot since then. The hot car was an accident, a momentary lapse. No one taught me how to be a good mother, but luckily I get a second chance.

'That's good to hear. And how do you feel about that?'

'It's the silver lining of this whole messed-up situation. It feels nice and vindicating to be back in Aspen's life after all this time.'

'That's right,' she says, her warm eyes on me. 'It *is* a messed-up situation. Something you couldn't control. Can you see how you're also a victim in all of this?'

I was fifteen when I hurt Asha, when I held her under water until the life drained from her. The pictures are still there for anyone to see. My eyes wide and manic, the trace of a smile on my lips. What's not visible is how, just out of the frame of the photo, Anton was urging me on. I often think about that day. Anton, Adrienne and the minders gathered around, forcing me to punish her. It was my fault she had run away, they said. I was responsible for her, and that meant it was my responsibility to administer the realignment. They said the Devil had her and only I could make him leave. But I held her under too long. I still remember the feeling of the child's life evaporating through my fingers as her body became limp. How can I be a victim?

'No. I hurt Asha. I brought this on myself.'

She considers this for a moment. 'Did you have a choice, Freya? Did you *choose* to hurt Asha? I don't think you did. I don't think anyone in your position would have acted differently.'

Adam tried and tried to revive her. He slammed her chest with his hands and blew air into her lungs. He cut her open, taking pressure off the brain. He electrocuted her. He did everything he could think of to bring her back. It was hours before he gave up, and let his head fall into his hands defeated.

Twenty years later he would be found hanging near the spot we took her from with a note in his pocket.

'I don't know. I guess that's for the legal system to decide.'

My lawyer is convinced nothing will come of the images showing what I did to Asha, but we are ready. Jonas is awaiting his own trial. He didn't get bail and it looks like a reasonably clear-cut case. When they raided his farm, they found an exact replica of the Clearing had been constructed, with half-a-dozen adults living on site and half a dozen children. One of them was Billy. Another was the girl taken from New South Wales. The rest were made up of children from those adults living there. Jonas knew Adrienne didn't have many years left. He was hastily pulling together a new twelve.

•

After my session with Olivia, I go straight to Billy's school. It was his first day back and his return was greeted warmly. His ordeal had been all over the news. He's not quite up to a full day yet, so we've agreed I'll pick him up at lunchtime.

Olivia has me painting again. I've started my first piece in years and maybe this time I will be able to finish it without the black square obscuring the scene. I've captured the anguish in my face as I carry Asha's legs and the stiff jawed determination in Anton's face as he carries her arms. Olivia is also helping me to work through the fears I have as a mother, the need to protect Billy all the time. I'm not there yet, but eventually I hope to let him live a normal life without me watching over him day and night.

I see him walking towards the school gate, guided by a teacher. I climb out of the car.

'Hey, Billy,' I say, squatting down to pull him into a hug. I squeeze him tight for a few seconds then make myself let go. 'Come on.'

We follow the familiar route home. Billy is tired but seems happy to have returned to his regular routine. As we roll down the driveway, Rocky bounds towards us, barking. He's not used to the new car.

Inside, we change into our bathers and head down to the river with Rocky. There can't be many more hot days left. Soon the river will be too cold for swimming.

I hurl Rocky's ball out into the water and watch as he rushes in. Billy dips a foot in, his arms wrapped around his bony body.

'Go on,' I say. 'It'll be nice once you're in.'

I walk out without hesitation, diving under, floating there as my hair fans out.

When I surface I ask, 'Are you excited to meet your brother?' Aspen is coming to dinner tonight.

'Yeah,' Billy says.

'Me too.' The current pulls me along gently. The sky is clear and beautiful, and for the first time in weeks I feel no eyes on me. It's just us out here: me, my dog and my kid.

THE WATCHER

I SEE YOU. Even now, when you believe things are back to normal. When you believe the threat is gone.

Do you ever wonder why I never called or wrote? Do you ever wonder why I came so close without ever seeking to speak with you? It's simple. I wanted to watch you. I wanted to know what sort of woman you are. I wanted to see what Anton saw. He was right. You were treading water, pretending to be something you're not. He knew you had abandoned the cause. They say we never really change; we just learn to act differently. You killed Asha, and you would have killed me.

As I watched you, I saw the moments when you reverted to that girl they told me about, the girl you were at the Clearing. When your anger and frustration bubbled over and you hurt Billy. I wanted to help with the collection. I wanted to see you suffer. I took such delight in sending you those flowers and seeing the look on your face. It was my idea but Uncle Anton approved.

We've been in contact for years. Receiving the email from him was the most exciting moment of my life. At first I really thought it was you, but it turned out it was much better than that. Uncle Anton helped me to understand the truth about you, the truth about Grandma. I knew only they could keep Billy safe and raise him the right way. We need to prepare him for what we all know is coming. Uncle Anton introduced me to our cause and I am so grateful to him.

I see you, *Amy*. Now, as I walk down your driveway with my girlfriend, as I hand you the bottle of wine we brought. I see you. When I called, you sounded excited. Slowly, surely, I will work my way into your life. I will get to know Billy. You will trust me, your lost son, and then we will all disappear together.

ACKNOWLEDGMENTS

I WOULD LIKE to first acknowledge all those who were affected by The Family cult that was active and prominent from the sixties to the nineties. Although *In The Clearing* is fiction, the seed of the story was born out of my fascination with the cult, the resilience of the children survivors, and the enigmatic leader. For further reading, *The Family* by Rosie Jones and Chris Johnston is a great place to start.

Once again thanks to the best agent/therapist/life-coach in the world Pippa Masson. Also to those tireless agents working to get my novels out in other territories – thank you Dan Lazar, Gordon Wise, and Kate Cooper.

I am grateful to have Robert Watkins in my corner to help me see the bigger picture and for supporting my career. Thank you to Brigid Mullane who saved Wayne's life on multiple occasions (he didn't contract leprosy, or grow a hump, he wasn't stabbed, shot or drowned. He probably owes you a beer.) I extend my gratitude to the rest of the team at Hachette in Australia and in New Zealand for your ongoing support and belief in my work, especially those who did such an incredible job in getting *Evie* out into the world – Daniel Pilkington, Sean Cotcher, and my amazing publicists Lydia Tasker, Tessa Connolly and Tania McKenzie-Cooke.

I am also grateful to Marion Barton for providing deep insights into the psychology of cult members, and Sue Werry, Antoni Jach, Tiffany Plummer, Russ Hogan and Lynn Yeowart along with the various other Tiffaneers.

Thank you to my broader circle of friends and family, including my siblings and father, Bill, for whom those book is dedicated and my late mother who made me believe I could do anything. I would also like to mention my mother in-law, Jackie, who is one of my first readers and certainly my most encouraging.

And finally Paige Pomare, my wife. When I can't seem to make anything work and the story is falling apart, she's always there with gentle words, a cup of tea, and a needle and thread to put it back together.

Reading Group Guide

IN
THE
CLEARING

by

J. P. Pomare

MULHOLLAND BOOKS

A CONVERSATION WITH J. P. POMARE

What inspired you to write *In the Clearing*?

I became obsessed with Anne Hamilton-Byrne, the leader of The Family, a new age cult that was active in Australia from the sixties to the nineties. Hamilton-Byrne would likely be considered the most *successful* female cult leader — success in this case measured by level of influence, achievement of overall goals, and membership numbers. Most of the cult was made up of upper-middle-class white Australians; many former members described her as having a sort of charm that could attract newcomers from the academic and medical world. Hamilton-Byrne also escaped with a relatively small fine and time served. She went on to live to be ninety-seven years old, dying in 2019 in a retirement home. I had so many questions about the wealth she accumulated, what really happened to the children involved in the cult, and most importantly: *why?* This book allowed me to formulate my own ideas and conclusions.

Tell us more about your own background. Did you always want to be a writer?

I grew up on a horse-racing farm in a small rural town in New Zealand. By the time I came along, my parents' attention was divided among four children, so we were often left to entertain ourselves, which wasn't hard to do on a farm with motorbikes and air rifles. We never had many books in the house, and there wasn't a real focus on reading or academic achievement, so it wasn't until I was a teenager that I fell in love with writing. I was reading the Harry Potter books when I realized I had been making up stories in my head most of my life. I had been imagining new worlds, and from there a dream of writing my own books formed.

In the Clearing is your second novel. What was different about the writing process this time?

With *In the Clearing* my vision was clear from very early on, and I didn't share it with anyone until I was happy with the story, at which point it became a case of simply problem-solving a couple of plot holes and tightening everything up. This was completely different from my first novel, for which there were always a number of voices contributing to the process, with a range of different editors and agents involved. With my first novel I wanted to please everyone, but with *In the Clearing* I wrote for myself first.

What kind of research did you do?

The most important part of my research was interviewing a former member of another Australian cult, which I did while her psychologist was present. This helped me to form the basis for the character Freya. I also read a lot of books about cults, in particular *The Family* by Rosie Jones and Chris Johnston. To capture the sense of place, I visited locations where The Family was active.

Did anything surprise you while writing or researching this novel?

I was surprised to find that Julian Assange had been involved with The Family as a child. Assange's mother got involved with a prominent member, and he subsequently was brought in and interacted with the cult's other children. There is a lot that we don't know about his involvement, but it was clear that it spanned the course of at least a year, and after his mother left and dragged him away from the cult, they were pursued and monitored, moving house to house and hiding their identities to escape. Of course, I could never put such an obvious reference to a real political figure in this work, as it is only *inspired by* a real-life cult and not necessarily *based on* The Family.

Was there a narrator you started writing first—Amy or Freya? Did you always know you wanted the story told from these two perspectives?

I started with Freya first. As soon as I had her narrative structure, everything else fell into place. I knew then that the story was going to be told from two perspectives: one had to be Freya and the other had to come from inside the cult. Eventually I settled on Amy.

What was it like to write about a cult? How much of your novel is based on real events? Was it difficult to fictionalize true history?

It was fun and scary. Fun because cults are so subversive but also so secretive, and this allowed me to fill in lots of blanks with my imagination. Scary because through my research and speaking with psychologists, it became clear to me how easily people fall into cults. Many underestimate their own gullibility—or rather their own preparedness to believe fantastical things if delivered to them, in a way that is consumable, by people who are influential and charismatic enough. Gaslighting is a common term these days, but it's important to understand that this is a real tactic employed often by powerful people to gain control over others.

For me, it contextualized a lot of what was happening in the world politically—namely, the rise of populism.

It was easy enough to fictionalize a true story. I took inspiration from books like *The Girls* by Emma Cline. A lot of the story is based on real events and real places, but ultimately the narrative is my own invention.

What do you hope readers will take away from *In the Clearing*?

I hope readers are shocked enough to interrogate their own assumptions about cults and cult members. People are born into the world of cults, but many are also attracted to it. Good people join cults. Most people, given the right circumstances, would join one.

Without giving anything away, did you always know how the story would end?

I did and I didn't. The ending of this novel was the original ending, but through the process of drafting and editing, I did try a couple of other variations out. Nothing worked quite so well.

What's next for you?

I recently released an audiobook with Audible that is out at the moment, but next up I'm working on a novel called *The Last Guests*. After a couple lists their place on Airbnb, guests find that when they go home things are not quite as they seem. It should be in stores in 2021.

QUESTIONS AND TOPICS FOR DISCUSSION

1. What did you think *In the Clearing* was counting down to? Were you surprised by who went missing?

2. Did you like Freya when you first met her? Did your feelings toward her change over time? Were you able to relate to her experiences? Why or why not?

3. Discuss how motherhood is explored in the novel. Is Freya a good mother? How is her approach to motherhood different than that of her own mother? How is motherhood interpreted in the Clearing?

4. How does losing Aspen shape Freya? Did learning what happened to Aspen change the way you felt about Freya's character?

5. Amy has never known anything besides her life in the Clearing. Is it wrong for her to expect new children to be happy there, too? Discuss how accountable Amy is for her role in the kidnappings.

6. Amy writes this question in her diary (p. 154): "If the world outside is so awful, why was Asha trying to return to it?"

Why *is* Asha trying to escape? How does Amy understand the world outside of the Clearing? Do you think her view is entirely wrong?

7. How much did you know about the real cult behind *In the Clearing* when you began the novel? Do you feel differently about the characters or the plot, knowing they are inspired by real events? Did the novel change the way you think about cults in our world?

8. The novel begins with the epigraph "I love children," as stated by Anne Hamilton-Byrne. Why do you think the author chose this quote? Does it change the way you read the novel?

9. Were you surprised by how the story ended?

10. What will you remember most from this novel?

ABOUT THE AUTHOR

J. P. Pomare lives with his wife in Australia, where he writes fiction and hosts a literary podcast. He is the author of one previous novel, the highly acclaimed *Call Me Evie*.